REVELATIONS AT POTTERS POND

Other Books by Carol W. Hazelwood

Fiction

Assume Nothing
Dead End
Dark Legacy
The Beastly Island Murder
Twilight in the Garden
Coyoacan Hill
Rising Mist (ebook)
My Grandmother the PI (ebook)

Non-fiction

A View from the Jury Box
Tiger in a Cage, the Memoir of Wu Tek Ying

REVELATIONS AT POTTERS POND

by

CAROL W. HAZELWOOD

Author's notes

I have taken great liberty with the Rhode Island coastline. The history of the area is true, although several names have been changed. The name of Quamscutt is fictitious. The Matunuck Oyster Bar owner consented for me to use the restaurant's name.

Many thanks to
Adele Kopecky and Bonnie Willacker for their input and editing.

Cover photograph
By
James Hazelwood

Copyright © 2015, Carol W. Hazelwood
First Edition

Without limiting the rights under copyright reserved above,
no part of this publication may be reproduced, stored in or introduced into
a retrieval system, or transmitted, in any form or by any means
(electronic, mechanical, photocopying, recording, or otherwise),
without the prior written permission of the copyright owner of this book.

Published by Aventine Press
55 East Emerson St.
Chula Vista CA 91911
www.aventinepress.com

ISBN: 978-1-59330-897-1

Printed in the United States of America

ALL RIGHTS RESERVED

2014

Chapter 1

The Victorian rental suited Diana's purpose for her three months of self-inflicted exile or punishment. She hadn't decided which. Perhaps both. The house with faded black paint, a steep-pitched roof, peeling dull green trim, bay windows, and a large front porch sat low between two sandy hillocks above the shoreline of Potters Pond.

While they stood on the gravel driveway, realtor Cora Jacob's words of praise about the home washed over her. "It's quaint, has that New England charm, yet it's wired for WiFi." Cora faced her client, a frown on her lean, tan face. "I can show you something smaller, but you said you wanted quiet. Your nearest neighbor is Ursula Von Reiter, the artist. She's owned the house across the pond for years. She moved to New York, but came back off and on. About five years ago, she returned to live here permanently. You've heard of her, I'm sure."

"I'm sorry, I don't know of her," Diana said.

"Perhaps only New Englanders know her work. She's had shows all over the world. She's in her eighties now."

Diana studied the quiet waters of the pond and the gray Cape Cod beyond, but said nothing.

"Yes, well…." Cora turned toward the house. "You'll love the inside."

Diana followed Cora up the sandy path to the wood door with its etched glass window. The door creaked open, and they stepped inside the dark interior that held the pine scent of recently scrubbed wood. Cora hurried to the windows and pulled back the heavy velvet green drapes. No dust arose. Clean.

"Marlene Schukart comes in once a week to clean and sees that everything's in working order." Cora seemed intent to add the information as if this would be an enticement for Diana to rent. "She was Mrs. Feeney's housekeeper for years. When Mrs. Feeney died, her nephew, Grant Cranston, became the owner and he's kept Marlene on."

Light streamed into the room showing an eclectic style of furniture. A long couch against the bay window faced a coffee table of distressed walnut. The furniture consisted of three chairs, a Windsor, a rocker, and a mid-century yellow-upholstered wingback and a long sofa. A large roll-top desk dominated a far corner.

"I doubt I'll need the woman's services."

"She's on a salary and would take offense if she couldn't come and check on things. Feels it's her duty. Of course, if you want her to do something special, you'd have to pay her."

"So, she's a fixture."

Cora shrugged. "You could say that. Come see the kitchen. It's been updated and should fit your needs." She flashed a smile, then walked through a swinging door, held it open for Diana and waved her hand at the spacious kitchen. A breakfast nook looked out over the backyard.

Diana nodded. "Quite modern for the vintage of the house. Is there a washer and dryer?"

"In there off the mudroom." Cora motioned. "When you're so close to the beach and the pond, the mudroom is a bonus. The water heater is tucked away behind that wall. Just in case something should go amiss. Not that it will, of course." She pointed out the kitchen window. "The backyard has a tool shed, and you can enter the mudroom from the driveway." She walked back to the living room. "There's a main bedroom and bath on the first floor."

Diana followed her guide, noting the queen-size bed and the full bath. She and Paul shared a king-size bed. Her reflection in the full length mirror, attached to the back of the bathroom door, gave her pause. Her eyes were red with fatigue, her beige pantsuit wrinkled, her shoulder-length black hair hung in limp strands about her pale face. As she left the room, she stood straighter hearing her mother's voice in her head: stand tall, don't slouch, what will people think, always look your best. Diana wanted to put her hands over her ears as if that might drown out the harping. To distance herself from the hold her mother had over her, she'd call her mother, Beatrice, instead of Mother.

"A second bathroom and three bedrooms are upstairs. Shall we take a look?" Cora started for the stairs.

"I doubt if I'll use them, but I'd like to see the entire house." Upstairs there was one small room unfurnished and two bedrooms with a Jack and Jill modern bathroom between them. Diana glanced at stairs leading upward. "Where does that go?"

"To the attic. Not much up there but a few suitcases. I'll have them removed if it bothers you," Cora said.

"That's not necessary." Diana followed Cora back to the living room and took in the desk. "I was looking for something smaller, but the price is right." Actually, she was surprised by the low rent for such a large home. Was there something wrong with the house that she didn't see? Finishing her latest murder mystery, her last in a series she'd contracted to write, was her excuse to get away. She could work here. Would she? "Will the owner accept a three-month rental?"

"I believe so. It was rented during the summer for a short time. Grant Cranston is overseas and won't be back until Christmas."

"I'll take it until the end of November. Do you have the rental agreement with you? When I called, you told me you'd accept a check for the first month's rent." She pulled her wallet out of her purse. "I'd like to move in now. My luggage is in the car."

"Oh, well, of course. There's a cleaning deposit, too. I have the paperwork in my car." Cora hurried out to get her briefcase.

Diana stood in the middle of the living room and gazed at the pond and the weathered Cape Cod beyond it. No other homes abutted the property on either side and this rental was the last house on a dead end road. Isolation, just as she'd wanted.

Now that she was here she wondered if she was doing the right thing, but staying in her Philadelphia home had become impossible. Her marriage was in shambles. Gossip had swirled. Paul said it didn't matter, but it did to her. How could she face her friends? Her mother had ranted that she hadn't raised Isabel or Jeffrey properly. Was she right? Is that why as adults her children had turned away from her? Or had Diana been at fault? Guilt rode her like a pack of wolves after their prey.

Family had been important to her. Family? No longer a family, only adults living different lives, in different states and countries. How could she have been so blind to her children's characters? Instead of understanding them, she had tried to mold them to her preconceived ideas. In retrospect she realized she'd allowed her mother's ideas to supersede hers. How had her life gone so wrong? Through misty eyes, she gazed at the large pond outside the living room windows.

Would three months away from Paul, away from friends, make a difference? She didn't know. Time might heal. She wasn't sure. She was scared, scared she'd never see her children again. Scared Paul would find someone worthier, younger. Scared everything that had gone wrong was her fault. Scared because she didn't know how to fix the mess she'd created.

Chapter 2

The following day Diana walked around Potters Pond enthralled with the serenity, the chirping birds and the lapping water against the reeds. A light breeze stroked the water. When she reached the narrow cement bridge that led to the Cape Cod home, she branched off the path and turned toward the beach, hiking over the sand dunes to the ocean. At the water's edge, she breathed in the salty air. A man threw a ball for his black lab. She envied a couple strolling hand in hand and nodded to them when they passed.

Could Paul and she be like that again? Once they'd been happy, hadn't they? The arguments over Isabel and Jeffrey had raged until they both had withdrawn into silence. Was it all her fault? She'd been unable or unwilling to withstand her mother's view of the world, an old fashioned view, a critical and prejudicial view against anyone or anything that didn't conform to Beatrice's idea of what was right. Diana had always backed down trying to keep the peace. But peace had come at a price.

As the week went by, Diana established a routine, walking to the beach in the morning, to the local mini mart in the afternoon to buy small items, anything to keep moving, stop thinking. She listened to the local gossip, smiled cordially, but didn't participate. She never looked at a newspaper, never listened to the radio or turned on the TV. Fear nibbled at her. Unable or unwilling to write, she avoided the desk and her laptop. Disconnected. Numb. A state she found lonely yet comforting.

That was how she existed until the day of the storm.

It was Monday morning, the earlier breeze had strengthened and stirred the surf into angry waves. Diana bent her head to keep her hat from flying off. As she approached the pond, a gust peppered her face with sand. She turned sideways and caught sight of splashes of bright red and gold. Curious, she made her way through a narrow opening to the edge of the marsh's rippling water. A tiny woman with a vibrant multicolored shawl over her shoulders sat hunched over an easel.

The woman's gray hair, woven into a braid, hung down her back. She sat on a canvas camp stool among the rustling reeds and sedges. The artist must have sensed Diana's presence, for she glanced over her shoulder, nodded, then made two quick brush strokes on her work. Without turning around the woman said, "Welcome to Potters Pond, Diana Bellfore. I'm Ursula, your neighbor."

"Oh, yes, Cora told me you lived in the Cape Cod across the pond."

"Since you're here, would you help me?"

Diana hesitated, then stepped forward. "Of course."

Ursula stood and turned to face Diana. Her face was weathered, thin, angular, with a determined look, despite the wrinkles of age. "The wind came up suddenly. A storm's brewing." She motioned to the canvas chair, "Would you carry it, please?" She stowed her easel, covered her painting with her shawl and put it under her arm.

Diana folded the chair, picked it up, and followed Ursula to the artist's home. The elderly woman took short, purposeful strides. Both women bent into the strengthening wind. The sting of tossed sand, the smell of salt air and the sound of pounding waves obliterated attempts to speak. They crossed the bridge, turned north and arrived at a copse of pines protecting the lane leading to the house. Ursula entered a side door to a small room under the back of the house. After placing her things on a bench, she took the chair from Diana and stowed it in the corner.

Ursula looked up at Diana, her blue eyes sparkled with only a slight yellowing of the sclera. "Thank you so much. You'd best hurry home before the wind gets worse. Tomorrow come for tea at three. The storm will have passed. Maybe a little rain. I'll expect you."

It was a statement, a command, not a questioning invitation. "A... that's kind of you, but—"

"No buts. I've watched you walk and walk. Goodness, what miles you've put in and for what purpose? It will be good for both of us. Come and let that be the end of it."

Diana felt like a chastised child, unable to find the words to respond in a meaningful way. Diana left, shaking her head in wonder. The woman was forthright to the point of rudeness. Part of her was angry at the woman's intrusion into her retreat and yet, she knew she'd go. With a writer's curiosity, she was always interested in unusual people, and Ursula seemed to fit the role.

The woman had a subtle European accent, probably German or Austrian given her name. Diana's thoughts tumbled to her daughter. Isabel would have been able to discern the woman's origin by her accent. Languages were her forte. From a very early age, she had mimicked the French au pair and babbled in French. Then when a woman from San Salvador joined the household as a cook, Isabel learned Spanish. She was a sponge with languages. After 9/11, she'd studied Arabic and Persian dialects at the university. Now she was stationed somewhere in Central Asia, acting as a translator for her Marine unit.

Diana wrestled with anger, fear, resentment. Why had her daughter chosen to go to war as a Marine? Diana couldn't comprehend the decision. Loyalty and patriotism were fine virtues until your child joined the fight. Paul thought they should be proud of Isabel. Men could feel that way. War was their domain. War was not a game and this particular war between tribes and religious zealots seemed unnecessary and futile.

Diana hadn't talked with her daughter since she'd left home over two years ago. Paul kept her apprised of their daughter's whereabouts. He'd gone to her graduation from Officers' Candidate School at Quantico. Diana couldn't bring herself to attend. A coward's way out. Now Isabel was with her unit in Afghanistan in danger from a barbaric enemy. No, Diana couldn't think about that and refused to face any of it.

She walked along the pond, recalling the last conversation she'd had with Isabel. She'd stood in Isabel's bedroom watching her daughter pack.

"I won't need much. Everything is government issue," her daughter had said.

"Why are you doing this?" Diana had asked, wringing her hands the way her own mother did. "You have a college degree. Dad can get you a job at the university. You can live here, save money. Meet a nice boy."

Isabel rolled her eyes and ran her hands through her short brown hair. "You don't get it, do you?"

"I'm trying to."

"Look, Mom. I want to do something with my life. If I stay here, I'll smother. All those silly bridge meetings, cocktail parties, do-gooder events. God, it's so boring. There's more to life than golf, parties and…" She threw up her hands.

"You could get a master's or a doctorate. Join the State Department." Diana groped for a reason to make her daughter want to stay. "Why the Marines?" She hoped to thwart Isabel's decision. "It seems an extreme reaction because you're bored."

Isabel sighed. "Mom, why can't you understand? They need people with my language skills. I want to make a difference, but I can't do that here."

"There are many ways to use your talent. Tutor, work for a language professor, many companies need language experts. What about the United Nations?"

"You sound like Grandmother. Why do you do whatever she wants?"

"I don't!"

"Yes, Mom, you always do. You repeat what Grandmother says. Do you ever think for yourself? I want you and Dad to be happy, but my staying isn't going to solve your problems. I'm sorry, but since I'm leaving, I had to say what I've been thinking for years." Isabel stopped folding a blouse. "I've got a brain. A damn good one. I'm not you. Joining the Marines is the best thing for me. I'm physically capable and have a skill they need. I will be doing something worthwhile with my life."

Stung by her daughter's hurtful tirade, she pulled back, trying to comprehend how Isabel could talk to her that way. Gathering herself and refusing to descend to anger, Diana murmured, "I know you'll do well. You've always been athletic." When her own mother had heard about Isabel's plans to join the Marines, she'd asked, "Is my granddaughter gay?" That question now echoed in Diana's ears. Was she? The thought had never occurred to Diana. Her daughter was tall, athletic, had boyfriends, but never a steady. Should she ask? Could she accept the answer? "I need to ask." She stared at her daughter's comely face, short brown hair, and trim muscular frame. "Do you prefer…women?"

Isabel closed her suitcase and laughed, then collapsed on the bed and stared at her mother. "Me? That's a laugh. You are a trip, Mom. Grandmother put that idea in your head, didn't she? You're so blind and so is Dad. You're asking the wrong person. Ask Jeffrey that question."

And that was when Diana's life had tumbled out of her comfort zone.

Chapter 3

Diana hurried up the steps of the Victorian with the wind playing havoc with her hair. She was about to open the door when she noticed a man in a camouflage uniform walking toward the house. An iron fist closed around her chest. A military man. Is this how they notify next of kin about loved ones' injuries or deaths? She remained paralyzed, one hand on the door knob, the other shielding her face from the wind. No, no one knew where she was, except Paul. He came closer, limping, head down, carrying a large duffle bag. At the bottom of the stairs, he kept his eyes riveted on the treads and slowly climbed the steps. It wasn't until he was on the porch in front of her that he looked up. His eyes widened.

"What do you want?" Diana's question was swallowed by the swirling wind.

A gust of wind slammed into the wicker furniture sending various pieces across the porch toward Diana. He grabbed one of the chairs, blocked the other one with his duffle and motioned with his head for her to open the door. She had little choice and walked into the living room. He shoved the furniture inside, tossed his duffle onto the floor, and shut the door behind him. The quiet was unnerving after the roaring chaos of the wind.

He ran a hand over the top of his crew cut. "What are you doing here?"

"I live here."

"That's not possible."

"Excuse me?" She stood erect, hoping her five-ten height would intimidate him, but she was still several inches shorter than the man. "I'm renting the place."

"Oh? Captain told me the house was vacant. Gave me the key."

"Are you sure you have the right house?"

"Yes, ma'am."

Diana hadn't been called ma'am in years. It felt odd and a little disconcerting. The man was polite but didn't look as if he had any intention of leaving. "There's obviously some mistake. The rental agent told me it was available for three months this fall. I have a lease agreement."

"That's Cora Jacob, right? Captain told me he wrote and told her not to rent it. That I was going to stay here until the first of the year. He knew I had no other place to go during my leave and rehab."

Leave? Rehab? Is that what Isabel would say when or if?

They remained mute facing each other in the entryway to the living room until he said, "Ma'am, I'm not going out in that storm today. It was a long walk from town. I got a bum leg. Mind if I sit down?"

"No. Yes. I mean, of course." She moved aside.

He limped toward the couch, turned, took an envelope from his jacket pocket and held it out to her. "This should explain things." He sat, his eyes fixed on her.

She took the envelope, opened it and read a short note addressed to Cora Jacob. *This is to introduce Sgt. John Morgan. As I wrote in my last letter to you, he will be staying at my house until the first of the year. Please afford him every courtesy and help him get acquainted with the area. Cordially Yours, Captain Grant Cranston.*

Diana handed the note back. "This is unacceptable. I've already paid the first month's rent and a cleaning deposit. Cora told me the owner wouldn't need the house until after Christmas."

"Looks like a stalemate, ma'am."

Diana stood. "I'll call Cora."

"Ma'am, I'd like to be in on the conversation."

She went to get her cell phone from the other room and returned. After punching in Cora's number, she put it on speaker. A recording came on. While she paced the room, Diana held the phone so he could hear the message she left. "This is Mrs. Bellfore. Sergeant John Morgan has arrived with a note from the owner, Captain Grant Cranston, saying he wrote to you not to rent the place since the sergeant would be living here till the first of the year. I have rented this house in good faith. Please call me back to resolve this matter."

She clicked off. "Now what do we do?"

He shook his head. "You're Mrs. Bellfore, Diana Bellfore, the writer? I can't believe the coincidence."

"It's not a coincidence. It's a mistake."

His brown eyes narrowed. "I'm staying." His square chin jutted forward.

She wanted to argue but thought it would be useless. Where would he go in the storm? "Okay, there are bedrooms and a bathroom upstairs. I'm not sure if the beds are made or if there's linen or towels."

"There are. Captain told me. In the hall closet."

She nodded, but remained perplexed. What could she do? Her stomach growled and she realized she had to feed this unwelcome guest. "Would you like a bite to eat? It's," she glanced at her watch, "after one."

"That would be great, ma'am. We can sort this out."

"Yes. There's obviously a mixup."

"Well, if I can't stay here, I don't know where I'll go or what the captain will think."

Diana wasn't sure what to say to that, so she turned and went to the kitchen. Despite his six four rugged build, he seemed harmless. She had no idea which branch of the military he was in. His camouflage uniform and patches were meaningless to her. Army? Air Force? Marines?

She heard his uneven footsteps on the stairs, a thump told her he'd dropped his duffle bag. She heated the vegetable soup she'd cooked the day before, made sandwiches of ham and cheese on rye, then placed them on the breakfast table. She wiped her hands on a towel, swung open the kitchen door and called up the stairs. "Lunch is ready in the kitchen." It reminded her of when she'd called her son who'd always dawdled.

The sergeant came downstairs, followed her to the breakfast nook, sat and looked out the window. "Even in the storm, it's beautiful…just like Captain said."

She sat across from him. "The soup might be very hot."

He nodded and picked up his spoon. "What should I call you, ma'am?"

She found herself blushing. "Mrs. Bellfore."

"Mrs. Bellfore?"

"That's what I said."

He gave a lopsided grin. "Amazing."

"Why?"

"Ah, no reason. It's a nice name. I'm Sergeant John Morgan."

"Yes, I know from the letter."

He gazed at her, smiled, then picked up his spoon.

As they ate, they watched the wind race through the pines sending needles against the panes. The house remained relatively quiet while the storm intensified, lashing the trees and sending anything not secured into the air. Neither said much, and whenever he spoke a few words, he called her ma'am or Mrs. Bellfore. She had no intention of allowing him to stay, and the less familiarity the better.

After he'd finished eating, he thanked her and took his dishes to the sink.

She went to stand next to him. "I'll clean up."

He smiled, nodded and went out through the kitchen's swinging door. She heard him treading up the stairs again. Knowing he had no place to go during his leave made her anxious about what to do. She'd paid. He hadn't. Surely Cora could find another place for him. What did he mean when he said, he wondered what the captain would think? Why did that matter? The man was out of the country.

A bang and the crash of glass in the front of the house brought her back from her ruminations. What now? She dried her hands and hurried to the living room. A shutter swung back and forth and the wind blew the heavy drapes, making them look like balloons. Window pane glass littered the wood floor.

The sergeant came downstairs. "I'll latch the outside shutters. Something's thudding in the rear of the house. Why don't you check on that?"

Diana stood transfixed for a moment, then went to investigate the noise in the mudroom. She found the back screen door hanging off its hinge acting like a wayward hammer. So much for Marlene Schukart keeping the place in order. She grabbed the screen handle, but found it difficult to close.

An arm came past her. "I've got it," he said. "Can you find a rope or something? We can tie it shut until I can fix it permanently."

She searched through the kitchen drawers, found a ball of twine and brought it to him.

He secured the screen. "That'll hold it for now. It's warped, needs planing."

The kitchen lights went out. She moved toward the wall and flipped the switch back and forth. Nothing. Although two in the afternoon, the dreary sky made the interior dark.

He asked, "Do you have a flashlight handy?"

"No."

"I have one in my gear. I'll be back in a second. See if you can muster up candles while I check the fuse box."

He was good at giving orders, just like a sergeant. In the dim light she picked up four candles in holders from the pantry and took them to the living room. A strong draft came through the smashed window. She closed the heavy velvet drapes and anchored them with a chair and a table, but it was only a temporary solution. Glass shards remained in the window frame, but removing them now was out of the question. She fetched a broom, swept up the glass littering the floor, then lit the candles with the long matches used for the fireplace. She placed two candles on the coffee table, one on the mantle and the other on a side table.

The sergeant came back with a flashlight, bent and lit the logs already stacked in the fireplace. "Hope there's more dry wood outside in the shed, cuz those," he nodded to the logs at the side of the hearth, "won't last through the day and night." He stood again. "The fuse box is in the basement." He turned and went to a door at the back of the staircase.

She hadn't given much thought to the door leading to the basement until now. Interesting that he knew his way around, but it must have been obvious that it led to the basement. She heard him bang around under the house. When he returned to the living room, he said, "Not the fuses, must be downed wires in the area." He stood by the hearth, then swung the beam of his flashlight over the blowing drapes. "I got an idea." He left and returned with a board and propped it against the wall. "Saw this earlier. Now all I need is a hammer and nails."

"I haven't seen tools in the house. Let me have your flashlight." She took it and went to the pantry, returning with a roll of duct tape.

"Great." He drew back the drapes. While she held the flashlight, he fitted the board over the shattered window pane and taped it securely in place. When he'd finished, he stepped back viewing his handiwork. "We're a good team."

She liked his attitude. "Yes, nice job." She extinguished the flashlight and sat in the chair by the fire.

He sat on the couch. "I don't much like wind, but I like rain, do you?"

"Not much. When our son was little, he'd hop in bed with us during a storm and the dog would cower under the bed. Only our daughter seemed unconcerned."

"Interesting for a girl not to be frightened. She must take after you."

Isabel was nothing like her. "Isabel was…is brave. Tough, resilient." As she said this, she realized she'd never told her daughter that she admired those qualities in her.

"Do you mind me asking, where's your husband and family?"

"Paul's in Philadelphia. As you seem to know, I'm a writer, mysteries. I needed some quiet time away…to write." Lately lying rolled off her tongue easily, and sometimes it sounded true even to her.

"So they're in Philadelphia?"

"My son is in Chicago, getting an advanced degree in architecture." That was true.

He gave her an odd look. "Your daughter?"

"Isabel is a linguist." Nothing more needed to be said.

They sat in an awkward silence, neither comfortable as though each feared overstepping an unseen boundary. The candles flickered; the fire consumed the wood with lapping flames. Outside the wind roared across the land.

She finally broke the silence. "You said you had no other place to go. What about your family?"

He hesitated, studied her, then leaned back. "I'm from Kansas. When I was fourteen, there was a tornado. Wiped out most of the town, killed my parents. After that I lived with an aunt until I got out of high school. She wasn't sorry to see me leave."

Diana's cell phone rang with its song: Greensleeves. She grabbed it off the table. "Hello. Yes, I'm fine, Cora. Did you get my message?"

Sergeant Morgan motioned that he wanted to hear the conversation, so Diana put it on speaker.

Cora's voice came over strong and clear. "I'm sorry there's a mixup. I haven't received a letter from Captain Cranston. Does Sergeant Morgan know how to reach him? Phone or email?"

He shook his head.

"Apparently not. What should we do? Sergeant Morgan has a letter saying the owner wants him to use the house, but I've paid for a month."

"I'm really sorry. This has never happened before. Can the two of you work it out until after the storm? Power's out all over, and driving in this storm isn't a good idea."

Diana sighed. "We'll handle the situation till then, but this needs to be resolved." She clicked off and stared into the fire. "Let's make the best of it until after the storm." She figured he'd move out in the morning.

He nodded. "Sometimes the mail takes a long time to get stateside. I heard the captain was assigned up north in the mountains. Communication to the states is almost impossible from there. It's a bad part of Afghanistan, but I never saw a good place there. Hot, dry, windy, sandy, and miserably cold in the winter. Every second you're out of the compound you can expect to get shot at or blown up. Inside the compound it isn't too bad, but you gotta expect the worst. All the time."

"It sounds awful. Why?"

"Why?" The fire's flickering glow played across his frowning face. "I don't get you."

"I know you're patriotic, we all are, but doesn't it seem futile? Why is it our war? Why should our young people get wounded or die in a fight that we can't win? What's it all for?"

"You a pacifist or something?"

"No. That's not it. I just don't see the reasoning behind fighting in a land that's not remotely connected to ours."

"Beg to differ with you. It is our business. I'd rather fight them there than here."

She'd had enough of these acrimonious arguments with Paul and Isabel. Even Jeffrey had chimed in. She searched for another avenue of conversation. "I wonder how Ursula Von Reiter is managing. She lives in the Cape Cod across the pond." Her nervous babble sounded inane, but she couldn't stop. "She's an artist, eighty some years old. Have you heard of her?"

He shook his head.

"I hadn't either. I met her the other day while she was painting. I'm going to tea there tomorrow." She tried another subject, then found herself back to the same issue that haunted her. "I'm sure the military is doing their best under terrible circumstances. I'm as patriotic as the next person and I support our troops, but—"

"That's okay, ma'am. A lot of people think like you do, even some politicians."

Diana clasped her hands together and sat straighter.

He seemed to take note. "You aren't afraid of the house or me, are you, ma'am?"

"Should I be?"

"No. It's just that with Mrs. Feeney's death, I thought you might be a bit squeamish."

"The house was rented this past summer. Just because a woman died in the house shouldn't be a problem."

"Miss Jacob didn't tell you?"

"About what?"

"When the summer renters heard about Mrs. Feeney, they told Cora that she'd breached the contract and they'd sue if they didn't get their money back."

"How do you know all this?"

"Captain Cranston, ma'am." The firelight flicked across his face. "I'm curious. Did someone tell you about this house or did you want to rent it despite its history?"

"Are you trying to scare me, sergeant?"

"No. Since you're a mystery writer, I thought you knew about how the former owner died."

She smiled. "All right, I'll bite. What's the story behind her death?"

"She was murdered. The police never solved the case."

Chapter 4

For Diana the night was long and sleepless. Several times she got up and untangled her sheets, sat on the edge of the bed, then lay down again. Her thoughts careened from Mrs. Feeney's murder, to the sergeant, to her door that had no lock.

Toward morning the wind abated, but a drizzling rain continued. She stirred, sniffing. Coffee? She glanced at the clock: a few minutes before six. She threw back the bedcovers and put on her robe and slippers. After removing the chair she'd propped under the doorknob, she stepped into the hall. "Sergeant, are you up?"

"Yes, ma'am," he called from the kitchen. "Electricity is back on. There should be hot water by now. I made coffee."

"Thanks. It smells good." Although she felt foolish about the chair, she nevertheless put it back against the door. Taking heed of the weather, she donned gray wool slacks, a navy blue turtleneck and sturdy walking shoes. She brushed her black hair, tying it loosely with a clasp at the nape of her neck.

Upon entering the kitchen, she found the sergeant at the breakfast table dressed in civilian clothes, a startling transformation. He wore a maroon chamois shirt and navy blue pants. When he stood, his heavy boots clunked on the wood floor.

"You're up early," she said.

"Not by my watch. Five is usually my wakeup time."

"Military training?"

"Something like that." He stood at the stove with a boyish grin on his face. "I made pancakes. Would you like a short stack?"

"Sounds good, thank you." She filled her coffee mug and took it to the table.

He slid the pancakes onto a plate and placed it in front of her.

"I'm not used to being waited on." She slathered on butter and poured syrup over them. "Where did you learn to cook?"

"My aunt. She might not have liked me much, but she sure could cook. I learned from watching her." He walked to the window that overlooked the backyard then turned toward her. "There's more batter. Would you like another one?"

"It's wonderful, but this is plenty."

While she sipped her coffee, he washed the dishes. "I was out in the shed this morning and found tools, so I can fix the back screen door. The wood pile seems okay, but we'll probably need more through the coming months."

She leaned back. "You're planning to stay no matter what Cora or I say?"

He walked over and sat across from her. "You shouldn't be here alone. Last night you shrugged off Mrs. Feeney's murder, so I didn't explain my other reason for being here. When the captain learned I was headed back to the states, had no family and nowhere to go, he asked me to look into his aunt's murder. In return I'd get a place to stay."

"What can you do that the police haven't done?"

"I've had training in criminal investigations, and a fresh look might help."

"Does anyone know the purpose of your visit? I mean besides the captain and now me? What about the police?"

"To my knowledge nobody knows. Wouldn't help my investigation if they did." He got up, brought the coffee pot to refill their mugs. After returning the empty pot to the sink, he sat again. "I'd ask you to leave except that might cause talk. I don't need that to happen."

"There might be more gossip about the two of us sharing the house."

He rubbed his hand over his short brown hair. "I hadn't thought of that. I wouldn't want to compromise you or cause you embarrassment."

She could hear her mother's carping voice saying, "What will people say?" But she wasn't in Philadelphia and refused to give in to past habits. "So I'm your cover, so to speak. The innocent who sits and twiddles her thumbs."

"Isn't that what you've been doing?"

"What do you mean?"

He held up his hand. "You said you were here to write, but you haven't."

"How do you know?"

"I checked your laptop. You don't even have an outline for your new book."

She wadded up her paper napkin. "You've got a lot of nerve."

"I snoop. That's my job."

"My life is none of your business. You seem to be under the illusion that you can come here and take over. That is not going to happen, and I can't have you here in this house."

He leaned forward and laid his broad hands on the table. "I'm staying whether you like it or not. And I believe the law will side with me." He shrugged. "Since you're here, you might be able to help me. You write mysteries, you've researched murders and know how clues might fall together. Wouldn't you rather catch a killer than worry about your daughter in Afghanistan?"

She leaped to her feet, shoving her chair back. Its legs scraped on the wood floor. "Who do you think you are? You have no right to bring my family into this. My life is none of your affair. Keep out of my life."

"I don't like being intrusive, but I needed to know more about you. Make sure I could trust you."

"And that allows you to pry into my personal life?"

"Yes. You're free to leave."

"Free to leave? I have a rental contract. You should be the one to leave."

"That's not going to happen. You'll get your money back. Cora can find you another house to rent." He waited and when she said nothing, he added, "But I could use your help. Don't you care that a murderer is roaming free? You seem to be the kind of woman who'd want justice."

She stood in the middle of the kitchen, shaking with fury, turned on her heels and marched out of the house, slamming the front door behind her. For several minutes she paced the porch. Rain puddled on the gravel path and splattered the pond's surface, casting a gray murky scene.

He'd invaded her privacy and found out about Isabel. He was military. If he read her emails and notes, he probably thought she was callous toward her daughter. She wasn't, but her inability to protect Isabel had made her withdraw into a shell. Did he also know about Jeffrey? He couldn't know. She clenched her fists at the violation, then gripped the railing. Tears of anger and frustration streamed down her cheeks. She was a coward and hated herself for that. Could she change? She was tired of running away from problems. If she had an ounce of gumption, she'd stay and fight for her right to rent the house. When the wall around her pleasant life in Philadelphia had imploded, she'd run from the problems, the hurt, the gossip, and her mother.

Faced with a difficult rental and housemate as well as a murder investigation, would she run away again? The irony of the situation was inescapable. Was this murder any of her business? Was the sergeant who he said he was? His sudden appearance had thrown her quiet retreat into chaos. Part of her enjoyed the disruption. It allowed her to forget her own problems.

She stared at the pond, letting her thoughts drift. Could she be of help, or was she deluding herself about her abilities? Could she walk away and let a killer remain free? She shivered, clasping her arms across her chest. Writing had been her escape, but now her fictional world collided with the real one. She was curious, a trait that might lead her into trouble. Still? What did she have to lose? She sighed, wiped away her tears, and took a deep breath of cool air.

The sergeant was cleaning the counters when she returned to the kitchen. "All right. You can stay. I'll stay too, but don't you ever dare violate my things, my laptop or interfere in any way with my life."

He held out his hand. "It's a deal."

She ignored his hand. "Easy for you to say." Her heart pounded. "What do I really know about you? You barge in here with a note from the owner and expect everything to go your way."

"I hadn't expected anyone to be here. I figured I'd talk to Cora after the storm. I wanted to find the house, settle in, not cause waves. I'm sorry you're caught in the middle." His light brown eyes softened. "I'm not trying to be difficult." He gave a hint of a smile. "I apologize for coming on too strong. Being gruff and abrupt is how I dealt with difficult situations overseas. Decisions needed to be made immediately, no wavering, no second-guessing or lives could be lost." He held out his hand again.

This time she shook it, feeling his strength.

"Let's discuss a plan." He motioned to the chairs in the breakfast nook.

As they sat across from each other, Diana noticed the lines on his face, the crow's feet, the drawn mouth, the flinty look in his eyes, all telling of trouble, pain and sorrow. "How old are you, Sergeant?"

"Thirty-two, ma'am." He studied her, his eyes crinkling into a smile. "I won't ask you the same question."

She shook her head with a slight upturn of her lips. "You probably already know, Mr. Snoopy."

"Yes, ma'am, I do."

"Could you stop calling me ma'am?"

"What should I call you?"

"Diana. After all we're going to be working together, living in the same house and formality seems, well, silly."

"Yes, ma'am...Diana, it does." His features softened. "Call me John."

"I'll stick to sergeant, just to show others we are not an item." He was twenty plus years younger than she, and she envied him. He had a cause—to find a killer. What did she have? A family dissolving.

He rubbed his forehead. "I want you to meet the locals like the artist Von Reiter you mentioned and talk to Marlene Schukart when she comes to clean on Thursday. The storm probably prevented her from coming yesterday."

"I'd forgotten she was supposed to be here."

"People will talk to a woman better than a man. You know, gossip."

"Is that your opinion of women, that we gossip?"

He shrugged. "Don't you?" He leaned back. "Men are more closed-mouthed. You can chat up the people in town about things they might know. What they say may give me, us, a lead." He rubbed the small scar on his chin. "I'll talk to Bert."

"Who's Bert?"

"Marlene's husband. He's a handyman."

"Marlene seems to be doing her job, but seeing the condition of the screen door and the outside trim on the house, I'd say Bert isn't doing his part."

"Right, but I need to have him around. Find out what he knows."

"Do you have a suspect?"

"No. The police report was sketchy. I've got a list of those who had opportunity and motive, but nothing points to anyone in particular."

"If I'm going to help, I'll need to know who these people are."

"It's better you don't. That way your judgement won't be clouded, and you won't screen what you hear." He paused before adding, "And...it will keep you safer."

She didn't like not knowing. The lack of knowledge might give her an edge, but it could also cause her to blunder into saying or doing the wrong thing. "There are some things I will need to know."

"Like?"

"How old was Mrs. Feeney?"

"Seventy-six, strong and healthy, according to the captain."

"Last night you said Mrs. Feeney was bludgeoned with a sharp-edged instrument. Any defensive wounds?"

"No. The report stated the weapon could have been a garden tool, given the dirt in the wound, but the police never found the murder weapon."

"I thought you said she was killed inside the house."

He took out a packet of photos and papers from a manila envelope and spread them out on the table. "These are photos of the crime scene." He put his hand over them. "You aren't squeamish, are you?"

"Depends how graphic they are."

"Not bad." He shoved them in front of her. "Her body was found in the living room. The coroner's report stated that the amount of blood found on the floor by her body was inconsistent with the size and depth of the head wound. He concluded that the body had been moved and placed inside at least an hour or two after the death blow. That's based on lividity."

"I know about lividity. Pooling of the blood in the body can denote how long it's been in a given position." She studied the photos. "So where was she killed?"

"The police couldn't find the kill site."

"No newly scrubbed area in the house or on the porch, no blood in nearby fields?

Did they search the pond?"

"They had a heavy rain during that time. They didn't use scuba divers, but did rake the pond's edges. If the murder weapon was in the pond, it would have sunk into the muck." He put his finger on one photo. "The report said she was wearing a housedress. I can't tell from the photo what they meant by that."

She smiled. "It's an old term for a simple dress a woman wears around the house. Obviously she wasn't going out or expecting guests."

He nodded. "That makes sense. Captain said his aunt was meticulous about how she looked and how the house was kept. Apparently she and Marlene Schukart had many arguments about how the house should be cleaned."

"Were the arguments bad enough to cause Marlene to strike her employer?"

"Captain thought not. Marlene was the one who found the body. Feeney had been dead for at least five days."

"If Marlene cleaned on Thursday, that means she was killed sometime on a Sunday," Diana said.

"Not sure the timeline can be pinpointed so exactly. I think it's more accurate to say she was killed sometime over the weekend."

"I see. That makes it more difficult. What do you know about Mrs. Feeney? Was she a church goer?"

"I don't think so, at least not when she was younger. Maybe you can find out more on that subject." He pointed to one photo. "The body was positioned to look like she fell and hit her head on the table. If you compare this photo to the living room today, you'll see that the rug has been removed."

"Blood stains are hard to get out. Do you know what happened to it?"

"No idea. Probably tossed. Cora might know."

Diana studied the photo. Mrs. Feeney lay on her stomach, her head tilted to one side, showing a gash on the side of her head. "I wonder what Mrs. Feeney normally did on weekends and with whom."

"That's one of the things I'd like you to find out."

Chapter 5

A few minutes before three that afternoon Diana stood on the porch ready to walk to Ursula's house when the sergeant came outside. "I think it would be better if you didn't tell Miss Von Reiter about my presence here."

"She'll find out sooner or later. This is a small town. She knew about me before I even met her."

"Cora probably told everyone she'd rented the house to you."

"It's no secret as far as I'm concerned, although I told Cora I wanted privacy." Diana's jaw tightened. "You didn't get that memo, did you?"

"I thought we buried the hatchet on that score."

Instead of responding, she studied the cloudy sky. "The rain's stopped. Any other advice about my visit with Ursula?"

He shook his head. "I'll be interested in what you learn."

"Me too." Diana walked down the steps and followed the meandering path around the pond and over the bridge. A stone walkway led to the front door that was painted a bright red. The paved road dead-ended at the driveway where an old Volvo was parked. There was no bell, so she lifted the brass knocker, letting its resounding whack announce her presence.

After a short wait Ursula, dressed in a vibrant orange smock over aqua blue corduroy slacks, opened the door. The small woman wore woolly slippers and beckoned her inside. "You can put your things there." She motioned to a hall bench. "Glad the storm didn't put you off. Any problems at the house?"

Diana followed Ursula into the living room. "You mean besides the power outage and banging shutters?"

"Ha. You get used to that sort of thing living close to the ocean." Ursula nodded to a low-backed modern white couch. "Please have a seat and I'll bring the tea, or would you prefer coffee?"

"Either is fine."

"Do be exact." The woman stood, regal in attitude. "Which would you prefer?"

Since frankness seemed to be Ursula's main characteristic, Diana matched it. "Coffee, then. Regular, not decaf."

"Good. I like coffee much better, even though I offered tea. I always think women want tea, but I prefer coffee and kuchen in the afternoon." She turned and went through a door to the kitchen.

French doors opened onto a wood porch that overlooked the pond with a view of the Victorian house. Despite the modern furniture, the living room was cheery with its color palette of orange, lilac, yellow and splashes of red. Diana studied the oil landscapes with painted silver frames. She was still enjoying the artwork when Ursula came back into the room carrying a tray with a pot, cups, and a plate with small chocolate cakes.

"Let me help." Diana removed several books from the glass coffee table. The titles were an eclectic selection—art history, the environment and astronomy. She put them on a side table inlaid with swirling mosaics of vibrant hues.

"Thank you." Ursula set the tray down and sat in an upholstered chair designed to fit her small stature. "I'm a little out of breath. Age is a damn nuisance. Would you mind pouring and serving the cakes?"

After they both had their coffee, cream for Ursula, black for Diana, and a plate with a dainty chocolate petit four, Ursula said, "I love this time of day. It settles my nerves. I can think about the painting I've done during the day."

"Your landscapes are lovely." Diana relaxed against bright teal cushions. "Are they all your work?" She gestured to the paintings on the walls.

"I have no room for other artists. I'm proud to have my children around me. I don't need others."

"I like them, but I'm ashamed to say I don't know much about art."

"Most don't." Ursula tilted her head. "However, since you're a fiction writer, you know the art of creating."

Diana wanted to avoid any conversation about herself. "I understand you're very successful. I'd love to see more of your work."

"Another time, perhaps." Ursula took a bite of cake and closed her eyes as if reveling in its taste.

Diana smiled, waited and sipped her coffee.

Ursula opened her eyes and dabbed at her lips with a pink linen napkin. "Was is the operative word. The art world has passed me by. I am no longer considered sale-able or some such words to that effect. Critics were unmerciful about my last show. My new approach to my work wasn't what they or the public expected or apparently wanted. I packed up and came back here."

"I'm sorry you had bad reviews. They go with the territory though, don't they?"

Ursula shook her head. "Never happened to me before."

Diana remembered the reviews of her first book that were less than flattering. Although she'd learned not to take them personally, it had been difficult. Unsure of how to continue, she sipped her coffee. It was strong and although she normally didn't add cream, she reached for it now. "You lived in New York. Have you been back here long?"

"Are you writing an article about me?"

"No." The woman's forthright question made Diana blush. "I didn't mean to pry, just curious."

"I'm a little sensitive. I wish I hadn't come back. The incident across the way changed everything."

"What do you mean?"

Ursula put down her plate next to her cup. "Didn't Cora tell you about Mrs. Feeney's murder?"

She should have anticipated this question, but hadn't. "I heard about it, yes."

"Thought you'd flee the moment you heard, but apparently you're made of sterner stuff. I was here when it happened, but I had the flu and hadn't been out in my usual painting haunts." She shrugged. "Even though Gloria Feeney had bought several of my paintings years ago, I didn't like her. Nobody did. She was a witch. Some would replace the w with a b in that word."

Diana found her comment interesting. "I was told that Marlene Schukart cleaned for Mrs. Feeney."

"I hope Cora didn't go into details about Marlene. Poor woman has had a difficult time since Gloria's demise."

Diana thought demise an odd word to use for murder. "The new owner kept her on. It's part of my rental agreement. She'll continue to clean every Thursday, but since I'd just moved in, I requested that she not show the first week. Then she missed yesterday because of the storm. I have yet to meet her. What's she like?"

"Good worker. Simple soul. I'm glad she's got the work. Ever since the incident, Marlene's husband has been drinking heavily. Not good for much lately." Ursula waved her hand as if she wanted to erase what she'd just said. "Please, don't repeat that. I don't want to hurt Marlene any more than she has been."

"How do you mean?"

"She found the body. Since she had violent arguments with the woman, the police harangued her. That made others think she was a prime suspect. Silly, really. She might be strong but she's incapable of murder." Ursula shook her head and gazed toward the French doors. "Of course, Marlene's happy the old woman is dead. Gloria Feeney gave her a terrible time, but Marlene needed the money. When she came here on Fridays, she'd complain about how rude Mrs. Feeney had been toward her."

"Did you have problems with Marlene or argue with her?"

"Me? Heaven's no. She's been wonderful. I tell her what I want done, and she does it. I never understood why Gloria gave Marlene such a hard time, but that woman was horrible to everyone. She'd find out your secret and spread it around until everyone knew your Achilles' heel."

"Did she do that to you?"

"At my age, I didn't give a hoot." She paused and took a sip of coffee, before adding, "I'm a celebrity here in Quamscutt. She lied about my recent work."

"The show you talked about?"

Ursula nodded. "Gloria wrote a letter to the newspaper claiming I'd become mentally ill. Without checking with me, the paper printed it. I could have sued, but what would that accomplish? More notoriety. I didn't want to give the woman the satisfaction. I just ignored her." She winked at Diana. "I had a heart to heart with the editor, and he wrote a full retraction. Still, the rumor persisted."

"Sounds like she was cruel and vindictive."

"Absolutely. Betrayal without remorse. That was her motto."

"I wonder what made her that way."

"Not sure. When I first knew her years ago, she was different. Not that I liked her even then. Her husband Hetch was a good man. Something must have occurred to turn her into a spiteful old woman." Ursula shrugged. "Maybe the divorce put her over the edge. Who knows?"

There was a loud bang on the front door. "That's probably my young friend, Penny. She drops in from time to time without so much as a by-your-leave. I love her visits. She's adopted me as her grandmother. Would you let her in?"

Diana rose, walked to the door and opened it. A tall, thin woman with red hair and freckles stood on the steps. Her mouth pursed at the sight of Diana.

She barged into the hall and twirled around toward Diana. "Who are you?"

The woman's outspoken manner matched Ursula's. "Diana Bellfore. I'm renting the Victorian across the pond."

"That monstrosity? How could you rent that place?" The young woman swept into the living room, her heavy plaid wool skirt swirling about her booted feet. "Ursula, you're entertaining and didn't include me."

"Get off your high horse, Penny, and meet my neighbor Diana. She's renting the Feeney house for three months. This is Penelope Nelson, wife of our quaint seaside town's Chief of Police, Charles Nelson."

Penelope made a face at Ursula. "You don't have to tell her everything about me."

"Dear girl, that would take an hour. Get yourself a cup and join us."

While Penelope clanged around in the kitchen, Diana resumed her seat on the couch, stunned by the two blunt-speaking women. A fleeting image of her mother's opinion about the importance of tact and tasteful talk flashed through her mind. She dispelled it, intent on being openminded to learn what they knew about the late Gloria Feeney.

Penelope returned with a cup, plate and napkin in hand. After pouring her cup of coffee, she took one of the small cakes and sat on the other end of the couch from Diana. "So you know about Mrs. Feeney?"

"I've just learned more about her from Ursula."

"No, I mean, the murder."

"Yes, I know about that, too."

"God, I hate the whole mess." Penny pulled at her skirt. "The town thinks Charlie should have caught the culprit even though they couldn't care a rat's ass about Gloria. They just don't like the idea of a murderer running loose. Of course, who would? Charlie was in an untenable situation." Penelope motioned to Ursula. "You tell her." She took a bite of cake.

Ursula smiled. "Penny is a little cryptic, and it's a bit complicated. Charles was the adopted son of Gloria's stepbrother. A few nasty people think Charles should have recused himself from the investigation, especially after no one was indicted."

Diana turned toward Penny. "That's rather a distant relationship to think that, isn't it?"

Ursula nodded to her friend. "Penny, tell her the full story. She'll hear it anyway. Better from you than others."

"Might as well." Penny put her empty plate on the coffee table. "You see, Gloria had gotten hold of some…" she glanced at Ursula, "incriminating history about me. When I was a teenager, I wasn't the model of decorum. Big-mouth Feeney found out I'd been arrested for drugs. Made a stink about it to the city council when they were about to appoint Charlie the new Chief of Police. It almost cost him the position. Thank God, the council knew how old Feeney distorted the truth." She gulped her coffee. "I'd have killed her myself if someone else hadn't beat me to it."

Chapter 6

Before Diana left, she exchanged phone numbers with Ursula. Afterward, instead of heading back to the rental, she walked over the dunes to the ocean, pondering what she'd learned from the women. Neither of them liked Mrs. Feeney and neither did the housekeeper, Marlene.

The sun dangled on the horizon in the western sky casting streaks of light through the clouds and onto the gray churning sea. She set a fast pace along the shore. The setting sun cast a shadow on a figure coming toward her.

Despite his limp, the sergeant was jogging. When he drew abreast of her, he stopped and bent over with his hands on his knees. "Out of shape."

"Should you be exercising so strenuously?"

"Need to get in shape as fast as possible. Can't do that sitting around." He stood erect and exhaled with a loud whoosh. "Thought you'd be back at the house by now."

"I needed to clear my head." She pointed west. "There's a little daylight left. I'll see you at the house."

She walked away, but he turned and joined her. "What did you find out?"

While they walked side by side, she told him about her visit with Ursula and how Penelope Nelson, wife of the Chief of Police, had arrived unannounced. "A very direct young woman. Said she'd have killed Gloria Feeney if someone else hadn't done it."

"Oh?" He stopped and picked up a shell.

"Not that she really meant it, of course." Diana talked over his head while he continued to kneel and study the shell.

"Is Penny on your list of suspects?" She frowned, wondering what was so intriguing about the shell.

"Ah, no. I do remember the captain mentioning her."

"Did he say anything of interest?"

He stood and looked toward the ocean. "Penelope is an unusual name."

Diana followed his gaze with the distinct feeling he was hiding something. "You seem distracted. What's bothering you?"

"Surprised at the woman's statement, that's all." He turned away. "It's getting dark. We should turn back."

"You're right. Hope we can find the path."

"I marked it."

"You're like a boy scout, always prepared."

His deep laugh sounded so much like her husband that she stopped.

"Something wrong?" he asked.

"No. I hadn't heard you laugh before. You should do it more often."

"Wish I had more to laugh about."

"Sorry. You've had it rough and that was unkind."

"Not at all. Laughter can get you through tough times."

Laughter had been sorely lacking between Paul and herself. Tough times? That's how she felt about her life now. Where had all her family's joy gone? Whose fault? She shook her head and knew it didn't matter. How to change or remedy the pain and hurt was the challenge.

They continued, leaving footprints in the soft sand. After entering the narrow path leading to the pond, they came to the bridge and turned toward the Victorian's hulking darkness.

He stopped, turned and stared at Ursula's house. The light from her porch reflected off the briny water. "How much can Von Reiter see of the Feeney house from her vantage point?"

"I didn't go out on her porch, but she has a good view despite the old pines and the porch overhang."

"With a telescope, she could see a lot more." He mounted the broad steps.

"I didn't see a telescope although she had books on astronomy." Diana looked across the pond. Dark thoughts about Ursula clouded her mind, but she shook them away. Silly to think the old woman could have committed a criminal act.

He flipped on the front lights, and they went inside. "If she has a telescope, she might have seen something the day Mrs. Feeney was murdered."

"She was sick that weekend. Besides, she couldn't have seen inside the house."

"True, but she might have seen someone come and go."

"She wouldn't lie."

"Wouldn't she?"

Diana shrugged. "True. I have no idea what she'd do."

He stood with his hand on the staircase's newel. "I making a casserole for dinner. There isn't much in the fridge or pantry. We'll have to shop tomorrow. I'll split the cost."

She smiled. "You do think of everything, don't you?"

"Try to."

Diana went to her room, tossed her cell phone on the bed and took a shower. The water soothed her body but her thoughts swirled between her family and the Feeney murder. It was easier to dwell on the murder. The housekeeper as a killer was an odd thought. A little like believing the butler did it. Marlene's husband was another matter. Did Bert's heavy drinking have any bearing on the case?

After toweling dry, she pulled her dark hair back, fastening it with a clip. As she dressed in slacks and a turtleneck, she smelled the aroma of frying onions and bacon. When she entered the kitchen, the oven was on and pans lay in the sink. "Smells wonderful."

He sat at the corner table reading what looked like files. "The casserole will be ready in about thirty minutes."

"The cupboard was bare. What did you find to cook?"

He looked up and grinned. "Bacon, onions, beans and rice, plus a few spices."

"Sounds interesting." She peered over his shoulder at the files. "More info on the case?"

He nodded and shoved some photos aside. "There are no clues or leads. I'm not surprised the police drew a blank."

She sat across from him and pulled a few of the photos toward her. They were shots of the living room, kitchen and mudroom. "Aren't the living room walls a different color now?"

"Yeah. Captain said Cora suggested they be painted."

"Why?"

"Probably to get the house ready to rent." He looked at the photos. "They look better now, don't they? Not so dark."

"Yes, but..." She took a photo, stood, walked through the swinging door into the living room with the sergeant at her heels. "Don't you see?"

"What?"

"What happened to the paintings?" She pointed to the photo and then the wall to the right of the fireplace. "There were two items hanging on the wall. See, the one in the photo looks like a painting of a landscape with a Victorian house. Where's the other one? The photo shows the distinct outline as if something had been hanging there for some time. The wall is lighter in an area the same size as that landscape painting." She felt the wall's surface. "There's been a patch job here where the landscape in the photo had hung." She moved to where the crime photo showed an outline of another picture. "There's a patch here as well."

He stood next to her. "The painting is probably stored and hasn't been rehung." He shrugged. "We don't know what was hanging in that other spot."

She waved the crime photo in the air. "Whatever was hanging on the wall was missing at the time the police found the body. The outline of the shape is the same size as the landscape. I'll lay odds it was another painting or something quite similar. It's been a year since the murder. Do you know when the walls were painted?"

"I'll have to ask Cora. The Schukarts became the caretakers, but she would have been involved with the redecorating. Maybe she forgot to have them rehung or thought they were too valuable to leave up during rentals."

"If that's true, where are they? Does she have them?" Diana felt like a dog gnawing a bone. "This could be important." She studied the photo. "The landscape in the photo looks like Ursula's work. She frames her work in silver painted frames. That's how that landscape is framed. Apparently Feeney had several of hers. Of course, I could be wrong about who painted it."

"Logical though." He looked over her shoulder. "Not sure Feeney would have bought art work. Doesn't seem to fit her profile." He paced the room. "I've been looking for a motive. Would a picture of Ursula's be worth killing for?"

"Have you heard about her disastrous show in New York?"

"I'll do an internet search and see what the paintings might be worth." He hesitated, then said, "Or you could ask Ursula."

Diana studied the living room's furnishings with a different perspective. All the walls were bare except for a clock and a framed map of Quamscutt. "Ursula said Feeney bought two of her landscapes a long time ago. Where are they? Was the one missing in the crime scene photo one of Ursula's? Was it removed before the murder or after?"

A buzzer sounded in the kitchen. "Casserole's ready. I'm really hungry. Let's search the house for the paintings after we eat."

He took out the casserole, while she tossed a small salad together. "I love salads," she said. "Not much in this one except a tomato and lettuce. Still it's better than nothing. There's a small amount of dressing left. She held it up. "French. Okay?"

He nodded and put the casserole on a trivet at the table. When they sat across from each other, he moved the files aside. They ate in silence until he said he'd found a place in Warwick that could cut a pane of glass to fit the broken window.

"Should we call Bert?"

"I can install it."

"You're handy to have around the house." She thought a moment. "Let's stop by Cora's office on the way to Wakefield. Even if she's not there, I can leave a note. Maybe that will get her attention. I need to speak with her about the rental agreement. It's odd she hasn't called."

"She might be worried you want your money back." He ate quickly, eagerly.

"It's not very professional of her to leave me dangling." She wiped her mouth with her napkin. "Do you think Cora would have information about the background of the paintings Ursula sold to Gloria?"

"Doubt it. Cora wasn't around then." He grinned. "I doubt the paintings were the talk of the town."

"You never know about what gossip or rumors have lingered."

"She'll probably have a simple explanation about where the paintings are." He looked at the remains of the casserole dish. "Would you like some more?"

"You finish it. It was good considering what you had to work with."

"I learned you can make a decent meal out of almost anything. Learned that from my stingy aunt." He scraped the dish, spooning it onto his plate.

"You didn't have it easy when you were young, did you?"

"It wasn't so bad. People take their families for granted. The Marines became my family. I lost buddies overseas. It does something to you." He pointed to his chest. "Inside. You don't want to get to know any new guys who come into your outfit. If you don't know them, you can't feel pain when they die. It never works out that way. You get close, because you depend on each other." He looked away and fiddled with his fork as if he'd said too much.

She understood the pain of loss, of separation. Isabel. Diana should write to her and tell her how proud she is of her bravery, her intellect, her beauty. Would her daughter read it after how Diana had acted? Why had she acted so aloof? Aloof, hell, she'd been downright mean to her daughter and just because her career choice wasn't the norm. Why had she followed her mother's example? Beatrice had never been a good role model.

And Jeffrey. Gay. God, why hadn't she picked up on that? He'd been an athlete, his high school's varsity baseball team captain. What kind of mother was she to be ignorant of her children's characters and actions? Jeffrey was intelligent, kind and loving. Did it matter that he was gay? She thought she was open-minded and accepted others, but when it was your own child, it was different. She'd blocked him out of her life. What a fool she'd been. Did it really matter? Why couldn't she accept his choice?

She glanced at the sergeant. "Sorry, I guess I wasn't paying attention."

"Or you were paying too much attention."

"Don't try to be my psychologist, Sergeant."

He pushed his empty plate aside. "Wouldn't dream of it."

She took her plate to the sink. "I'll clean up."

He crumpled up his paper napkin. "While you're doing that, I'll check the basement for paintings."

While she put the dirty dishes in the dishwasher, she heard noises from the basement. When he came back from his search, he said, "Nothing. I'll check the pantry and the mudroom closet." After a few moments he reappeared, shaking his head. "Let's try upstairs."

After a thorough search of the bedrooms, they walked up the narrow stairs to the attic. A lone bulb hanging from a frayed electrical cord cast a dim light. The dormer windows were covered with sheets and a heavy layer of dust covered the wood floor.

She peered into the dark attic from the doorway and pointed to a pile of rags. "Looks like no one's been up here in a long time. It's spooky."

He laughed. "That coming from a mystery writer."

She nudged him in the side with her elbow. "I write. I don't…" She sneezed.

"You want to go back down, while I poke around?"

"Thank you. I'll give you the honor of searching." She waited in the living room, hearing scrapes and thumps, then silence. What was he doing?

When she was about to go upstairs to see what was happening, he came down the stairs, his face grim, his eyes flinty. "You won't believe what I found."

"A nest of rats?"

"That would have been a better find."

She sighed and shook her head. "Come out with it. Don't keep the surprise all to yourself."

"Tucked in a corner of the attic. Remains of a baby in a small wooden box."

Chapter 7

Sergeant Morgan suggested they wait till morning to call the police. "The remains are mummified, must be years old. Another day won't make any difference." He sat on the couch, gazing into the fire he'd lit in the hearth. "The box was covered with dust. The police will bring in a forensic specialist and might ask us to leave the house. I don't want to do that tonight, do you?"

"No, of course not. Why would we have to leave? We've only been here a few days. It's not like it's mine or yours." She leaned back in her chair.

"You never know what the police will do." His fist rested against his jaw, then he put his hand on his knee. "There's something else we need to discuss. Why did we go into the attic? That will be a question we'll need to answer."

"We'll tell them the truth. We were searching for the missing paintings."

The firelight flicked across his face. "How did we know the paintings were missing?"

"Because of the crime scene photos...." She shook her head. "I see what you mean."

"They'd want to know why I have those photos, and why I'm interested in solving a murder that should be of no interest to me."

"They want to solve the murder, too."

"True, but do you really think anyone will confide in you or me if word gets out about why I'm here? They'll shun you, too."

"I don't like the idea of lying to the police."

"We won't lie. We tell them the truth. You're renting the house to have quiet time to write a book. I'm here on R&R out of the kindness of the new owner, Grant Cranston. We've called the rental agent about the mix-up, but she hasn't gotten back to us. We keep it simple." He paused. "We'll only lie about why we went up to the attic."

"So what reason do we give for going up there?"

He smiled. "A noise, a bang. After the storm we were concerned that a window might have been broken up there like the one in the living room."

"Makes sense." She settled back in her chair. "It's a small town. People will talk, especially since there's already been a murder committed here."

"The more people talk, the more we learn." He rose to stir the fire with a poker, then leaned against the mantel. "There's one problem I foresee. The press."

"I've thought about that, too. What can we do?"

"Nothing. Tell the truth and stick to it. Cover-ups lead to trouble."

After further discussion about who would make the call and when, he went upstairs, and she retired to her room. It was late, but she was sure her Paul would still be up on a Friday night. She sat on the edge of the bed, phoned him and waited for him to pick up. Instead, she got his voice message. Friday nights had been their date night. Where was he and with whom? She left a message. "Checking in to see how you are. I'm driving to Wakefield tomorrow to pick up a few things. Thinking of you and wanting to talk." She hesitated, then continued. "I left in a hurry. I'm sorry we didn't settle some things and talk about the children. Please call. Love you, Diana."

After getting ready for bed, she lay awake waiting for his call that never came. Could she blame him? It wasn't that they had anything to settle about their adult children. It was her attitude, her problem. She hadn't or couldn't come to terms with Isabel and Jeffrey's decisions about their lives. Her husband had accepted them. Diana and her mother, Beatrice, had fought the children's choices, denigrated them. Instead of trusting Isabel and Jeffrey to make their own way in the world, she had obsessed about what would become of them. Wouldn't any mother? Had she turned into her mother? Horrid thought.

The only request Paul had made before Diana left was that she tell Beatrice not to call or contact him. Beatrice accepted the arrangement and even appeared to be glad Diana was leaving town. "I'll tell my friends that you've gone to a writing symposium. That should cover any gossip," Beatrice had said. "When you return perhaps my grandchildren will have come to their senses."

Diana knew that was a pipe dream. Isabel was a Marine, serving in Afghanistan. Too late for that to change. Jeffrey was studying and living in Chicago with his partner. Nothing would change. Should she? Could she? She had to!

Eventually she fell into a fitful sleep.

In the morning she made the call to the authorities. Two officers responded and questioned them before Detective O'Reilly, blond, broad-shouldered and handsome with a toothpaste ad smile, arrived in an unmarked car. After introductions and more questions, the detective went up to the attic. Soon a coroner and a technician turned into the side driveway, making the area look like a parking lot.

Under the police directive, Diana and the sergeant waited outside on the porch. She clasped her arms in front of her. "It's overkill considering I'd reported skeletal remains and not a body. You'd think we'd found a massacre."

The sergeant leaned against the railing. "Now you know why I suggested we wait until morning to call."

"Should we call Cora? As the rental agent, wouldn't she have known what was in the attic?" She paced the length of the porch.

"Let's wait and hear what the detective has to say before we do anything."

Diana frowned and bit her lower lip. "Cora hasn't even responded to my earlier call. Not very professional. This rental is turning into a disaster." Lashing out at others wouldn't help, but she couldn't hold her tongue. "My husband suggested this town."

"I wondered how you came to this particular place."

"I don't mean it's his fault that I'm here. He got the recommendation from my daughter who knew about it from a friend."

"Oh. Now I understand." He walked to the end of the porch. "You're upset. I get it."

She babbled on. "I wanted to write a mystery set in Rhode Island. Each of my previous novels have had a different New England location. I certainly put my foot in the right or wrong place depending on your viewpoint." She walked down the length of the porch to stand next to him and gazed across the pond. "I bet Ursula can see the police cars and wonders what's going on over here."

"I'm sure everyone in town will hear soon enough. The police cordoned off the end of the street. That'll keep the media at bay for a while."

The front door opened and Detective O'Reilly came out. His slacks held traces of dust, and his tie was askew. "We're removing the box and the baby's remains. Glad you didn't move it after you found it." He looked at Diana. "How are you holding up?"

"Edgy, but okay. It's not as if this is a recent death, is it?"

"No. The body was mummified like Sergeant Morgan said, but I'm not sure how long it's been in the attic. The house was searched after the murder. My officer couldn't or shouldn't have missed the box."

"So someone could have put it there recently." Diana said.

"Hard to tell. We'll know more after the forensic team finishes. The lab tests on the box and the remains might give us a clue, too," the detective said.

"Will you talk to the officer who searched the attic?" the sergeant asked.

"I don't see the need. Angie Murphy retired from the police force last year." The toothpaste smile was replaced with tight lips.

Ignoring the detective's reaction, the sergeant pressed his point. "Since you're not sure when the remains were put there, shouldn't you question her."

"The police will handle this matter."

Diana stepped forward. "Since I signed the lease, I've learned there was a murder here a year ago and now there are remains of a baby. I wonder if I should stay."

"It might be best if you moved out," the detective said.

"Is that necessary?" the sergeant asked.

"No, but Mrs. Bellfore might be more comfortable." He put on the toothpaste smile.

"Cora Jacob is the rental agent. Shouldn't she be notified?" Diana asked.

O'Reilly nodded. "Her office said she's in Boston. I left a message on her cell for her to contact our department. She's supposed to be back on

Tuesday." He glanced from one to the other. "Since you seem intent on staying, don't cross or take down the police tape we've strung across the stairs to the attic."

The sergeant checked his watch. "If you don't need us for anything else, we'd like to pick up a new window pane in Wakefield before the stores close."

"We're finished for now. No need for you to hang around." The detective nodded to Diana. "I hope the rest of your stay in Quamscutt is quieter."

Diana sat on the porch rail. "There is one thing, detective. I've been told that Mrs. Feeney's murder has never been solved. Is that true?"

His smile disappeared and his eyes narrowed. "It's a cold case, but we never give up."

"Was there something special about Mrs. Feeney that would cause someone to murder her?" she asked.

Detective O'Riley frowned. "Why the interest?"

"The killer might come back for something he or she wasn't able to take earlier." That wasn't what she thought, but she wanted to know what information the police had.

His jaw tightened and his body stiffened as if he begrudged giving out the information. "According to those who knew the house and Mrs. Feeney, nothing was missing. Right now only a chair and an empty trunk are in the attic."

Diana put on her innocent face. "Could you be more specific about the Feeney case? Unlike the locals, I'm in the dark and would appreciate understanding some of the details. I don't want to say or do something I shouldn't."

The detective grimaced and looked from the sergeant to Diana. "According to her estate lawyer, no specific valuable items were listed in Mrs. Feeney's papers. After our investigation of her murder, the house was boarded up. When the estate was settled, the heir hired Bert and Marlene Schukart to be caretakers. I'll be talking to them about this recent find. Cora Jacob was hired to have the place fixed up so it could be rented. The new owner is in the military, stationed overseas." He tapped his notepad. "Mrs. Feeney's death occurred a year ago. If someone had wanted something, it's long gone. You're quite safe and we maintain regular patrols in the area."

"That's reassuring."

The sergeant stood at the front door and watched O'Reilly leave, then turned to Diana. "That went better than I expected. Let's hope the press doesn't show."

"I keep forgetting the vultures," she said.

"Never forget the media."

They gathered their things, locked the front door and went out through the mudroom to her sedan. On the drive to town, Diana's thoughts reeled through the morning events. *A mummified baby is a bizarre find. If I wrote something like that, the readers wouldn't believe it. That's the trouble with fiction. It has to be believable even though what happens in real life sometimes isn't.*

The sergeant turned to her. "I was afraid you'd give away the store when you asked the detective about Mrs. Feeney."

"I thought I was rather clever. When he said there was nothing valuable in the house, I immediately thought of the paintings. The police have no idea about them. Isn't that strange?"

"Yeah, I was thinking the same thing. I don't have a full police report though. They might have noticed the missing picture on the wall, but didn't give it much credence. I'm glad you weren't more specific."

"Cora is the one to ask." Diana passed a line of slow trucks. "If the baby's body has been up in the attic for decades, the police would have found it when they searched the house after the murder. If it was brought in afterward, who did it and why?" She glanced at him. "You were rude to O'Reilly when you questioned him about the officer who did the attic search."

"Wanted to see his reaction. I plan to find and talk to Officer Murphy. I also want the names of the other officers on-scene at the murder a year ago."

"I could ask Penelope Nelson."

"Be careful if you do. I don't want to arouse her suspicions."

"You're right. She's sharp." She turned off the highway and drove into the center of Wakefield. "I'd like to know more about Gloria Feeney, too."

"Is that necessary?"

"There's always a reason why people act the way they do. It might tell us who had a reason to kill her. Why was she so meddlesome and vindictive toward everyone? At least that's the impression I've gotten from talking to Ursula and Penelope." She sighed. "Who do you think is the mother of that baby?"

"That's the concern of the police, not mine. I'm interested in Mrs. Feeney's murder." He studied the street signs. "Turn left at the next street. The store's down the block."

After they bought the glass for the window and shopped for groceries, he asked Diana to drop him off at a used car lot. "I need my own transportation."

"Do you want me to wait?"

He grinned. "I'm a big boy, Mom."

She laughed. "Force of habit. Sorry."

"Don't wait up. I'll have dinner out." He closed the car door and walked away favoring his injured leg.

It was dark when Diana returned to the Victorian and opened the back door. The silence gave her pause. She hadn't thought about it before, but the sergeant's presence had been reassuring. She left the glass pane in the backseat, brought in the groceries and turned on the radio tucked away in a corner of the kitchen. It was almost six o'clock. She switched on the porch and living room lights, then lit the logs in the fireplace. With the house flooded with light, she returned to the kitchen and placed the kettle on for tea.

While waiting for the water to boil, she puttered in the kitchen and stopped when the local news announcer said, "The Feeney Victorian house on Potters Pond is again the site of a mystery. A year ago Gloria Feeney, age seventy-six, was murdered and the case was never solved. Yesterday the remains of a newborn were found by the renter, mystery writer Diana Bellfore of Pennsylvania."

Diana whirled around and glared at the radio. "Damn it."

The announcer continued, "According to police, the skeletal remains of the baby were taken to the state laboratory for testing. In other news—" Diana clicked off the radio.

When the doorbell rang and rang as if stuck, she went to the front of the house. Through the side window, she saw two men standing on the porch. One had a camera. Without opening the door, she called out, "Who is it?"

"We're from the South Kingston Weekly, ma'am. We'd like to talk to you about the recent finding of the dead baby."

"The police told me not to speak to the press until they've finished their investigation." A lie, but they didn't know that. "I will not open the door. Thank you. Goodbye." She switched off the porch lights. She heard them grouse and shuffle along the porch. Were they going around to the back door? Surely they wouldn't do that. She hurried to the back and slid the bolt into place.

The kettle whistled. She poured water over a jasmine flavored teabag in a large mug. The back door handle rattled. "How dare you," she screamed. "Go away."

"We just want a statement, Mrs. Bellfore."

"If you don't leave, I will call the police and make a formal complaint."

They swore, but minutes later they drove away. She took her tea into the living room, sank into the chair and watched the fire.

Her husband still hadn't phoned. Should she call him again? She'd left her purse in the kitchen, went to get it and took out her cell. Back in the living room, she held the phone in her lap. Why hadn't he called? Was he so angry with her that he'd found solace elsewhere? She thought about the eligible women he knew at the university. She had always been jealous of his popularity with women and felt insecure even though Paul had never strayed. Look, but don't touch is what she'd say to him, and he would laugh.

When her phone rang, it startled her. Finally. The number wasn't one she recognized. "Hello?"

"Diana, this is Penny Nelson. I got your number from Ursula. I hope I'm not disturbing you at this hour, but I just heard about the baby. I need to come over. Now, tonight. Please say it's okay. I must talk to you."

Chapter 8

Penny had sounded desperate, her words rushed, her voice strident. Although still apprehensive about the press returning, Diana turned on the porch lights again, kept watch out the back window and waited for a car to pull into the gravel driveway. Headlights streamed across the yard, a car stopped, and Penny emerged. She ran around the side of the house and up the front steps. Before she could knock, Diana opened the door.

Penny hurried inside. "Terribly sorry to bother you." Her words tumbled out. She wore a black jacket that came down to her hips, tight black leggings and high-heeled boots. She stared around the room, seemed to remember her manners and managed a half smile. "You must think I'm bonkers."

"Since I don't know what's bothering you, I don't know what to think." Diana motioned for the young woman to sit down. "Would you like some tea?" She hesitated, then added, "Or perhaps something stronger. I have a bottle of red wine open."

"Wine, thanks." Penny abruptly sank into the chair by the fire that Diana had occupied earlier.

"I'll just be a moment." Diana went to the kitchen and returned with two glasses and the bottle. After pouring the wine and handing a glass to Penny, she sat on the couch. There was an awkward silence while Diana waited for Penny to explain.

Penny clutched her wine glass and stared into the fireplace. "I never liked this house. It gave me the creeps. Still does." She looked at Diana. "How can you stand it?"

"I haven't found the house a problem, although the events that have happened in it are alarming."

"Yes, well, there is that, too."

"I gather you lived here when you were younger."

"Me? No. I visited, that's all." Penny downed her wine and glanced at the bottle. "May I have another?"

"Of course, help yourself."

"Thanks." She got up and filled her glass, took a sip, then paced the room, glass in hand. "Here's the thing. I'd like to go up in the attic and have a look around. I wouldn't ask, except it's very important to me."

"I can't let you do that."

"What? Why not? You're renting. It's no skin off your back."

Diana held up her hand and shook her head. "The police explicitly said no one should cross the yellow tape they strung across the stairs leading to the attic. You of all people should know to obey that directive."

"Oh, God." Penny slunk back to the chair. "Maybe I could take a peek. You know, without messing with the tape."

"Absolutely not. I'd be guilty of abetting you and I won't do that." She leaned forward. "Tell me what you're looking for and perhaps I can help."

Penny waved her hand as if shooing away a fly. Her thin shoulders slumped. "Had you been up in the attic before? I mean before you found the…baby?"

Diana was unsure how to answer. "No. I had no reason to go up there until I heard something banging and went to check. I didn't find anything else, if that's what you're asking." She studied Penny, trying to determine what she was after. "I gather your husband told you about our…my discovery."

"Charlie? God, no. He stays mum about police business. I heard it on the radio. Charlie doesn't know I've come here. Please, don't tell him." Penny studied her fingernails as if she didn't like the color of her crimson nail polish. "Who was the officer in charge?"

"Detective O'Reilly. Do you know him?"

Penny pursed her lips. "A little."

"Has he been on the force long?"

"About five years. He was here before Charlie was hired as Chief. He investigated Mrs. Feeney's murder. Not sure he's any good. All he did was accuse innocent people, making their lives miserable." Penny sprang to her feet and set her half-full glass on the side table. "I've got to leave. Thanks for letting me come over."

"I'm sorry I couldn't help you." Diana stood. "I wish you'd tell me what you're looking for." She put forth her best motherly voice. "What's bothering you?"

"I had an idea that Mrs. Feeney found out about my past through letters I'd written. I don't need more rumors spread about me. Poor Charlie. It's strained our marriage. I'd do anything for him." Penny opened the front door, letting in the cold night air.

"If it's any consolation, if I find something pertaining to you, I'll give it to you. No questions asked." A sympathetic smile played on her lips. "Does that help?"

"Yes, thanks."

Diana closed the door, leaned against it and listened for Penny's car to leave. What could Penny have written and why would Mrs. Feeney have her letters? Her stomach growled, and she went to the kitchen to find something to nibble on. A car came into the driveway again; its headlights swept across the window. Had Penny forgotten something? She closed the fridge door. If it was those reporters again, she'd call the police. The back door rattled.

Her voice wavered. "Who is it?"

"John Morgan. You've thrown the bolt."

She hurried to the door and slid back the bolt. "I thought you had a key."

"I do, but it doesn't work when the bolt's thrown. Why the extra safety?" He entered with a small suitcase in his hand.

"A reporter and a photographer came earlier and tried to get in." She followed him into the living room. "They'll probably come back tomorrow."

He put his suitcase down at the bottom of the staircase and studied the room. "You had a visitor."

She raised an eyebrow. "You are observant. Penny Nelson came by. She was very upset and wanted to look in the attic. I refused her request."

"Did she say why?"

"Something about letters that Mrs. Feeney may have had that would cause trouble for her."

"Interesting."

She nodded to the suitcase. "You went shopping."

"Needed more civilian clothes." He picked up his suitcase, stopped and asked, "Did you tell Penny I was living here?"

"Of course not, but she'll learn that eventually."

"Yeah." He went on upstairs.

Diana took Penny's glass to the kitchen. It was late and she decided to have crackers and cheese. While she was cutting the cheese, the sergeant came in, walked to the breakfast nook and tossed a small bundle tied with twine onto the table.

"This may be what Penny was after."

With her plate in one hand, Diana walked over to look at the packet. The top letter was addressed to Grant Cranston with a return address of Penny Tanner, 172 Baker St. Providence, RI. "Have you read them?"

"Nope and I don't intend to. You can give them to her."

"Why didn't you say something about these earlier?"

He shrugged. "It was between the captain and her."

"Odd, that after all these years you found them. Where were they?"

"In the trunk, not where I found the box with the baby."

She fingered the twine and studied the postmark. "Sixteen years ago. Could these have any bearing on Mrs. Feeney's murder or the identity of the baby?"

He stared out the window. "I'm not going to muck around in the captain's past."

"What if they have some bearing on the present? Penny's about your age. She would have been a teenager then and old enough to have had a baby."

His jaw tightened, and he glared at her. "You want to give these to the police? Stir up trouble between Penny and her husband? Accuse her of something that might not be true?"

"Absolutely not. Besides, I told Penny I'd give her anything pertaining to her." She took a bite of cracker. "I'm surprised the police didn't find them in the search after Feeney's murder. Detective O'Reilly's toothpaste smile gave me the impression he wasn't truthful about what they found in this house."

He laughed. "White teeth gave you that clue?"

"It's the way he smiled. Off and on like a switch." She glanced at the packet of letters. "She'll think it odd that I have the letters when I said I didn't."

He shrugged. "You found them in a drawer."

Diana picked up a piece of cheese. "You're very good at making up stories."

As he left the kitchen, he said over his shoulder, "Only when it helps the innocent and convicts the guilty." As he left, the kitchen door swung back and forth on its hinges.

Diana bit into a chunk of Gouda and chewed. She took her plate of cheese and crackers into the living room, sat and sipped her wine. Although Rhode Island wasn't the safe harbor she'd anticipated, she was intrigued with the people she'd met and the mysteries surrounding them. Ursula was the most eccentric and interesting of all of them. She had accepted Diana's invitation to Sunday brunch at the old inn on Route One.

She went to the desk, set her wine glass aside and turned on her laptop. With the password to access the internet, she checked her email. She sighed and leaned back. Her shoulders drooped. Nothing from Paul or any of her friends. Had she been excommunicated from all invitations in Philadelphia? What had she expected? Her mother had warned her. Her so-called friends were acting as if she had a social disease. To them perhaps having a gay son and a daughter in the Marines might be just that. She took another sip of wine. Where was Paul? Should she call him again? No. One message was enough.

Putting aside her hurt feelings, she turned her internet search to Gloria Feeney. In the archives of the local newspaper site she found an old article.

The body of Gloria Feeney, age 76, was found by Marlene Schukart when she went to clean the woman's home located on Potters Pond. The police believe Gloria Feeney was murdered several days before the gruesome discovery. Mrs. Feeney had no children. Thirty-one years ago she and Henry (Hetch) Feeney, owner of Hetch Electrical Company, divorced. The investigation is led by Detective Joe O'Reilly, formerly with the Providence Police Department.

She thought for a moment and then searched for information about Henry Feeney. He was owner of Hetch Electrical Company of Wakefield, Rhode Island, now living in a nursing home in Pawtucket. The sergeant might not be interested in Gloria's past, but she was. The more you knew about your characters' past, the clearer their lives and the lives of those around them became.

Perhaps her mystery writer's perspective would pay off.

Chapter 9

Thursday Marlene called to say she was unable to come, but would be there the following Thursday. The days rolled by with the sergeant and Diana holding to their separate routines. He ran every morning, while she took long walks. Both in their own troubled worlds.

On Sunday morning Diana woke to the familiar aroma of brewing coffee. She checked her clock—6:30—and groaned. The sergeant's early hours bedeviled her. The first rays of the autumn sun crept through the foliage and shone through her window. After showering, she dressed in a cotton skirt that swirled around her ankles, a cream-colored blouse and a navy blue cardigan. While brushing her hair, she noticed new streaks of gray intertwined with the black ones.

Perhaps the gray had been there earlier, but she'd ignored it. Now her age ate at her. Was Paul seeking younger women? Damn. She had to stop envisioning things that might not be true. But the little green devil on her shoulder whispered—what if they are true? She slammed down the brush and went to the kitchen.

The sergeant sat at the table eating scrambled eggs and toast. "You're dressed up. Off to church?"

"I'm taking Ursula to brunch." She poured a cup of coffee.

"Good idea." He took a bite of toast.

She sat across from him. "I'm doing all the work to learn who might have killed Mrs. Feeney. What are you doing or do you have a Tom Sawyer complex?"

He grinned. "You're good with words. I'll have to read one of your books. Do you have one with you?"

"A few in my car. I was told to always have them handy. I'll bring one in later."

After a gulp of coffee, he wiped his mouth with his paper napkin. "Last night I was at a local bar and met Bert, Marlene's husband, the caretaker. I showed him a letter from the captain that instructed me to have Bert help me with repairs."

"You had such a letter?"

"Of course not, but he didn't know it wasn't real. He'll be here early Monday morning."

"Did he say anything interesting that might give you a clue about the murder?"

He shook his head. "Too blurred with booze. I warned him to show up sober or the captain might stop paying him to be caretaker."

"That got his attention?"

"Oh yeah, he understood me. I told him if he wasn't sober I'd have a talk with Marlene." He took a bite of his eggs, then added, "His reaction to my mentioning his wife was interesting. He started to stammer and shake. And it wasn't DTs."

"He wouldn't be the first husband to be afraid of his wife."

"Are you speaking from experience?"

Her eyes narrowed, her lips tightened. "You're out of line, sergeant. I resent your innuendo. Paul and I do not have that kind of a marriage. I told you to keep out of my private life." She stood, grabbed her coffee cup and stormed through the swinging door.

"Sorry," he called after her.

Out on the porch Diana paced, anger exuding from every pore. Her marriage was no one's business. She banged her fist against the rail. Why hadn't Paul called her back? Was he so angry with her that he no longer would take her phone calls? She'd left in a hurry with their relationship in turmoil. After taking a deep breath, she made a deliberate thought shift to Mrs. Feeney's murder. Nothing like a mystery to keep you sane.

The sergeant came outside. "Look, I'm a brat, a bastard. I apologize. Your life is your affair. I have no right to make judgments or make unkind remarks." He ran his hand over his chin's day old stubble. "In my defense, I can only say that my past relationships with most women have been stunted." He stopped and smiled. "But I met a great gal, so I'm changing, slowly. Still, I'm not good at tact. A shortcoming the Marines couldn't change. It isn't right to take out my anger at the world on you."

She stared at him, her anger ebbing. "That's quite a confession."

"Yeah, well, I don't often explain my life to others."

"Most of us don't or at least don't want to. We'll call a truce." She held out her hand.

He clasped it in both of his, then moved to the steps. "I thought I'd take a run on the beach."

He was wearing shorts and a gray sweatshirt. She glanced at the puckered red scar that ran the length of his leg.

He caught her look. "It's ugly, isn't it?" He fingered the edge of the scar below his shorts. "It's healing."

"How were you injured?"

"Mortar fragments." He must have seen her grimace. "Don't start thinking about your daughter."

"I wasn't. I.... How can you be so perceptive?"

He tilted his head. "I invaded your privacy, remember. Your laptop. I know Isabel's a translator in Afghanistan. Her unit will protect her. We had a woman translator assigned to us. She was fantastic. Brave. Carried her share of the load. Never asked for special favors. Most of the guys would have died for her."

"You said was."

His face went blank. "Talking about my past, not hers." He hurried down the steps and jogged down the path toward the beach, his injury affecting his stride.

She watched until he disappeared. Something inside her caved, and she leaned against the porch rail. With deliberate steps, she went inside to write a long overdue letter to her daughter.

At the desk she pulled out a sheet of stationery from her briefcase.

Dear Isabel,

I'm writing to you with a heartfelt apology for my inability to accept your career choice of joining the Marines. It was my fear for your safety that prompted my inexcusable behavior and words. I am ashamed that I didn't attend your graduation ceremony from officer training school. I'm very proud of you, and your bravery astounds me. Your father understood the choices you've made. I'm grateful that the two of you remain close.

All I want is for you to be happy and fulfill your dreams, not mine or your grandmother's. Of course, you were right in that, too. I never could stand up to her.

I've gone on a sort of vacation and am seeing things more clearly. I'm writing this from a house in Quamscutt, Rhode Island, close to the ocean. Your father said you'd suggested this area. The rental is a dreadful looking Victorian with plenty of ghosts. Perfect for my stories. A young sergeant, wounded in Afghanistan, is also staying here. Although he's often rude and intrusive, I'm learning from him that military personnel work as a team and look out for one another.

Please know how much I regret my behavior. Forgive me if you can. I hope to hear from you soon. Keep safe.

Love, Mom

After mailing the letter, Diana picked up Ursula and drove to the quaint inn's restaurant. From their table by large windows, they enjoyed the view of pines and the autumn colorful foliage. The sun shone through the branches dappling the greenery in shadows. An oriole gorged itself at a bird feeder, while a squirrel chattered nearby.

Ursula took another sip of her mimosa. "Thank you for this invitation. I haven't dined out in a while. I always liked coming here. This old building has a lovely New England charm, although some floorboards creak and one or two doors stick. In New York my partner Evelyn and I ate out almost all the time. We had so many friends and knew many fellow artists." Her smile deepened her facial wrinkles, and her dark red lipstick ran into the lines around her lips.

Had Diana heard correctly? She hesitated, but recovered quickly. "What made you move back? I mean besides the critics' reviews of your last exhibit."

Ursula held the stem of her glass, her hand poised in midair. "You're both kind and naive. I caught your expression when I mentioned my partner. I thought you knew. Everyone else does." She frowned. "Maybe I'm just used to being accepted in New York."

Unsure what to say, Diana waited.

Ursula sighed, then said, "Evelyn died of cancer five years ago. We had many happy years together. After she died my paintings changed. The critics expected the same old style. I couldn't do it anymore. Instead, I threw my emotions on canvas, lashing out with anger and frustration. After the exhibit and the harsh criticism, my rage at the world waned. I realized the remaining days of my life should be spent in Quamscutt where I'd lived when I first came to this country so many years ago." She finished her drink and set it on the table.

"Would you like another?" Diana asked.

"No thank you. One at my age is enough to loosen my tongue." Her face took on a shrewd expression. "Now tell me, why did you invite me to brunch?"

Ursula's abrupt question caught Diana off guard. Thankfully, the waitress appeared with their food, giving her time to think. "Your Eggs Benedict look good," Diana said.

"I considered the quiche you ordered." Ursula tasted her food. "This is very good."

"Do you know where the name Quamscutt came from?" Diana ran her finger down the side of her sweating water glass.

Ursula put down her fork. "The Narragansett Indians lived on these lands long before the English settlers came, and they sold it to four wealthy Englishmen around the mid-sixteen hundreds. That deal was known as The Pettaquamscutt Purchase. Our small seaside town took the name and shortened it." She hesitated, tilted her head and winked. "Now what do you want to know about? Gloria Feeney, her house? Me?"

"You are direct." Diana clasped her hands together at the edge of the table. "I gather you heard about the baby's remains found in the attic."

"The entire town knows."

"Penny came by the other night after hearing about it on the radio. What can you tell me about her?"

"Dear Penny is a lost soul. She's adopted me as the grandmother she never had. It's a role I don't mind and enjoy her company, but sometimes she becomes obsessive about me, my paintings, my problems. It's not mentally healthy for her, but what can I do? Things that I believe should be ignored, she wants to take on as a crusade."

"Like what?"

"The house you're renting for one. She's rather morbid about it. And my paintings for another. She's believes my work should be treasured by everyone." She took another bite, eating European style with fork in one hand and knife in the other, relinquishing neither. "Penny grew up in Providence, led a rebellious life, did drugs, straightened herself out and went to college. Her father raised her after her mother died. A decent man, according to Penny."

"What did she do after graduation?"

"She became an accountant and works freelance for private individuals. That's how I met her. I needed someone to help with my accounts and taxes. Evelyn had always done that. After she died, things became a mess. Penny is an organizing wonder."

"Glad to hear it." Although her food was excellent, Diana wasn't concentrating on her quiche as much as she was on Ursula. "Did you know Gloria when you lived here before?"

"Yes, but we weren't friends. She was more of an acquaintance I'd meet now and then. A simple person, reasonably pleasant, went to church, socialized. Her husband was a big, tall man, very sure of himself. Started as an electrician and eventually opened his own business. Self-made man as they say. I was in New York at the time, but I heard she became pregnant, but the child died. Rumor had it that the baby was so deformed its death was a blessing. Years later, when she and Hetch were both in their late forties, I heard they divorced. When I returned to Quamscutt, she had become a recluse—spiteful and vindictive."

"Sad." That's all Diana could think to say, and they ate in silence for several minutes.

An elderly well-dressed couple came by their table. "Good to see you, Ursula," the man murmured. The woman turned to Diana. "You're the mystery writer renting the Feeney house, aren't you?"

Diana smiled. "Word gets around."

"It's a small town." She gave a toothy smile. "I'm Corrine O'Reilly, and this is my husband, Peter."

"Nice to meet you," Diana said. "Are you related to Detective Joe O'Reilly?" They had to be, given their fair looks.

"His parents," Corrine said proudly. "I hope the ah…findings in the house haven't upset you."

"It's been a bit disconcerting, but I'm managing."

"Good for you," Peter said and gave his wife a nudge in the back. "Table's over there, dear." He nodded to Ursula. "See you at the Brecks next Saturday."

The couple moved off to be seated on the far side of the room. Ursula let out a soft sigh. "That's the problem with going out. You bump into people."

Diana laughed. "True. Sometimes that's fun."

Ursula cleared her throat. "Used to like it. Not anymore."

"Who are the Brecks?"

"Hoity-toity, art lovers and big spenders. They're having a show of my work at their house in Newport."

"That's fantastic."

"I guess."

"You aren't thrilled?"

"God help me, yes. You know what it's like loving your children. My paintings are like children to me. Putting them on display is both wonderful and frightening. You have to have ego and courage." She finished her meal and gave her plate a slight push to the side.

Diana took the last bite of quiche. "You told me that Gloria owned two of your oils. I haven't seen them in the house. Do you have them?"

Ursula's eyes narrowed. "Why would I have them? Of course, if the witch needed money, I would have bought them back." She shook her head. "I have no idea what became of them."

Their conversation dwindled after that and nothing more was said about the Feeney's or Penny. They finished their meal and drove in light traffic along Route One with its riot of autumn colors. Diana's dark glasses enhanced the reds and yellows. She loved the northeast's change of seasons despite the bitter Philadelphia winters. Her thoughts roamed to her house in the suburbs of Philadelphia. The garden probably needed tending even though she'd given the gardener specific instructions before she left. Paul never bothered with the flower bed or the vegetable plot. That was her domain. Even barbecuing was not something he did, although he enjoyed going to their friends' cookouts.

Diana stopped in front of Ursula's Cape Cod. Before getting out of the car, Ursula turned to Diana. "Thank you for the brunch and the conversation. Why don't you come to the Brecks as my guest? Of course people might think you're my new partner. Would you mind that?"

Diana's mouth must have gaped because Ursula laughed. "I'm joking, Diana. Anyone can tell you're heterosexual. I've even wondered if that young man staying with you is not what he pretends. Your lover, perhaps?"

Ursula was out of the car and walking to the red door of her house before Diana could respond.

Chapter 10

Monday night Diana awoke with a start to the music of Greensleeves coming from her cell phone. She fumbled in the dark, switched on the bedside lamp and grabbed her phone. Paul.

"You sounded worried when you left your message," he said. "Hope it's not too late to call."

She looked at the clock, a few minutes before midnight. "It's late, but I've been waiting for your call. Where have you been?"

His clear, sonorous laugh echoed over the phone. "I can't believe you forgot. It was my men-only weekend."

"Oh, my gosh. I'm sorry I bothered you."

"Well, you couldn't really bother me since we don't take phones with us. You sounded worried, upset. Is everything all right?"

She hitched herself upright against the headboard. "I left with so much unsaid between us. It wasn't right. I miss you."

"Okay." His voice was hesitant. "How's the rental? Is it what you wanted?"

She laughed. "Not exactly. It's an old Victorian on a pond near the ocean with historical mysteries." She smiled at her understatement.

"Sounds like it's right up your alley."

"In a way. I've been talking to a young man, a wounded sergeant, who's returned from Afghanistan. He knows about Isabel's assignment. He's very outspoken. We argued."

"So you've met your match?"

Perhaps she deserved that dig. "Paul, I've had time to think. I...I wrote Isabel, apologizing for my behavior. Will she ever forgive me?"

"I'm glad you wrote her. Sounds like your time away has been good for you."

"Have you heard from her recently?"

"Yes." The warmth of his voice eased her worry. "The men in her outfit call her Izzy."

"That is an awful name."

"You sound like Beatrice."

He was right. Would she ever get over acting and talking like her mother? Bad habits are hard to break. "They must like her if they've given her a nickname, right?"

"Oh, yeah. She says the camaraderie makes life bearable. It's hot, sandy and scary. They were caught in the middle of a battle." There was a silence. "They lost a few soldiers. Your letter will help her."

Diana closed her eyes, her heart thudded. "You said, 'she says.' Does that mean you talked to her?"

"You haven't lost your acute listening skills. I talked to her the week you left. I didn't call you since I know how worried you've been and didn't want to upset you. Their unit was sent back to a safe zone."

"Was Isabel injured?"

"Nothing serious."

"What does that mean?" She scrunched the sheet in her fist.

"Shot in the shoulder, but released back to active duty yesterday."

Diana squeezed her eyes shut, trying to blot out the picture of an injured Isabel.

"I debated whether to call you right away, but then I left town. It's better you know what she's going through. I know you worry, and so do I, but they take precautions to keep as safe as they can."

"I'm scared out of mind for her. I know it's her choice, her life, and I shouldn't have been so...so willfully negative."

"Isabel will be pleased to get your letter. Have you made any other decisions?"

He was talking about Jeffrey. The slow disintegration of her relationship with her son hadn't healed. Her lack of a response must have told Paul what he didn't want to hear.

"Diana, I just got back and have to unpack and be ready to lecture in the morning. Why I ever accepted an eight o'clock slot, I'll never know."

"You like getting up early."

"Maybe I'm getting old."

"Paul, never you." She hesitated, then added, "I love you."

"It's been a while since you've said that. We both need to say it more often. Take care, Diana. Let's talk next week. Sunday afternoon, okay? Bye."

"Talk to you then. Bye, love." She clicked off and mulled over the conversation. How could she have forgotten his "men-only" weekend? Paul and five of his friends went off three times a year, leaving all communication devices behind. No wonder he hadn't told her earlier about Isabel being wounded. "Oh, God, please keep her safe," she murmured to the quiet room. She turned off the light and thrashed about most of the night.

In the morning the now familiar aroma of coffee filled the air. When she went into the kitchen, she saw the sergeant outside in the backyard poking around in the shed. She turned on the radio, hoping the local news was about something other than the recent events at the Feeney house. Instead of news, rap music blared. She turned the radio off.

She stepped out the back door holding her coffee mug. A slight breeze chilled the air, and she pulled her cardigan tighter about her. Scattered clouds skittered across the sky, but the sun stretched across the small lumpy grass lawn by the shed.

The sergeant waved and walked toward her. "Good morning. You slept in."

Diana glanced at her watch. "I wouldn't call seven-thirty sleeping in."

He smiled and shrugged. "I'm going to attack the shed today. Clean it out, see what's worth saving. It's a mess. I don't think anyone's been in it for years."

"Bert should have done that."

He grinned. "I don't think Bert has done much of anything."

"Perhaps you should let the captain know what a deadbeat caretaker he has."

"In due time. For now I want Bert here so I can pump him for information."

Diana nodded and looked at the driveway where he'd parked his used pickup truck off to the side to allow her car an easy exit. She pointed to the silver Ford Ranger vintage '90s truck with a few dents. "Did you get a good deal?"

"Not bad. Only 94,000 miles but has new tires. It'll do great till I leave the first of the year." He nodded back to the shed. "I can haul stuff to the dump with it."

"Are you sure you should do that? What will the captain think when he returns and finds something he wanted has been taken away?"

"I'm only getting rid of junk, not anything worthwhile. Besides, he gave me the authority to fix up the place." He squinted at the house. "I'm going to power wash the entire outside, sand and repaint."

She, too, studied the house. "Hope you choose a lighter color than black."

"You bet I will. Perhaps you can help with the choice."

"I'd be glad to. What will Cora have to say about your plans for the house?"

"She has no say. I have the captain's authorization. I'm more interested in what she knew about the item in the attic."

"We won't know till tomorrow." The morning cold seeped into her bones, so she went back inside. At nine o'clock she called the retirement home in Pawtucket where Hetch Feeney lived.

When the switchboard operator put her through to him, she said, "Mr. Feeney. This is Diana Bellfore—"

"Oh, yeah, the mystery writer. Heard all about the hoopla at Gloria's house. You gonna write a book?" He coughed. "Hey, I don't care what you write."

"I'm not planning to write a book about that, but I would like to talk to you. Are you free today?"

"Hell, I'm free everyday. Need a break from the monotony. Come on out."

"This morning then, about ten-thirty?"

"Good." He hung up.

She stared at her cell. That was easy. The abruptness of the New Englanders she'd met continued to surprise her. Ursula, Penny, and now Hetch.

At ten she backed out of the driveway and almost rammed into a van coming in. The man pulled over, and when she drove past, he nodded to her with a dour expression. It had to be Bert. Although tempted to stop and introduce herself, she continued on her way. There'd be plenty of time to meet him later.

The retirement home was a converted old estate set back from the road. A covered walkway connected the wood-shingled manor to a new red brick building. She parked in the lot reserved for guests and made her way to the entrance. The doors opened automatically, and she walked to the reception desk.

"I'm here to see Henry Feeney," she said to the chubby woman behind the counter.

"You mean Hetch." The woman gave her a broad smile. "He doesn't get many visitors. Are you related?"

"No, I'm from out of town. What room is he in?"

"It's in the annex, one three three. Sign in here and sign out when you leave." She pushed a ledger forward and gave Diana directions. "Enjoy your visit."

Diana went through the lobby and past several doors marked: Reserved. There were signs for Art Class, Music, Dance. She nodded to elderly men and women using walkers while others dozed in chairs. Not the way Diana wanted to end her life, but then none of these people had wanted this end either.

The new annex smelled fresher, and the air wasn't as stifling. She stopped at room 133 and knocked.

"Door's open," came the voice she'd heard on the phone.

She entered a living room with a small kitchen nook. Hetch Feeney sat in a wheelchair, his legs covered with a throw blanket. He had a thick head of white hair, broad shoulders and a barrel chest.

"The mystery writer," he announced in a booming voice. "Glad you came, Mrs. Bellfore. Heard you were renting Gloria's house. How's it going?" He gave her a hearty handshake.

"Please call me Diana."

"Fine. I'm Hetch." He nodded to a small patio visible through a wide doorway. "Let's go outside." He wheeled outside and she followed. "That chair over there is comfortable, or so I'm told. I'm stuck in this thing." He pounded the arms of his wheelchair.

"You seem quite fit. Do you mind if I ask what happened?"

"Crane fell on me. Happened about four years ago. Crushed my legs. I can stand, but it hurts like hell. I lost the use of my legs, my wife Lilly died, and my son took over my company at a young age. Never thought he'd be able to handle it, but he did."

"You've had a difficult time. I'm sorry."

"Yeah. Hell of a future, huh?"

"I didn't realize you'd remarried."

"When I divorced Gloria, I was fifty, she was forty-four. I met a younger gal. Lilly and I had a son, Sam. Lilly died a year after my accident."

"Gloria got the Victorian in the divorce?"

"Yeah. I wasn't angry at her…well, maybe a little. She blamed me for our baby daughter's deformity." He stared at Diana. "Don't act like you didn't know about that. Figured you'd done research before coming here. Wouldn't be much of a writer if you hadn't."

"It's sad when something terrible happens to your child."

"You got children?"

"A girl and a boy."

"Then you know how parents feel. It was real rough. Gloria never got over it. We stopped talking to one another. I couldn't stand the quiet. She must have known I was going to leave her, cuz she got real sexy, we reconnected, and I had second thoughts about a divorce. Then like a hot and cold spigot, she turned to ice, so I packed up and left."

"Was Gloria jealous that you had a healthy baby with Lilly?"

He shrugged. "Lilly wanted a child, so I took the chance that our child would be okay. He's almost thirty now, a big strong fella, smart enough to keep the business on an even keel even during bad times. Wish he'd come visit more often. It gets damn lonely. I get updates on the business via the computer, but hell, I'd sure like to be there."

"This might sound like an odd question, but what did you do with your baby's body?"

He leaned back, his eyes narrowed. "I know what you're thinking. That skeleton sure isn't Gloria's and mine. Let me tell you, we gave the baby a decent burial at Saint John's, and she's still there unless some weirdo dug her up. Gloria visited the grave every week. I couldn't stand it. Tore me apart to see her mourning forever and not put it behind her, but there wasn't anything I could do or say to help."

"People say Gloria changed."

"Yeah, she did. About a year after our divorce, I saw Gloria. She was real thin, and there was something eating at her, making her say awful things about everyone and acting mean." He shrugged. "I turned away and left it all behind. Nothing else I could do."

"Did Gloria ever see a doctor to deal with her loss?"

"Wouldn't go. God knows, I tried to make her."

"Was she heavy at one time?"

He chortled. "Nope. She took care of herself. Proud to be average height and small boned. She did gain weight while we were getting the divorce, wore big blouses that hung down to her thighs. Never saw her dress so awful. Stress does strange things to people's appetite. But, as I said, she looked thin a year later."

Diana decided there wasn't much else she could learn, but didn't want to leave abruptly. "How are you faring?"

"Can't complain. I'm eighty-two. I sure would like a dog though. They let you have 'em here if they aren't too big. Sam, he's my son, doesn't think it's a good idea."

"You're the one who wants the dog, not Sam."

He grinned and his gray eyes sparked. "You got that right, but how do I go about getting one when the only time I get out of this cage is when Sam takes me out to dinner once a month?"

"Can't this place provide you with transportation?"

"They'll take you, and drop you off someplace to shop, go to the doctor, things like that, but getting a dog might be a push for them. I know for certain Sam's put the bug in their ear not to help me get a pet. I could handle the financial aspect. You gotta pay extra if you have a dog, cuz of the cleaning."

"Would you be able to take care of a dog? I mean, walk it and pick up after it?"

"Sure. It's Sam who's making it impossible. He hates dogs. Claims he's allergic and couldn't visit me anymore. Course that's a crock. The truth is Sam is scared to death of dogs. Got bit when he was about three and never got over it. When Sam doesn't get his way, his fearful temper erupts. I hate to rile him."

"What kind of dog do you want?"

He thumped his palms on the arms of his wheelchair. "You're thinking of helping me, aren't you?"

The idea hadn't completely taken form, but she thought everyone needed a companion. Her mother would never allow her to have a dog and when she and Paul had gotten a puppy for the children, her mother had been furious. Sam sounded like the same controlling type of person as

Beatrice. The puppy incident had been one of the few times Diana had rebelled against her mother. "The thought has occurred to me." She grinned.

"You're an angel." He lowered his booming voice. "It can't be a puppy and it can't be too big or scared of things or people. I'd have to take it to the vet now and then." He hesitated. "I could manage that."

"You've thought it through, haven't you?"

"Think about it all the time." He rolled back into the living room, and she went with him. He held out a paper to her. "Take a look at that ad. What do you think?"

Need a good home for our four-year-old cocker spaniel, Shelly. Our family is moving out of the country, and we can't take her with us. She's had all her shots, and the veterinarian will vouch for her temperament.

The address was in Wakefield not far away. The ad was a week old.

Diana was not one to do impulsive things but something goaded her. "Call them. See if the dog's still available. If it is, I'll drive you."

His mouth fell open, then he grabbed the phone.

Chapter 11

During the drive home, Diana felt a warm glow, something she hadn't experienced in a long while. Hetch had his dog companion, and the family had found a good home for their pet. It had taken a few hours for the family to warm to Hetch as the possible owner of their beloved spaniel, Shelly. When the dog jumped onto Hetch's lap, the situation was resolved. Afterward Diana had delivered Shelly, with all her doggy necessities, and Hetch back to his apartment at the retirement home and promised she'd visit them soon.

It was after four o'clock when she pulled into her driveway. Since the van blocked her way, she parked on the grass. Bert and the sergeant stood by the Ford pickup loaded with junk.

Stepping out of her car, Diana approached to view the stuff to be hauled away.

"Looks like you've been busy. Hard to believe there was that much in the shed."

"Bert, this is Mrs. Bellfore," the sergeant said.

Bert wiped his hand on his jeans and shook her hand. "Please to meet you."

"I'm looking forward to meeting your wife on Thursday." Diana had expected Bert to be a burly sort, but he was reed thin, tall with a horselike face and a prominent red-veined nose that told of heavy drinking. At the moment he was sober.

"I'm sorry my wife couldn't come the other day. I always drive her, but she didn't feel up to it."

"I understood. The news of the baby's remains was upsetting for everyone."

The sergeant stepped forward. "We're attacking the attic tomorrow, then when Marlene comes, she can clean it. Right, Bert?"

"Yes, sir. She'll come. I'll be here at ten tomorrow."

"Wait a minute." Diana frowned. "What about the police tape? You can't cross it."

The sergeant picked up a box and put it in the back of his truck. "Detective O'Reilly came by, searched the attic again, then took down the tape."

"He and his men were here a long time, Mrs. Bellfore." Bert looked down at the ground.

"Bert did a good job today." The sergeant put his hand on the man's shoulder. "The police didn't bother us." He smiled at the older man. "I'll see you tomorrow. Remember my rules."

"Yes, sir." Bert nodded to Diana and walked to his van.

"You seem to have him under your thumb." She watched Bert back out of the driveway.

"He's been a lamb. Didn't want to go into the shed at first, so I tossed things out to him. After a while he got into the swing of things. Come take a look. I'm interested in what you think about something I found."

The shed was bigger than it appeared from the outside. They had not only cleared out debris, but wiped down all the surfaces, hung tools and stacked garden items in a corner. There wasn't a cobweb in sight.

"Take a look at this." The sergeant picked up a silver painted picture frame. "Remind you of anything?"

"Ursula's paintings have the same colored frames." She fingered the wood and the back. "Shreds of a canvas?" She shot a questioning look at the sergeant.

"That's my guess. If we had access to a lab, we could determine the type of paint, even the type of canvas and how long it's been here." He shrugged. "But we don't have a lab. Giving it to the police at this point isn't a good idea. I'd have too much explaining to do."

"I could ask Ursula, but I'd like to find out more before I do. I wouldn't want to upset her. What about talking to the art department at the local university?"

He grinned. "You're sharp, Mrs. Bellfore."

"Glad you finally realize that."

They both laughed.

Once out of the shed, the sergeant pointed to the grass. "Some of the topsoil washed away in the last storm. I mentioned to Bert that more needed to be added and he clammed up. I kept at him. He told me that new topsoil had been ordered from Cramer's Compost Company last year. He couldn't remember if it had been delivered before or after Mrs. Feeney's murder. He was lying. Not sure why. I'll check with the company."

"It's strange he'd lie about something so mundane."

"Exactly."

As they walked toward the back door, she asked, "Find out anything else?"

"He and Marlene were questioned by O'Reilly and Officer Murphy."

"You're going to talk to Murphy, aren't you?"

"If I can find her." He held up his hand. "I'll be discrete."

She shook her head. "I hope so or you could cause unnecessary trouble." She went into the kitchen and left him while he removed his boots in the mudroom.

Later he walked into the kitchen in his stocking feet. "I'll get more info from Bert in the next few days. I wanted to win his confidence without him getting skittish." He glanced at his feet. "He follows his wife's orders. He wouldn't enter the house without taking off his boots."

"Marlene must rule the roost in their household." Diana took out a a bottle of wine. "What about the trash in your truck?"

"Too late today. I'll take it to the dump tomorrow morning." He glanced at the wine.

"Tough day?"

"Not at all. I'm celebrating. Join me."

"After I take a shower." He turned to leave. "By the way it's your turn to fix dinner."

"Easy to do." She put two baking potatoes in the oven, prepped a loin of pork with barbecue sauce, set the timer and put the broccoli aside to cook later. Humming, she took a plate of cheese and crackers, the wine and glasses into the living room and sat to enjoy the pleasant glow of the fire. She mulled over the sergeant. He seemed pleasant, efficient and considerate, so why did she feel that he had a hidden agenda, other than finding Feeney's murderer?

She leaned back and stared into space. In spite of her concern for Isabel, her unhappiness over Jeffrey, and her unresolved issues with Paul, she was pleased with her good deed for Hetch. She sipped her wine and thought of Ursula who had been so open about being a lesbian and it didn't matter to Diana, so why was she upset with her son's choice? Jeffrey was handsome, intelligent and caring. Had he questioned his sexual orientation growing up? She'd thought that she and Paul had a good relationship with their children. Obviously, that wasn't the case. Or perhaps Jeffrey had intuited that she wouldn't have understood?

A clean-shaven sergeant came downstairs wearing gray slacks, a blue shirt and V-neck sweater. His crewcut was beginning to grow out, making him look less like a military man. "You look content." He poured himself a glass of wine.

"Except for a few chaotic thoughts, I am."

After taking a cracker and spreading it with Brie, he sat on the couch, his drink on the nearby table. "I know better than to ask what those thoughts might be."

"I talked with my husband last night." She hesitated, then added, "Isabel's been wounded."

"What?" He flinched and caught his wine glass before the contents spilt. "How bad?"

"According to Paul, superficial. I wouldn't be sitting here relaxing if it had been serious. She's been pulled back to a safe zone."

"There are no safe zones in Afghanistan. Even Kabul is dangerous." He stared at her. "What about the rest of the outfit?"

"Some wounded, a few deaths." She frowned. "It's terrible. Even though they aren't your men, I can see you care."

"God, how could I not?" He clasped his hands together, bit his lower lip and stared at the floor.

The wall clock's ticking resounded in the silence. He stood and paced, hobbling on his bad leg, his face twisted in anger. "I hate hearing that my…my guys, our guys get it and I'm not there to help."

"It seems so useless, especially when the people you're trying to help are the enemy. Does it solve anything?"

"Jesus, I'm not sure, but since we're in it, we damn well better finish it and not do a half-assed job like we've done in other places. It makes me sick. All our efforts down the tubes because of politics. Jesus. What's our country coming to?"

"That's why I oppose these recent wars. They make no sense. Look what happened in Iraq and is still happening. Tribe against tribe. Our leaders lied to us."

"I might agree with you on some points, but if every time the military disagreed with its commanders and announced it wouldn't fight, we'd have chaos, anarchy."

Not wanting to get drawn further into an argument about politics and war, Diana switched the subject. "I learned from Hetch Feeney that the baby's remains in the attic couldn't have been his and Gloria's. Their baby was deformed, died after birth and buried in the local graveyard."

He nodded, but seem uninterested. "I need the password to the house's internet."

"I should have given it to you earlier." She went to the desk, wrote it on a piece of paper and handed it to him. "I sometimes wonder if knowing what's going on over there is good or bad. I'm so worried about Isabel, and now you're upset with the news, too."

He noted the password and looked at her. "I might be able to contact a buddy and find out exactly what happened to your daughter and her outfit."

"Isabel is going to be okay. I'm sad about the others. Will it do us any good to learn how many soldiers were wounded or killed and who they were?"

He slumped into the couch and put his head in his hands. "Shit. What a friggin' mess."

Not wanting to witness his anguish, she took her wineglass and went to finish preparing dinner. As she set the table, she wondered if she wanted to know the details of Isabel's injury. Would it matter? She couldn't do a damn thing about anything that happened over there and neither could the sergeant. So what was the point? She placed her hands on the counter, allowing her emotions to overtake her. Fierce tears streamed down her face.

When the broccoli boiled over, she turned down the heat. She took a breath, dabbed at her face with a paper towel, pulled out a tissue and blew her nose. "Damn it," she said to the empty room. After getting herself under control, she pushed open the kitchen door. "Would you bring the wine and the plate of cheese? Dinner's ready."

By the time he came into the kitchen, she had dinner on the table. He commented on how good the simple dinner was, and she nodded. Diana talked about what she'd learned about Mrs. Feeney, but didn't mention Hetch's new pet. The glow of helping Hetch had dwindled. Since the sergeant remained withdrawn, nodding and eating, she gave up her one-sided conversation, and they finished their meal in silence.

After they took their plates to the sink, she stood next to him. "What's done is done." She put her hand over his. "I can't dwell on what happened to Isabel, her unit and all the others fighting or I'll go crazy. You shouldn't either. You're here and you can't change what's going on over there."

He refused to meet her eyes. Instead he bent to the chore of washing the dishes. Unable to dislodge his dour mood, she left and went into the living room. Someone banged on the front door. What now? God, it's probably the damn reporters again.

"Mrs. Bellfore," an angry voice yelled. "I'm Sam Feeney."

As Diana opened the front door, the sergeant came out from the kitchen. Sam pushed his way into the house, thrust his hand against Diana's shoulder and shoved her. "You're the bitch who stuck her nose into my business." The heavyset man raised his fist.

Before she could recover from stumbling backwards, there was a blur to her right. If she'd blinked, she wouldn't have seen the sergeant grab Sam's arm, twist it, and send the man sprawling face down on the floor.

"Get off me. Let me go," Sam screamed.

"No way, scumbag. Who do you think you are barging in and assaulting a woman?" The sergeant increased his leverage on Sam's arm.

"Shit. You're breaking my arm."

Diana, having caught her breath, stepped forward. "Sergeant, maybe you'd better let him up. You will behave yourself, won't you, Sam?"

"Yeah, yeah."

"We should call the police." Although the sergeant sounded serious, he winked at Diana.

"No, really, I won't hurt anyone, honest. Let me up."

The sergeant eased up on his hold and let Sam struggle to his feet, but kept a tight grip on the man's arm. "One wrong move and you'll be eating wood again. Got it?"

"Yeah. Let go." Sam Feeney remained bent over.

"Ask nice."

"Please."

The sergeant released his hold.

Sam stood erect, then staggered back against the far wall, rubbing his shoulder.

"All right." Diana's put her fists on her hips. "What's this all about?"

"Can I sit down?" His voice was now a whimper. He edged toward the couch and sagged onto it while the sergeant and Diana stood over him. Sam glared up at her. "Look, my dad shouldn't have a dog. I don't like dogs. When I heard some lady helped him get one, it freaked me out. Then I find you're the same woman staying in this house, the house that's supposed to be mine." His nostrils flared. "What do you expect me to do? Give you a medal?"

The sergeant's face showed interest, not anger. "What do you mean this house was supposed to be yours?"

"What's it to you?"

"You're the one who has the explaining to do," the sergeant said.

Sam's eyes narrowed, but after a glance at the sergeant's face, he said, "I'm Hetch Feeney's son. Gloria was his ex-wife. About nine years ago, I got to know her when I rewired the place. She promised she'd leave the house to me if I helped her out now and then, so I did. Instead she gave it to some nephew she hadn't seen in years."

"So what?" the sergeant asked. "The estate's been settled. You have no claim."

"I do." He gripped the edge of the sofa cushion. "She said it would be mine." Sam's facial muscles twitched. "The bitch lied. You watch. I'll get the house."

"If you thought this house was rightfully yours, why didn't you act sooner?" Diana asked.

"I got new information. I'm filing a lawsuit against Grant Cranston."

The sergeant laughed. "On what grounds?"

"Because he's an impostor. He's not her nephew."

Diana lost her patience. "That might be true or not, but it has nothing to do with barging in here and assaulting me."

"You helped my dad get a fucking dog. Turned him against me."

"Yes, I helped your father get a dog because he needed a companion. You only visit him once a month. And for the record, I don't know you and never said a word against you, but maybe I should." She hesitated, before adding, "You live up to your reputation of having a vile temper."

His chin came up. "I can't babysit my old man. I run the damn business."

"Exactly. You aren't around. That's why he needed a dog." Diana was so angry that her thoughts poured out uncensored. "Temper combined with greed can be a powerful motive for murder. From what you've said, you're a prime suspect for Gloria Feeney's murder."

Sam's mouth gaped, his dark eyes widened.

The sergeant smiled.

Sam refused to apologize and his whining claims against Diana and Captain Cranston continued in a steady drone of vindictiveness. The sergeant yanked the man up by his arm and escorted the recalcitrant man to his car.

When the sergeant returned, Diana said, "I appreciate the rescue. I thought he was going to hit me."

"I thought so, too. That's why I acted."

"You were amazing. Thank you. I hope I don't have to meet him again." Her voice was calm, but her heart raced with fury and fear. "Perhaps you should notify the captain of Sam's intent."

"Difficult to do and besides I'm not sure Sam's lawsuit is credible."

Tired and confused she sat and leaned her head back. "I wonder if he did kill Gloria Feeney. Perhaps he should be on your suspect list?"

The sergeant rearranged the cushions on the sofa. "I wonder if the police questioned him. Before the guy drove off in his new BMW, he gave himself an alibi. Claimed he was in New Hampshire the entire weekend and has buddies to prove it." He grinned. "You sure scared him."

"He deserved it. What a temper. No wonder Hetch was worried about his son's reaction to him getting a dog. What a fuss over a dog."

"So you acted the good Samaritan? Good for you."

"I'm not known for spur of the moment acts, but this one felt right. I told Hetch I'd visit him to see how he was getting along with Shelly. Now I have more questions for him about Sam."

"I presume Shelly is the dog." He started toward the kitchen. "I'm going to get a beer. How about you?"

"There's a bottle of red wine. I'd love a glass of that."

He returned and handed her a glass of wine. "Let's discuss the murder. We've got a few leads, but they're nebulous and disconnected. We've got Ursula's frame and two missing paintings." He relaxed on the couch, taking a swig of beer from the bottle. "There's Sam who has a motive but claims to have an alibi, a caretaker who's jumpy and lies about a topsoil delivery, plus a detective who seems to be inept, hiding something or corrupt."

"And there's the baby's remains that might be decades old, but it's not the Feeneys'," Diana added.

He frowned. "So what was it doing in the attic? How long has it been there and who put it there?"

She'd slipped off her shoes, stretched out her legs and sipped her wine. "Don't forget Penelope's letters, and how she wanted to get into the attic." She studied him. "Those rightfully belong to Captain Cranston since they're addressed to him."

"Not sure I want to go there." He put down his beer bottle.

"There are a few things we have yet to explore. You're going to question Bert some more and check on the topsoil dealer. I'm going to check with the University of Rhode Island's art department and then visit Ursula. I'll take the frame with me." She thought about Penny. The letters could be related to the murder. If they weren't, she'd return them and say nothing about their contents.

"We still have to talk to Cora and Murphy," he said. "I don't trust Detective O'Reilly. He acts as if he's covering up something."

"In a small town the Chief of Police would be involved with the case, wouldn't he?"

"He should have, but I don't want to stir up trouble with him or give away my mission."

"Maybe you can't act in an intrusive manner, but I can. Just a meddlesome mystery writer, snooping around asking everyone questions."

"Questioning the wrong people could get you into trouble."

"Isn't that what you asked me to do?"

"Yes, but I don't want you to get hurt."

"Moi? People have a tendency to forgive and forget an old lady."

He grinned and shook his head. "You don't look or behave old, so you might not get away with the act."

She smiled. "We'll see."

Chapter 12

The light from the bedside lamp created shadows on the far wall. Dressed in her nightgown and robe, Diana sat on the edge of her bed with the small bound packet of letters on her lap. From the envelopes' furrowed sides, it appeared that the old twine around them had been retied. When? A year ago or earlier? Had the sergeant read them?

She unknotted the twine. The letters were in chronological order, the oldest on the bottom. She scooted back against the headboard, inverted the stack, and opened the oldest letter dated September 1998.

Dear Grant,
Ever since I returned home, I've been wanting to write, but wondered if you'd want to hear from me. You came to my rescue when anyone else might have turned away or blabbed about my situation. I was desperate. I know you got in trouble for leaving camp to take me to that doctor. I heard through the grapevine that you had to clean bathrooms the rest of the summer. Sorry. My father accepted my excuse of being sick and coming home early from camp.
I hope this letter doesn't get you into trouble with your aunt. Let me know if it's okay to write again. I have a job at a small dress shop in Providence. Of course, I lied about my age. Earning money makes me feel good, and Dad likes the added income. I owe you big time. Pawning your father's watch and your clarinet was a super thing to do. I'll try to send you money soon, so you can get them back.
You'll be a junior now. You said you liked baseball and track. Will that help you get into Annapolis? Even though your father's dead, will you be able to use his contact with the senator? Write if you can. Your friend forever, Penny

Diana folded the letter and put it back in the envelope. She felt sad for Penny and proud of Grant, although she didn't know him. The boy had courage and been a true friend. It was obvious that Penny had had an abortion. Had Grant gotten Penny pregnant or had he just been a friend? She thought about the skeleton in the attic and shuddered. Diana remembered that Penny said she'd been in this old Victorian house before and hated it. When had she visited? If Gloria Feeney had this letter, she could have caused trouble for Penny, and according to Penny, she had.

Diana picked up the next letter dated November, 1998.

Dear Grant,

I was so pleased to get your letter, typed no less. I'm glad your aunt helped you get your watch and instrument out of hock. She sounds much nicer than you told me she was. Maybe she's softened toward you. I've been clean for four months. It's been hard. My grades are better and I'm studying harder. Maybe I can go to college after all, or at least a trade school. You told me I was good at math and had a good mind. Not many would agree with you.

Since you and I talked at camp, my relationship with Dad is better. I'm earning a good commission on sales, and Dad is letting me put money aside now that he knows I'm serious about the direction of my life. Thanksgiving and Christmas are the busy times, so I won't be able to visit you over the holidays. Maybe this summer we could get together. Let me know. Thank your aunt for inviting me to Thanksgiving dinner. That was sweet of her. Your friend, Penny

Diana put down the letter. Penny's letter sounded as if she and Grant hadn't gotten together again. Penny's version of Gloria Feeney was at odds with all the other things Diana had heard about the woman.

She read through the rest of the letters sent monthly through June. Then they stopped. The last letter caught her attention.

June 1999

Dear Grant,

I'm so excited to visit you at last. I plan to get a ride with a friend. Don't you have a car anymore? You said you'd never give it up no matter what your aunt threatened. I look forward to meeting her. She seems to have done a 180 about you and helped you so much. I'll try to be there in the early afternoon, but my ride makes my time-line iffy. Your friend, Penny

She placed the letters on the side table and turned out the light. What had happened that summer between Penny and Grant, and what part had Gloria Feeney played in their relationship?

Diana sank into a deep sleep and awoke to what she thought were people arguing outside her window. She sat up, feeling groggy. The noise wasn't from outside, but came through the heating ducts. She flipped on the light and checked the time: three o'clock. She put on her slippers and robe and went into the hall. The screams and yells came from upstairs. "Sergeant?" she called. She hurried up the steps and switched on the lights in the upstair hall. When she stood in front of the sergeant's room, the screams were hoarse and terrifying. She knocked, then opened the door.

The light from the hall streamed across the bed where the sergeant lay writhing, tangled in sheets and sweating. His jagged voice ripped through the air. "I'm coming. You'll be okay. Hang on. I'll get help. My leg, my leg." He screamed as if he were in agnony. "I can't feel it. We're dying. God, we're dying. Gotta retreat. Keep firing." He sat up, the sheet falling away from his bare torso. "God, don't die, Johnny. Please. Don't die."

She moved to the bedside and put out her arms to comfort him. He grabbed her. When he collapsed back onto the mattress, he pulled her down on top of him. She pushed away and tried to be calm and firm. "Sergeant, wake up. You're dreaming."

His head rolled to the side, his eyes opened, but remained unfocused.

"It's all right. You're safe. You're in the States, in Rhode Island." She reached over and turned on the bedside lamp. "Nothing can hurt you here."

Releasing his grip on Diana, he threw his arm across his face. His breath came in gasps.

Diana went to the bathroom and soaked a towel in cold water. At the bed again she wiped his forehead, removed his arm from across his face and placed the wet towel over his eyes. He moaned.

"It's all right. You had a nightmare." She leaned over and placed her cool hands on either side of his face.

He sighed and reached up, circling his arms around her back, pulling her down again. She lay with her head on his bare chest, listening to his racing heart that gradually slowed to a fast yet steady beat. When his arms slid away, she sat up. The scar across his chest was raw and puckered. Tracing it with her fingers, she felt anger at how the viciousness of war tore human flesh.

He yanked the towel from his eyes, squinting in the light.

She turned out the lamp, allowing only the hall light to filter into the room. "You're going to be all right. It must have been horrible for you."

"Yeah."

Neither moved. The silence grew. She shifted her position as if to rise, but he grabbed her arm. "Thank you. Sorry. Stay for a few minutes, please."

"All right." She sat still. "Do you want to talk about it?"

"Yes." Silence. "No." More silence. "Christ, I'm a mess."

"Who's Johnny?"

"Sergeant Johnny Morgan."

"But that's you."

"Yeah, that's me." He held her hand against his chest.

She waited, her emotions reeling between horror of his wound and caring about his distress. "My son had nightmares when he was young. What you experienced was far worse and real." She took a deep breath. "My husband would get him up and have him shower, while I heated hot chocolate. Later we'd talk and eventually he'd go back to sleep."

He released her hand. "A shower's a good idea." He sat upright, not looking at her. "Although I'll have a cup of tea, instead of hot chocolate."

"I'll get clean sheets." She left the room and waited until she heard the shower running, then returned and remade the bed. Back downstairs she went to the kitchen and put on the kettle. While the tea brewed, she pondered Grant's physical and emotional condition. How many returning veterans had similar reactions to their war experiences? And then her thoughts jumped to Isabel.

When she heard him come downstairs, she put the cups on a tray and went into the living room where he sat on the couch wearing gray sweat pants and a T-shirt. The lamps glowed, casting a dim shadow over his drawn face. His dark brows obscured his eyes.

She set the tray down, poured the tea, adding a dollop of honey, and handed it to him. "Maybe tea laced with rum would be better, but we don't have any."

He nodded. "Thanks. This'll do."

She took her cup and sat in the chair. "Is this the first time you've experienced such a vivid nightmare?"

"No, but I thought I was getting over them." He took a long sip of tea. "When the docs released me, they said I might have a relapse. I thought I wouldn't."

"Fighting Sam and hearing the news about your fellow soldiers could have brought the dreams on."

"Yeah." He put his cup on the coffee table. "I think it would help if I explained about Johnny."

She nodded, but remained silent.

"Johnny was the best sergeant and friend a man could have. He saved my life, but I couldn't save his." He stared into the dark recesses of the room. "He lay next to me while the fighting continued. I couldn't do a damn thing for him or for my men. We were getting slaughtered. My radioman was dead, a few yards away. I bellied over to him and called in an air strike on our position. It was our only hope, but it killed some of my company. What does that make me?"

"For those who survived, you're probably a hero."

"That's not how I see it."

"How did the army see it?"

He shrugged. "They don't always get things right."

"You were decorated. Am I right?"

He looked away. "I was full of hate for the enemy. I deal with that every day. A poem I read helps some. Walt Whitman wrote it during the Civil War. It's called 'Reconciliation.'

Word over all, beautiful as the sky,
Beautiful that was and all its deeds of carnage must in time be utterly lost,
That the hands of the sisters Death and Night incessantly softly wash again, and ever again, this soiled world;
For my enemy is dead, a man divine as myself is dead,
I look where he lies white-faced and still in the coffin—I draw near,
Bend down and touch lightly with my lips the white face in the coffin."

Silence hung between them until Diana asked, "If you're not John Morgan, then who are you?"

"I thought you might have guessed by now. I'm Grant Cranston."

Chapter 13

They talked off and on letting silence fall easily between them before one of them began again. He finally asked, "You read the letters, didn't you?"

She nodded.

"Thought you might."

"With the murder unsolved, I felt it was necessary. I won't tell anyone about the contents."

"I'm glad you read them. It makes it easier to explain what happened here," he nodded to the room, "between Penny, Mrs. Feeney and me." He hesitated, staring at the wall. "You see, I never wrote Penny. It was Mrs. Feeney who wrote to her, leading her on, telling her about the wonderful things she was doing for me. In truth the woman was more vicious than ever."

"You never saw Penny's letters?"

He shook his head. "Not until the other day. I was stunned when Penny arrived here in the summer at the invitation of Mrs. Feeney. She believed I was the father of Penny's aborted child. She'd planned the whole meeting so she could rage at us. She relished the moment, screaming and throwing a torrent of obscenities at us in this very living room. When Penny learned the fake letters, she was hurt, demoralized. I think she'd fallen in love with me all because of those letters. Poor girl." He took a deep breath, before continuing. "I came close to killing Mrs. Feeney that day."

"How old were you?"

"Penny was sixteen and I was seventeen. That was the problem. I was under Mrs. Feeney's control until my eighteenth birthday in March the next year. She was my legal guardian with access to funds set up for me, but she used them mostly on herself. When she refused to continue paying for my car insurance, I had to sell it. I hid the money, but she found it and took it."

Diana was shocked at the cruelty of the woman. "That day, when Penny came here, what did the two of you do?"

"I walked her to the bus station and never saw or heard from her again. I went to the lawyer and told him how Mrs. Feeney took the money I earned. He said he'd send her a letter admonishing her, but unless I wanted to file charges and get into a lawsuit, I I was stuck living with her until I was eighteen."

"I can't believe an aunt would be so nasty to her nephew."

"I'm not her nephew. Sam was right about that."

"I don't understand. How could she have become your guardian?"

"My parents were friends with the Feeneys when they lived in Rhode Island. After I was born, they wanted to be sure I'd be taken care of if anything happened to them, so they made Hetch and Gloria Feeney my guardians until I turned eighteen. When I was five, my dad got a job in Wisconsin, and we moved away."

"They never changed that document?"

He shook his head. "A big mistake. When I was fourteen, my parents came back here for a visit and I remained in Wisconsin. They were killed in a car crash, a hit and run, on Route One. The police never caught the driver. Hetch Feeney was married to someone else by then and had a twelve-year-old son, Sam. They wouldn't or couldn't take me in. I assume that when Gloria found out about the money, she stepped forward and took control." He shrugged. "The rest you know from the letters."

"I'm so sorry. Yet in spite of her, you went to Annapolis."

"After that episode with Penny, a friend let me use his home address, otherwise she would have intercepted my mail. Before I turned eighteen, I had contacted the lawyer and the senator, both friends of my father's who put my name up for Annapolis. At age eighteen I rented a room near the high school with money from the fund my parents had set up for me and Gloria could no longer manage it. I was free. After that things were better."

Diana glanced at her watch, stood and pulled back the heavy velvet drapes. The morning sun was just creeping above the house across the pond.

He moved next to her and put his arm across her shoulders. "Thanks for listening." He kissed her cheek.

A warm glow spread over her. "Hungry?"

"Starving."

She turned and smiled. "Good. Let's make breakfast."

Over pancakes and bacon, Diana said, "I've been calling you Sergeant. You must have resented that."

"No, I didn't. It made me feel Johnny was here, helping me. You've got to continue calling me that. If you call me Grant in front of people, my cover is blown. It would make the investigation awkward and more difficult."

"I understand your position, but it'll feel strange calling you Sergeant instead of Grant. I'll compromise. When we're around others, I'll call you Sergeant, otherwise it'll be Grant. Is that your full name?"

"Grant Alan Cranston."

She looked out the window at the pines and small meadow in the backyard. The house held so much evil, yet its surroundings were lovely. "What about Penny and other people in town?"

"I'll avoid Penny and for the others…well, there aren't many who would remember me. I left over fourteen years ago."

"Why would Gloria leave the house to you?"

"I've wondered the same thing." He finished off his pancake, wiped his mouth with his napkin and took a sip of coffee. "Maybe she wanted to rub it in. Make me remember what had happened here." He nodded as if he was certain that was the case. "I found a suitcase in the attic. Not the one with the remains, but another one with Penny's letters. It contained my father's watch and my clarinet."

Diana's heart plummeted. "She got them out of hock and never gave them back to you? It's hard to imagine such vindictiveness."

He sat back. "I've put a load of my problems on you. Are you sure you want to stay and see this through?"

She nodded. "I'm in way too deep to leave." She wanted to help this man who had endured so much and had succeeded in life despite everything. "Don't you know that a mystery writer has to tie up all the loose ends?"

"This isn't fiction." He glanced at his watch. "I think the dump opens at seven, so I'll take the truckload of junk then."

After they'd cleaned up the kitchen, Diana went to shower and change. It was still early when she called Penny. Although Diana didn't tell her why she wanted to meet, Penny intuited the reason.

"I gather you have something for me," she said. "Let's meet on the dunes in front of Green Street. Do you know where that is?"

"Down from Ursula's house?"

"Yes," Penny said. "No one should be on the beach this early. Can we meet now?"

"I have a few chores to finish. I can be there in about forty-five minutes." After clicking off, Diana thought about the trauma Penny had experienced. She must have been shaken when her husband took the job of Police Chief of Quamscutt. Had he known of Penny's past before Mrs. Feeney spoke to the city council?

Finishing her work around the house, Diana stuck the letters in her fleece jacket, walked around the pond to the path's right fork, and climbed over the dunes. Penny was already there, sitting on a dune facing the ocean. The breeze ruffled her red hair glinting in the morning sun. The young woman looked angelic dressed in a green wool sweater and a long plaid skirt tucked about her knees. Under that lovely veneer there existed a very outspoken and troubled woman. Diana now understood the cause.

Diana waved and felt the packet of letters in her pocket. She walked forward, her shoes churning through the heavy sand. "Good morning, Penny."

The woman looked up. "How do you do it?"

Diana frowned. "Do what?"

"It's early in the morning, and you're dressed like a fashion model, yellow scarf tied at the throat, white blouse, rust-colored fleece jacket and beige slacks. In a roundabout way I'm complimenting you. I don't do that very often. Not good at it." She patted the sand next to her. "Best sandy bench on a brisk sunny morning."

"It's lovely." Diana sank onto the cool sand. Without looking at Penny, she handed the packet to her. "I believe these are what you wanted."

Penny took the letters in both hands, gripping them as if her life depended on having them. "Thank you."

"I saw they were addressed to Grant Cranston. Would he want them? He's the new owner of the old Feeney house."

Penny shook her head, but kept her eyes riveted on the sea.

Diana waited, hoping for more of a reaction. Through the haze, she could just make out the outline of Block Island in the distance. "The envelopes date back many years. You were quite young."

"Too young. Too naive. Too rebellious and mixed up."

Diana remained silent. The same man who always walked along the beach with his black lab waved at them. A gull swooped down and caught a fish swimming too close to the surface. The never-ending waves rolled in, indifferent to the woes of humans.

Penny's tears splashed onto the old stationery. "It was a long time ago, and I don't think Grant would want them."

Diana put her arm around Penny's shoulders. "I'm sorry the letters upset you."

Penny gulped, sighed, then brushed back her tears. "I'm not a crier. I'm stronger than that." She sniffled and fingered the packet of letters. "It's what these represent."

"You were in love with Grant?"

"In a way, yes. He was good to me when I needed a friend. Mrs. Feeney was the one who ruined everything." She brushed the sand off her skirt. "She was cruel, mean and hateful. I'm so glad she's dead."

"With her murder unsolved, I'm not sure that's a good thing to be saying."

"Wanting someone dead and doing it are two different things. Feeney had so many enemies that it took the police a long time to sort through the list." Penny smiled. "Charlie knows I'm innocent and that's all that matters to me."

"How long have you been married?"

"Almost six years. Been in this town for four. Charlie loves his job, the area, the people. If we had a child, our lives would be perfect." She let out her breath and stuffed the letters in her skirt pocket. "I can't have children." She looked at Diana. "You read the letters?"

"With an unsolved murder, I thought it prudent. I'm sorry I intruded on your privacy."

Penny shrugged. "That's okay. Since you read them, you'll understand why I can't have children. We thought of adopting, but the cost is huge, and the wait is long." She turned to Diana. "You're lucky you have children."

"Yes, I am. The more I hear other people's problems with their children, the more I realize how fortunate I am. Isabel chose the military even though she could have gotten a state department job as a linguist. I…I didn't like that."

Penny gazed out to sea. "Grant went into the navy."

"You kept in touch?"

"No. I heard from a friend that he got into Annapolis despite his aunt. He was smart, hardworking. He'd do well in anything he pursued."

"Do you know where he is now?" Diana asked.

"Somewhere overseas." Penny sent a questioning look at Diana. "Why do you ask?"

"Just curious."

"I hope he sells the house, but I'd rather see it demolished. Maybe it'll burn down. He probably has insurance, so he'd make out all right." Penny traced a pattern in the sand with her fingers. "Ursula did a painting of that damn house and sold it to the Feeneys. Can you imagine? Ursula loved the landscape and the Feeneys ruined it." She shook her head. "I don't understand Ursula sometimes. She's so adamant about her work and yet refuses to do anything about the paintings Gloria owned."

Ursula's comment about Penny's obsessiveness came to mind, but she discounted it. "How about a walk along the beach. The tide's out."

"Great idea." Penny jumped to her feet, took off her sandals, then put out a hand to help Diana up. "I'll take the ocean side, so you don't get your slacks wet."

Side by side they walked toward the water then headed west, the sun at their backs. Neither of them said much for some time. Diana was startled when Penny took her arm and asked, "Do you get along with your daughter?"

Diana's heart skipped a beat, but she felt a need to be truthful. "I don't think I've ever understood her. It's only recently that I've reached out to make amends for my past…actions. I love her very much and admire her, something my own mother never demonstrated toward me. Unfortunately, I let my mother influence my actions toward my children."

"Sounds like you're changing."

Diana smiled and nodded. "It does, doesn't it? It feels good."

"What about your other child, a son, I think Ursula said?"

"Jeffrey is studying architecture in Chicago."

"You love and admire him, too?"

Diana stopped walking. "I...of course."

"My mother died when I was five. I often wonder what it would be like to have a mother, what she would think of me, and how she would act. I think about what it would be like to have a child to love. Sounds wonderful to me." She pulled on Diana's arm. "Keep walking. By now you know I'm blatantly nosey."

Diana laughed. "Yes, I've noticed and so is Ursula. I can't complain though, since I have the same trait."

They continued up the beach with Penny sharing what her life had been like growing up, and Diana explaining about her childhood. They watched a family playing catch with a Frisbee, then turned and walked back the way they'd come.

"I had a visitor the other night," Diana said. "Sam Feeney. Do you know him?"

Penny stopped, letting the cold water circle her bare feet. "God, do I." She stared out to sea. "Well, I'll amend that. I don't know him, but I know about him. When the news hit the papers ten years ago, I was pleased, thinking that Gloria deserved to have a criminal for a son. I read everything about his drug bust. When he wasn't sentenced to jail and only got probation, I was furious. It was only later when I learned he wasn't Gloria's son that I calmed down."

Diana asked questions about Sam's criminal past, but Penny didn't seem to know much more than the basics. They continued discussing Sam until they stood at the fork in the path.

"I plan to stop by and see Ursula." Penny looked over at the Cape Cod house. "She hasn't been feeling well. I worry about her."

"She appeared to be fine when I lunched with her on Sunday. She was her usual outspoken self." Diana was still miffed at Ursula's remark about the sergeant and her. "You and Ursula seem to be close friends."

"When Gloria tried to undermine Charlie's appointment as Police Chief by going after my reputation, Ursula denounced her. Many people knew Gloria was cruel, but Ursula was the only one who stood up in front of the city council and told them exactly what everyone knew: Gloria Feeney was a vindictive gossiper and liar."

Diana smiled at the picture Penny conjured up of Ursula. "Must have been a grand performance. Did Gloria ever forgive her?"

Penny shrugged. "I doubt if Ursula cared one way or another. No love lost between the two of them even before that." Penny leaned forward and hugged Diana. "Thanks for a great morning, and I don't mean just these." She nodded to the letters in her skirt pocket. "I enjoyed getting to know you better. Let's meet again soon." She walked away, turned, and waved.

The conversation concerning Sam made Diana's return visit to Hetch a necessity. Could Sam have killed Gloria? If so, what was his motive? The loss of the house didn't seem enough of an impetus, but the young man had a wicked temper.

Chapter 14

Diana sat at the desk, opened her laptop and searched the internet for information concerning the drug charges Sam had faced over ten years ago. She found the story in old issues of the Boston Globe and Providence Journal.

Sam and two brothers, Phil and Robert Yukovitch, were arrested for importing and distributing cocaine. Although some of the shipment had been recovered, ten kilos were unaccounted for. Phil and Robert were convicted and spent five years in prison. Officer Joe O'Reilly had testified on Sam's behalf, explaining that the boy was merely a naive pawn in the crime.

Diana made a star by O'Reilly's name in her notes. She leaned back, thinking of how Sam and O'Reilly's connection might relate to the present. Sam worked for Gloria, who promised him her house, but changed her mind, or else never had any intention of leaving it to him. O'Reilly had befriended Sam and investigated Gloria's murder. Had he been remiss in searching the attic and overlooked clues? Had Officer Murphy been at fault instead of O'Reilly? She rubbed a finger over her lips. "Interesting, very interesting." Her words echoed in the quiet room.

She went back to reading other articles. Since Sam had no priors and testified against the other two, he got off with probation. Robert died in a shoot-out with the police in South Boston a year after his release. Years later Phil was convicted of burglary and served another prison term. His second release from prison occurred only weeks before Gloria's murder.

Hard to imagine he had anything to do with her murder, but it was worth investigating.

She picked up her cell and called Hetch Feeney. "Hello. This is Diana Bellfore. How are you getting along with Shelly?"

"Great. Her previous owners are coming by to check how she's doing later this afternoon."

"Do you have time to see me this morning?"

"Hey, I'm getting popular."

"That's good, isn't it?"

"Maybe, but when the police want a DNA sample from me, I figure something bad's going on."

"It probably has to do with the remains found in your ex-wife's house."

"I told them the same thing I told you. It can't have anything to do with me." He let out a heavy sigh. "What the hell. I cooperated and let them take a swab."

"That was wise. It might clear things up, and they won't bother you again."

"So, what do I owe another visit from you? Not that I mind. You helped me out." There was a pause, then he asked, "Did Sam visit you?"

"Yes."

"He give you a hard time?"

"Some."

"I'm sorry about that. He went off like a rocket when he heard about the dog and that you were renting Gloria's house. I don't understand him sometimes."

"I'd like to talk to you about him."

"Not my favorite subject of late. Come before lunch, okay?"

"I'll be there by eleven." She clicked off. When Grant's truck pulled into the driveway, she went out to the backyard to meet him.

He got out of his truck and walked across the grassy area in a criss-cross pattern. "Hi." He looked up.

"What are you doing?"

He stopped. "What do you see when you look at this yard?"

She shrugged. "Grass, weeds, wildflowers, lumps and bumps in the soil. It's not smooth like a lawn, and the path to the shed is quirky. It would make more sense for it to lead from the back door to the shed in a straight line instead of a big arc."

"Exactly." He walked over to her. "Bert says he was supposed to keep the yard wild, but that's not true. I talked to the local company that delivers topsoil and sod. The manager went through his invoices and found that the delivery to this address was made on the Monday after the weekend of Mrs. Feeney's murder, but before the body was discovered on Thursday."

"Have you asked Bert about the timing of the delivery?"

"Haven't had a chance and I need to ask him why the slate slabs aren't set in a straight line."

While they were talking, Bert drove up in his van. "Don't mention any of this to him," Grant said. "I don't want to spook him."

Bert got out of his van. An oversized T-shirt hung from his lean frame, and his jeans were faded and threadbare at the knees. Marlene must not be in charge of Bert's work clothes.

Diana turned to Grant. "I'm visiting Hetch this morning to ask about Sam." As she walked away, she said over her shoulder, "By the way, I gave the letters to Penny and had an interesting conversation."

"Hey, wait, tell me what happened."

"Not now." She nodded toward Bert. "I'll fill you in tonight." She went inside to get her purse and notes from the old newspaper articles. When she left through the mudroom, Bert and Grant were sitting on the bench taking off their shoes. "It's good you're both housebroken."

Bert frowned. "Excuse me?"

"She means we're smart to take off our shoes when we come in from outside."

"Oh." His long face maintained a stoic expression. "My wife insists." He pushed his shoes under the bench. "It's a good habit."

"I'm sure Marlene appreciates it," Diana said. "The attic will probably be as clean as the shed when you're finished today."

"Shouldn't take long and then we can drag the storm windows out of the basement and sand them." Grant stood. "I plan to paint them and the house. Still haven't decided on the color."

Diana stepped over Grant's wayward shoes. "It's your turn to cook dinner, Sergeant." The screen slammed shut behind her.

On her drive to Hetch's, her cell phone rang its merry Greensleeves tune. She dug it out of her purse and saw it was Paul. "I'm in the car. Can I call you back when I get to my destination? It'll be about thirty minutes."

"Okay, but don't forget. It's important."

"Oh? I can pull off the road now."

"No. Call me back." He hung up.

Diana's heart accelerated, and she stomped on the gas pedal. What could be important? Isabel? Jeffrey? Twenty minutes later she was in the retirement home's parking lot. She rang Paul and waited for him to answer.

"That was quick," he said.

"I hurried. What's happened? Is Isabel all right?"

"Both Jeffrey and Isabel are fine. I called to tell you I'm putting the house on the market."

She almost dropped the phone. "What?"

"We talked about it before you left. We agreed the house was too big for the two of us."

"We talked about it, but we hadn't made a definite decision."

"Look, you're away for three months, and I'm rattling around in this house. It doesn't make sense. Janie Newcomb is a good real estate agent and knows the comps. She agrees that the price you and I discussed is in the ballpark."

The thought of young and attractive Janie in their house with Paul made Diana's jaw ache. "Can't you wait till I get back?"

"Janie says fall is a good time to sell. I want to do it now and be done with it. The kids aren't coming back home after all our arguments, and you've left."

Diana swallowed hard and tears sprang to her eyes. "This three months is only temporary. You know that."

"Do I?"

"Paul, what are you saying?"

"When you were here all we did was argue. I don't want to go through that again, do you?"

"We've had arguments before—"

"Diana, this is a separation and you know it."

"That's not what I want—"

"When you left, you didn't think about what I wanted. I've had time to think and this is what we should do."

"Maybe I should come home—"

"You're not listening. You went off. I'm here. I'm putting the house on the market. I'll send you the papers. We can talk further when we get an offer. In the meantime our three months apart may resolve some issues."

The line went silent for a few seconds. "I want more out of marriage than we have now, don't you?"

"Of course, yes. You're right. Shall I come home now?"

"Let's give it time. With this separation perhaps we can sort things out."

She stared out the windshield. "Is there someone else?"

"Oh, for crying out loud. Why do women always think there has to be another woman?"

Because that's usually the case, she thought, but said, "I love you. We can work this out."

"I hope we can. I'd like to, but in the meantime we sell the house. If it sells quick, I'll rent an apartment."

"But what about long term? Where will we live?"

"Time will tell on that score."

"I'll have to come home and pack. Isabel and Jeffrey still have things in the house they'll want."

"I can pack Isabel's things. Jeffrey said he has nothing here he wants."

"When we talked a few days ago, you didn't say anything about this. Why now?"

"Isabel was the topic of conversation then. By the way she's being reassigned to Jordan."

"You've talked to her?"

"No. Email."

"Why Jordan?"

"Our troops are helping with the refugees pouring across the border, and they need Arabic interpreters."

Diana's head was spinning with Paul's abruptness and his news. "I don't think it's fair for you to put the house on the market while I'm away."

"You should have thought about that before you left."

"This isn't the first trip I've taken to research my books."

"Never for three months."

"I'll come home this weekend. We can talk."

"If you do, then you can talk to your mother, too."

"Is she bothering you?"

"We had words. It didn't go well. According to her, I'm an evil man. You left me because I raised an irresponsible daughter and a gay son."

"That's so unfair. I'm sorry. I'll talk to her."

"You've never stood up to her before. Why should I think you'll do it now?"

"I will this time. She's gone too far."

"Everything's gone too far. If you're here this weekend, you can sign the paperwork Janie's preparing. If not, I'll send them to you." He paused as if waiting for her to say something, but she was tongue-tied. "I have to go to Chicago."

"Something's wrong with Jeffrey?"

"His partner David has a cancerous growth. They're operating this Friday. I told Jeffrey I'll fly out to be with him."

She groaned at this news. "Should I call him?"

"Not unless you're willing to accept him unconditionally."

"I'm trying." She was near tears.

"You don't seem to have a problem with other gay people, why him?"

"He's my son."

"So, treat him like a son." He paused. "Sorry to be so gruff, but there's a lot on my mind. Even things at the university are difficult. I have enough years in to get my pension. The present administration refuses to support the teachers. I've had it with them."

"There's no point in my coming home if you aren't going to be there. I'll come the following weekend."

"Fine. If you don't come, I'll send the real estate contract to your post office box."

"Call me when you learn how the operation went for David," she said.

"Okay. Till then." He clicked off.

She held her cell phone in her limp hand and stared at the retirement home. Tears that had been squelched for months cascaded down her cheeks. Paul sounded angry and worried. What could have happened in the few days since they'd talked about Isabel? Would his friends know what was going on at the university? Did she dare call Paul's best friend, George? Paul wouldn't like the interference, and it might make things worse.

She held her head in her hands, trying to think what she could or should do. Feelings of hopelessness swept over her. "Crap!" She took a deep breath. "I can't sit here dithering." With a heavy sigh, she folded her notes and jammed them into her purse. She got out of the car, hurried to the restroom inside the retirement home's lobby and reapplied her mascara and lipstick before walking to Hetch's room.

When she knocked on his door, a bark greeted her before Hetch called out, "Come on in."

A tail-wagging Shelly sniffed Diana. "You're a good guard dog." Diana bent down to scratch the dog behind the ears.

Hetch had a wide grin on his broad face. "She's a happy pup." He nodded to the patio. "Let's go out there." He hesitated and stared at her. "Want some water or juice? You look a little done in."

"Thanks, no. I'm fine." She walked outside and faced Hetch.

"Sam must have really shaken you," Hetch said.

"He did. If I hadn't had a friend with me, I think he would have hit me."

Hetch shook his head. "You pressing charges?"

"No. That's not why I came." She sat down. "I need to know more about him because I've learned that he had a motive for killing Gloria."

"Oh, come on. That's not possible."

"Sam claimed that Gloria's house belongs to him and not Captain Cranston. Why would he think that?"

"He shouldn't, but he does." He stroked his chin, studying her. "Okay, I'll give you some background. About nine years ago Gloria's house needed electrical work, and she hired my company. Sam needed to grow up, become responsible, so I let him manage the job even though he'd just turned twenty. Turned out the entire house needed rewiring. After he finished the job, he kept going back to do odd jobs. Since he'd been so loyal, she said she'd leave the house to him when she died. I told Sam to forget it. Gloria never honored a promise to anyone."

"He says he's going to file a lawsuit against Grant because he's not her nephew."

"Course Grant wasn't her nephew. I told Sam that. Why he thinks he can file a lawsuit is beyond me."

Diana shifted in her chair. "Ten years ago Sam was involved with men who were convicted of importing and distributing cocaine."

"You've been digging into the past." He studied her, then sighed. "I gave him the job at Gloria's to help him get his act together."

"One of the men sentenced for the crime was released a year ago. A Phil Yukovitch. Do you know him?"

"Yeah, from the trial."

"Could Phil have had anything to do with Gloria's murder?"

Hetch reared back and chortled. "I don't know. Why?" He nodded. "I get it. You think Sam might have wanted Gloria dead because of the house and had this guy Phil do it."

"Something like that."

"Sam's no angel, but he had no hold over Phil. Sam always felt guilty about testifying against the others. If anything Phil might want to get back at Sam, not the other way around. Why would Sam want to kill Gloria? He has plenty of money. The business is doing amazingly well."

"It must be. He drives a new BMW."

"Yeah, even I asked him about that. Company got a big contract from the town. Grabbed it from under Benton Electric's nose. So he gave himself and the men bonuses. He told me he doesn't owe money for anything. No credit card debt, nothing. I think he's pissed that the old woman conned him, and there isn't a damn thing he can do about it."

"I'm sorry I asked, but he scared me." She rubbed the side of her neck.

"I'll talk to him. He shouldn't be bothering you. After Gloria was murdered and the police inquiry was finished, Sam haunted the place. Cora, the realtor, had to get a restraining order against him." He sighed and shook his head. "Parents can't always control what their kids do."

"I'm well aware of that. I have two children and have no say in how they lead their lives."

"You shouldn't. I've allowed Sam to take over the business, and he's doing things his way. Turns out it's been for the best. He's gotten contracts that I'd begged to have in the past. He even got the contract to do the electrical work for the new police station. That was a coup. Benton Electric used to get all the public facility jobs. Sam undercut their bid and still made money." Hetch stroked Shelly behind the ears. "Times change and it's hard for me to accept the new stuff. I don't even like the music they play."

Diana smiled. "Neither do I and I'm younger than you."

"You're still young. Sam thinks I'm a crabby old curmudgeon, but he's no angel either. He comes in here, yells and screams and then doesn't come back for another month."

Diana wondered if her family viewed her as old, stuffy, uncaring of their wishes. "May I ask a personal question?"

"Hell, why not? You've practically accused my son of murder."

"I didn't, but after reading about his past, I needed to find out more about him to understand where he fits into the puzzle of Gloria's death."

She stood. "I've taken up too much of your time." She glanced at Shelly. "I'm glad it's worked out for you and the dog."

"Sit down," he ordered. "You can't leave before I know what the personal question is."

She sat and gripped her purse in her hands. "It's nothing, really."

"Then why did you ask and why were you in a dither when you arrived?"

She twisted her wedding band, then clasped her hands. "I had a distressing call right before I came." She felt like an idiot asking a man she barely knew, but she had no one else. What did she have to lose? "Do I come across as…stuffy, prejudiced, a difficult woman?"

He shook his head. "Oh, lady. You are nosy as hell, but I wouldn't call you stuffy. Prejudiced? Not sure. You're open and forthright. I like that. Some might find that hard to take." He smiled. "Now I have a question for you. Why did you ask me that?"

She broke into tears, grabbed a handkerchief from her purse and her words poured out. "I had an argument with my daughter and my son and haven't talked to either one since, and now my husband's unhappy. He might want to get a divorce. My life has turned upside down."

"I'm honored you confided in me." He wheeled nearer and patted her arm. "I guess you need to make things right, but remember there's another side of the equation. The other fellow. It might not be all about you, but some of you and some of them. That's what I've come to understand about Sam and me."

She sniffed. "I shouldn't have blurted out my family problems. You've got your own problems." She glanced at him. "You've been very kind in spite of my questions about Sam."

"Wish I could be more understanding with my own son. I guess that's the way it is between parents and kids." He looked down at Shelly. "At least the dog doesn't talk back and obeys most of the time."

When she put her handkerchief into her purse, she saw the notes she'd stashed in it. Pulling out the paper, she read the last item. "There is one more thing. How well do you know Joe O'Reilly?"

"He's a good friend of Sam's. They've known each other from when we lived in Providence. Helped Sam out of that mess ten years ago. Both Sam and I owe him big time."

Chapter 15

When Diana drove into her driveway, she couldn't remember anything about her trip back. She'd been focused on Paul, the children, the sale of their house and felt overwhelmed. She sat in the car, then looked over at Bert and Grant sanding and chipping paint off the storm windows. Their clothes were smudged with dirt, their faces streaked with sweat.

She got out of the car, passing them on the way to the back door. "Looks like you've been in the coal mines."

"Feels like it." Grant dusted off his pants. "Cora called. I asked her to come by tonight to discuss the rental arrangements."

"What time?"

"Seven. Okay?"

She nodded. "It's your turn to make dinner, but seeing your condition, I'll do the honors."

"Angel thou art." He saluted and returned to his work.

Diana went into her bedroom, shut the door and collapsed on the bed. Her mind spun. She loved her family and felt a grinding hurt that none of them seemed to love her. The letter she'd written Isabel might take a long time to get to her. Now that she was in Jordan, she might never get it.

Diana sat up. "Idiot." She hurried to the living room and opened her laptop.

Although she'd sent brief one line emails to Isabel since she'd enlisted in the Marines, this was the first one that had meaning. She shook her head, knowing she'd been stubborn and self-righteous. Communication was key. God, if anyone knew the power of words, she should. In the email she reiterated what she'd written in her letter and added how much she wanted to hear Isabel's voice. I don't know when to call you. Can you call me? Could we Skype? She clicked send and sat back. One step done. Now for the next.

She called Jeffrey and after two rings he answered. "Mom?" His voice was tentative, strained.

"Jeffrey, it's good to hear your voice. I talked to your dad, and he told me about David. I'm so sorry. How are you holding up?"

"It's difficult." There was a long pause. "I'm surprised to hear from you."

"I've been wanting to call, but I didn't have the nerve. Our quarrel was unnecessary. My fault. I love you, Jeffrey, and always will." Her words tumbled out. "If David and you want to be together and you're happy, that's all that matters." She waited, hoping he'd say something. "Can you forgive my earlier stupid rantings?" As she waited for his reply, her heart beat increased, her face flushed.

"It's hard to get my head around your sudden acceptance. Right now I'm focused on David. I'm not sure what I'll do if he doesn't make it."

"I wish I could do something for you. I'm glad your dad will be with you. He's a rock in a crisis."

"Yeah, he's been real understanding."

The implication was clear. She wasn't. She couldn't deny the truth of that. "Will you let me know how the operation goes, or have Dad call me? I do care. I love you."

"Okay, Mom. Thanks for your call. I appreciate it." There was another long pause as if he was trying to gather his thoughts. "Isabel was wounded. Have you talked to her?"

"No. I wrote a letter and just emailed her. I hope she replies soon."

"Let me know if she does and find out exactly what's going on. She's been less than candid."

"What exactly have you heard?"

"The soldier who saved her was badly injured and he didn't make it. I think she feels lucky, but guilty since she only took a bullet in the shoulder. That's all she'd say, but I could tell she was hiding stuff. She always has. Never wants to let anyone know how she really feels."

"You talked to her?"

"She called me from the Landstuhl Hospital in Germany. Didn't want to worry you or Dad. I finally persuaded her to call Dad."

Jeffrey had always been close to his sister and knew her better than either Paul or she did. "Thanks for the insight. Could you ask your dad to call me when he has a chance?"

"Sure. Are you and he on the outs?"

"Why do you ask?"

"It's obvious, isn't it? You're in Rhode Island, and he's got trouble at the university."

"I'm only away for a few months." She swallowed, trying to decide exactly what to say. "Your father wants to sell the house."

"Yeah, he told me. Sounds like a good idea, especially if he's not going to teach anymore."

"What? Don't be silly, he's got tenure. He's just unhappy with the present dean."

"Didn't he tell you?"

"We haven't had a chance to talk much. We're getting together the weekend after he gets back from visiting you. What did he say about his job?"

"Not much. I got the impression he was angry about something that happened. Says teaching isn't worth what the administration wants to put him through."

"Are you sure? Teaching has been his life." She felt the cold grip of fear. Fear for Paul and herself. Being a professor had been his identity, his joy. What would cause him to give it up? Jeffrey's voice interrupted her thoughts.

"I've got to cut this short. I'm taking David to have blood work done before his operation. Nice to talk to you, Mom. Bye."

She hung up and the word "nice" hung in the air. Repairing her relationship with Jeffrey would take time and work on her part. At least she'd started to mend the chasm she'd created between herself and her children. The hold Beatrice had on her was fading. Would she have the courage to be her own person when she came face to face with her mother? At the age of fifty-two she finally understood what was important—Paul, Isabel, and Jeffrey.

"Thought you were going to make dinner."

At the sound of Grant's voice Diana spun around in her chair. "I got involved with communicating with my family."

"Good thing to do." He stood in his stocking feet, staring at her. "Are you okay?"

"Yes, well, maybe a little distracted." She fumbled with her cell phone and tried to smile. Glancing at her watch, she was surprised to see it was almost six. "I'll start dinner."

"I'll be back and help after I shower." He took the stairs two at a time.

During dinner they discussed what she'd learned from Penny and Hetch. Diana was glad to focus on things other than her family. "Sam has motive for the murder. Although Detective O'Reilly helped Sam ten years ago, would he risk his job and his reputation for Sam?" She wiped the condensation off her water glass with her finger.

"We need to know more about O'Reilly." He took his dishes to the sink. "Bert was closed-mouthed all day. I asked about the stone path from the backdoor to the shed. He said he thought it looked artistic."

Diana laughed. "That doesn't sound like Bert."

"More like a female perspective."

"Marlene?"

"Could be, but why?" He rinsed the dishes and put them in the dishwasher while she brought the cooking pots to him.

"Why don't you move the stones on a direct path to the shed and see how he reacts?"

"Thought about that, but wondering if it's too soon. I need his help to get the place shaped up. I hope to power wash the outside tomorrow. Then Marlene can clean the windows Thursday."

Diana leaned against the counter. "You seem obsessed with the house and the murder. Why do you care?"

He sighed and wiped his hands on a towel. "I like things neat, no loose ends." He hesitated. "And I have to keep busy so I won't think about," he threw the towel down, "you know, the past, the battles, my outfit, my…my friends." He abruptly left the kitchen.

After putting away the last few dishes, she went into the living room and found him standing by the front door, staring at the floor. "What are you thinking?" she asked.

He shrugged. "About her, about how much I hated her."

"Gloria?"

"Yeah." He ran a hand across his face. "I keep wondering. Why did she leave this place to me? As an act of repentance or an act of revenge?"

"Does it matter? It's how you accept it and what you do with it, not what her motive was."

He studied her. "You're very wise yet you seem to have trouble understanding your own family."

She sat in the chair next to the unlit fireplace. "I'm dealing with my problems. I emailed Isabel and called Jeffrey."

"Great. So you know Isabel's in Jordan."

She frowned. "Yes, but how do you know?"

"I told you. I have a buddy over there. We email back and forth."

"Why didn't you tell me?"

"I planned to, but it's better you learned it from her." He sat on the couch.

"I found out from my son, I haven't heard back from her."

When the porch doorbell rang, Diana looked at her watch. "Cora's prompt."

Grant opened the door to Cora, who was dressed in jeans, a turtleneck and corduroy jacket. "You must be the sergeant Captain Cranston mentioned." She shook his hand. "Glad to meet you." Cora turned to Diana who'd remained seated. "I'm really sorry about the mixup." She glanced from one to the other. "Have you come to a decision about how to work this out?"

"We've agreed that both of us will stay," Diana said. "Since he's Captain Cranston's guest, I can't throw him out and I don't want to leave. I'll continue to stay for the three months." As Diana said this, she thought about Paul's desire to sell their house. This rental might be a haven even with all the turmoil surrounding it.

Cora put a hand to her chest. "I'm so relieved. This house has been a nightmare from the start." She sat at the far end of the couch and fiddled with one of the throw pillows. "When Detective O'Reilly told me about the remains in the attic, I almost fainted. You must have been upset, and I certainly don't blame you."

Grant drew up a chair across from the couch. "It seemed odd that no one had been in the attic even though the entire interior of the house had been repainted."

"I saw to that. All the mattresses and bedding have been replaced. If I hadn't done that, no one would want to rent the place."

"But what about the attic?" His voice was insistent.

"It was going to be a rental not a sale. I saw no reason to go up there. Oh, I took a peek, but there were only a few suitcases, trunks and a box. It wasn't my business to go through those, and after hearing what was in one of them, I'm glad I didn't."

"How did you end up as the overseer of the house?" Diana asked.

"Through Chief Nelson. When the police were finished with their investigation, the place became a haven for squatters and vandalism. After Feeney's murder Ursula would call the police whenever she saw a light coming from this house. Nelson got tired of sending patrols and talked to the lawyer handling Gloria's estate. The estate hired a security guard. A deal was struck that the house could be repaired and painted inside before the close of probate. I was available and had experience in redecorating. I kept the Schukarts on and hired a carpenter and a painter."

"Why the carpenter?" Grant asked.

"Vandals had torn off wall paneling upstairs. It was a mess. I also needed to get a restraining order against Sam Feeney to prevent him from entering the house."

"The security guard didn't do his job?"

"Her, not him. Angie Murphy had the night shift. I thought the days would be okay since we had crews coming and going. I should have put a guard on days as well, because Sam was persistent and clever."

"Angie?" Grant asked. "Was that retired Officer Angie Murphy?"

Cora nodded. "Since she knew the area and the local officers, I didn't object to O'Reilly's recommendation."

Diana and Grant exchanged glances, but Diana only said, "I heard Sam thought the house belongs to him."

"Sam totally frustrated Angie. He had keys to the house, so I changed the locks, but he still came around. It didn't matter how often the police rousted him, he'd always return. Claimed it was his right." Cora took a deep breath. "He's a difficult person."

Diana nodded. "He came to the house the other night and claimed the place belonged to him and not Captain Cranston. If the sergeant hadn't been here, I'm not sure what Sam might have done."

"The man's a menace," Cora said.

"He calmed down," Grant said. "I don't think Mrs. Bellfore or I want to make a big deal about it. After blowing off steam, he left quietly."

"Well, if he comes around again, report him. He shouldn't come here bothering either of you."

Diana thought further talk about Sam was pointless. "You did a good job on your choice of paint colors. I noticed there aren't many pictures on the walls."

"It's a rental, not a home. If you want to hang something, use those quick removal tape things."

"That's not what I meant. Ursula told me Gloria owned two of her paintings, yet they weren't in the house." Diana nodded to Grant. "I had him look everywhere."

"I have the framed photographs at the office, but Ursula's painting is at my house. I thought it too valuable to be left lying around, especially after the problems I had with vandalism and Sam."

"It? Ursula said there were two paintings." Diana glanced at Grant.

Cora shook her head. "The police took an inventory of everything before I redecorated. I have a copy of the list. There was only the one painting of Ursula's. I heard there was quite a history of a feud between Gloria and Ursula about it. After I took it down and stored it, even Penelope Nelson got into it. Said there was bad karma around that particular painting of the house. Penny has become a little too obsessive about this house and Ursula. She demanded I return the picture to Ursula, but of course, I couldn't do that. Penny became irate about the whole matter. I told her that when the Captain returns, I'll hand it as well as other items left in the house over to him."

"I didn't mean to insinuate anything was amiss." Keeping Cora on her side was important. "It's only that I understood that Gloria had two of her paintings, and I wondered what happened to them."

Cora shrugged. "If there was another, Sam might have gotten his hands on it. He's impossible and intimidating." She ran a finger around the inside of her black turtleneck sweater. "If there's anything you need, call." She stood to leave.

After they saw her to the door, Diana turned to Grant. "What do you think?"

"Sam seems to be a problem for everyone." He rubbed his jaw. "Interesting that Angie Murphy was the security guard. That's a lead we need to follow, but not sure I'm the one to do it."

"Oh, don't look at me," Diana said. "I've got enough to do." Diana stared at the walls. "The paintings could be important. I hope to meet with the head of the URI art department first thing tomorrow. I'll visit Ursula afterward."

Grant paced the room. "Cora's right about the panels upstairs. I could see where the repairs were made."

"What happened to Gloria's personal belongings?" Diana asked. "She must have had jewelry, or books, or special objects."

"I sure don't want them."

"I understand your reluctance. However, they might give us clues about who would want her dead and why. If her personal effects weren't in the attic, the police might have impounded them or her lawyer may have them. Do you know who he is?"

"Clayton Morris. He's in Providence. I've only been in contact with him through letters and emails."

"Maybe it's time you visited him."

"That means blowing my cover as the sergeant."

"Does it? If he isn't local, how would anyone know?" She studied him. "Besides, don't you think it's about time you gave up the masquerade?"

Chapter 16

Wednesday Diana awakened to dark clouds that reflected her mood. When she entered the kitchen, Grant was finishing breakfast. "I haven't seen you in a suit before," she said.

"Going to Providence. I was going to power wash the exterior but with another storm brewing, I'll have to wait. I told Bert to take the day off." He glanced out the window then picked up his dishes. "I'm taking your advice and made an appointment with Clayton Morris."

For a moment she forgot that Morris had been Gloria's estate lawyer. She poured a cup of coffee and sat at the table. "He might be able to explain why Gloria left the house to you."

"Maybe, but I'm not expecting any big revelations." He reached for his jacket on the back of the chair. "Perhaps he'll clear up where Sam got the idea that the house belongs to him." He pulled on his jacket. "I'll stop by the police station on the way back to get Angie Murphy's address and any information they might have on the identity of the baby's remains."

"Are you going to ask as Grant Cranston?" A clap of thunder and a flash of lightning startled her.

He sighed and gave her a small smile. "I'm not learning much as the sergeant." He nodded. "Yeah. Captain Grant Cranston has arrived."

"I'm glad. I'm tired of calling you Sergeant in front of others. I began to feel schizophrenic." She paused and added, "How do you think Penny will react?"

"I don't think she's relevant to the situation. What happened between us has long since passed. I'm hoping that Chief Nelson will let me see the entire case file on Gloria's murder."

"That might help." She went to the fridge and took out the orange juice. "Ursula asked me to go to the exhibit of her paintings at the Brecks. I plan to accept, since Joe O'Reilly's parents will be there. Between our separate inquiries, we might learn something new."

"Hope so. See you tonight." He went out the door.

Before leaving to visit the university, Diana went to the shed, took the frame with the attached canvas fragment and put it in her car. Driving down the road, she spotted a BMW parked on a dirt lane. There weren't too many of those in town. She continued past, pulled into a driveway and watched out her side window. The BMW edged onto the street and turned in the direction of the Victorian. "What are you up to, Sam?" Her voice resonated in her car. She debated whether to call the police or investigate herself. She made the safe choice.

While she waited for the police, she wondered why Sam had such an affinity with the Feeney place. When the police car passed by her parked car, she followed it back to the house. The BMW was parked in the driveway. The officers introduced themselves, and after conferring with Diana, they entered through the back door while she waited outside. Soon they reappeared with Sam in handcuffs.

"He didn't put up a fight," one officer said.

Sam glared at her. "It's gone. What happened to it? Bitch!"

Diana frowned. "What are you talking about?"

"She stole it. Bitch!" He spat on the ground. "I'll get her."

She swallowed. "Who? Me?" She turned to the officer. "Can we add his threat to the breaking and entering charge?"

Officer Daniels nodded. "File a complaint at the station."

As he was led to the patrol car, Sam yelled over his shoulder. "It's not breaking and entering if it's your own house."

While one officer put Sam in the patrol car, Officer Daniels came over to her. "Would you look to see if anything is missing. We didn't find anything on him, but I'd like to be thorough."

She nodded and Officer Daniels followed her into the house. She wondered what Sam was looking for. She saw nothing unusual until she entered her bedroom. The drywall had been bashed in above the outlet, leaving a foot-wide hole. "Stupid vandalism."

"That wasn't there before?" Officer Daniels asked.

"No. What could he have been after?"

The officer reached into the hole, but found nothing. "As you said, vandalism. We've had trouble with him here at the house before." He turned to go. "If there isn't anything else, we'll take him in and book him. Come to the station and file a complaint."

After he left, she phoned Grant's cell. When he didn't answer, she left a message explaining what had happened.

At the police station she signed the paperwork and was about to leave when she met Detective O'Reilly in the hall. "Sam Feeney hasn't gotten over his interest in the house I'm renting," she said.

"He's obsessive about that place, but he's harmless."

"He didn't sound harmless. Ask your officers. He made threats. This is the second incident I've had with him. Are you defending him?"

O'Reilly stepped back. "I'm not. Vandalism is wrong, but law enforcement has other things to do beside house sit. There's no sense in making a big stink about a small infraction of the law. We have a low crime rate here in Quamscutt, and there's no reason to blow it out of proportion."

Diana felt her face pale. "Since he's been a friend of yours for years, I understand why you'd like to make light of his actions, but it's your job to enforce the law for all citizens."

His eyes narrowed. "Don't tell me how to do my job. Maybe you'd be happier in another town, another rental. Sam's case will be treated like any other." He turned on his heels and strode away.

"Damn," she muttered. She'd handled that badly. Although it was stupid to make an enemy of O'Reilly, Chief Nelson should know about the man's connection with Sam. As an outsider, she'd be pegged a troublemaker if she said anything, but O'Reilly's background could be pertinent to the investigation.

In the afternoon Diana knocked on Professor Irene Jamison's door with the silver-painted frame in her hand. After a voice called out to come in, Diana entered a light-filled office with stacks of books on one bookshelf and a screen and projector propped against another wall. A tall, willowy woman with dark hair stood behind a desk piled with papers and folders.

"Mrs. Bellfore, come in. I'm Irene." The woman had a small mouth with deep lines on either side as if she wore a permanent smile. "I've read some of your books. Enjoyable reads. What brings you to my department?"

Diana held out the frame with the small piece of attached canvas. "I'm hoping you might give me some information about this. I found it at the house I'm renting and wondered if you could tell me something about it."

Irene moved from behind her desk, took the frame and placed it on a nearby table. "It's seen better days. Old."

"Very old?"

Irene shrugged. "Hard to tell. It looks familiar. Local. Hmm. I know. Ursula Von Reiter frames her work this way. Of course, that doesn't mean this is one of hers." Irene looked up. "Have you asked her? She lives in the area."

"I know nothing about painting. What about the piece of canvas connected to it?"

Irene took out a magnifying glass. "Today, linen is popular with professional artists. It comes from the flax plant and is more expensive than cotton. Cotton duck canvas is more economical. From the tightly woven threads I'd say this piece is cotton. If this is from one of Ursula's paintings, it was some time ago. She uses linen now."

Irene pointed to the piece connected to the frame. "This was attached with a spline at the rear of the frame. That way the artwork can be displayed without a frame. See how the paint goes around the sides?"

"Can you tell anything about the paint?"

"Not without lab tests." She smiled at Diana. "What's this all about—a mystery novel you're writing?"

Diana hated lying to the kind woman. "In a way. I hope you don't mind."

"I'm delighted to help an author." She looked at her watch. "I'd love to hear more about the story, but I have a class in twenty minutes."

"I appreciate the help. I'll let you know what comes of my inquiries."

"Please do, and if you see Ursula, tell her I'm looking forward to seeing her at the Brecks."

"I'll tell her."

Diana drove to Ursula's, wondering how her unexpected arrival would be received. She parked next to Ursula's Volvo and left the frame in her car. A ten-speed bike leaned against the side of the house near the front door.

After she knocked, Penny, dressed in stretch pants, an emerald green pullover and sneakers, opened the door. "Well, what a surprise," she said. "Come in. We were just talking about you."

"Oh? That doesn't sound good." Diana went into the colorful living room.

Ursula sat on a chaise lounge, a throw rug over her legs and a scarlet scarf at her throat contrasting with a vibrant aqua blouse. Her face was pale and her voice had a raspy quality, but her eyes were alert. Pushing away the feeling that the old artist could read her mind, Diana sat on the couch. "Am I intruding on a gossip session?"

"It's not gossip," Ursula said. "We were discussing the latest events at the Feeney house. All the elements for a mystery writer."

Penny stood behind Ursula's chair, wringing her hands. "I told her about Grant and the letters you found."

Diana nodded, but didn't know where the conversation should go. Did Penny know that Grant was home? How could she? She glanced at her watch. He should be finished talking to the lawyer by now. "I dropped in to see how you were. Penny said you haven't been feeling well."

"At my age there's always something. You go to bed one way and wake up with something you didn't have the night before. How do you get a cold overnight?"

"Will you be able to go to the Brecks on Saturday?" Diana asked.

"Absolutely. It might be my last hurrah."

"Don't say that." Penny moved to an ottoman near Ursula and took hold of the woman's small hand.

Ursula smiled. "Don't fret. I'm going to be fine."

"I've decided to take you up on your invitation to the Brecks, if it's still open," Diana said.

Ursula pulled herself to a more upright position. "Good. Do you mind driving me?"

"Not at all."

Penny smiled in what Diana took to be relief. "Charlie and I were going to take her, but we can't get there till later, and she should be present at the beginning."

"What time Saturday?" Diana asked.

"Two," Ursula said, then coughed.

"Their house is near the old Newport mansions." Penny stood. "It's a bit of a drive. I'll write out the directions."

"Will an hour allow enough time to get there?"

"Plenty," Ursula said. "I don't want to be too early."

A loud clap of thunder shook the room. Ursula looked out the windows. "Penny, you should leave or you'll be caught in the rain."

"Is that your bike outside?" Diana asked.

Penny looked up from the note she was writing. "My car's in the shop till Tuesday."

"I can give you a ride home."

"That'd be great." Penny handed the directions to Diana before turning to Ursula. "I'll heat the soup I brought before I leave."

Ursula shook her head. "It's too early. I'll stick it in the microwave later." She looked at Diana. "She thinks I'm an invalid because I have a cough." The small woman tilted her head back. "Did you come to ask me something special or was it only to say you plan to go to the Brecks?"

Diana blinked. "You don't miss much, do you?" She pointed to the paintings on the wall. "I found an old picture frame in the shed much like the ones you use. I was wondering if it might be yours. You said Gloria had two of your paintings, but Cora Jacob said there was only one."

Ursula closed her eyes. "So?"

"Ah, I was wondering if you could identify the frame as yours. There's a bit of canvas attached."

Ursula sighed heavily and opened her eyes. "I don't care if it's mine or not. So what? She bought them and could do what she wanted with them. Get rid of the frame. Donate it to a thrift store, or something."

Diana was surprised at the dismissal of the frame, since she remembered how Ursula had spoken of her paintings as her children. "Of course. That's a good idea."

"Now you two leave and get home before the storm lets loose."

"You're sure you'll be all right?" Penny frowned.

"Fine. I have my cell phone. If anything happens that nice husband of yours can send one of his officers."

Penny gave Ursula a kiss on the cheek, and Diana said she'd pick Ursula up at one on Saturday. As they walked out the door and stowed Penny's bike in the trunk, the rain began.

Concerned that the bike might fall out, Diana drove slowly. "Is Ursula very ill?"

"I'm not sure." Penny's face crumpled. "I found medication in her medicine cabinet. One was a blood thinner and another for angina. I think she has a heart problem, but she claims she has no health issues other than age. Still, I'm concerned."

"Has she seen a doctor?"

"She says doctors just prolong life. Says she has regrets and wants to leave before her reputation is tarnished."

"Because of the bad reviews of her work? That doesn't sound like her."

Penny nodded. "That's why I can't stand to leave her alone. She hasn't been to a doctor in two years. Do you think she'd do something…stupid?"

"God, I hope not." She hesitated and glanced at Penny. "Don't take on that burden. There's nothing you can do if she makes up her mind to end her life. You can't be with her every minute. She's her own person, and from what I've learned about her, she's always lived life her way. Don't judge her or try to become her savior. You'll only hurt yourself."

Penny stared at her. "It sounds like you've been in this situation."

Diana gripped the wheel tighter and nodded. "My father. A long time ago. He couldn't face his life and killed himself."

"I'm sorry."

"Eighteen years now. It never really goes away. I know the experts say to get the person help, but that isn't always possible. Ursula is stubborn. That's why I'm warning you not to take on her burdens. It will bring you nothing but sorrow and drive you nuts."

"She's like a grandmother to me."

"I understand. It's hard to see someone you love suffer." She took a deep breath. "Sometimes we can't help them."

While Penny stifled her sobs, images that Diana had suppressed skimmed through her mind. Her father and mother's incessant arguing, her father's depression, and her mother's nagging came back in a flood. She thrust them aside. "On another subject that you might find interesting, Sam Feeney broke into the house. I spotted his car and called the police. They caught him redhanded. He'd banged a hole in a wall."

Penny shook her head. "I'm not surprised. They should burn that house down. It's no good to anyone, even Grant. Why would he want it or want Ursula's missing painting? You said Cora has one of them. It doesn't belong to her. It's Ursula's."

"How do you know Cora has only one of the paintings?"

"You told us that. She painted two landscapes for the Feeneys. Maybe Cora has both of them. Ursula feels her paintings are like children. Did you know that?"

Diana nodded, but decided not to give an opinion, since Penny seemed to be getting worked up about it. "I met Detective O'Reilly at the station, and he made excuses for Sam. Do you have any idea why?"

"No. Joe's usually Mr. Law and Order."

"You'd think after Cora got a restraining order against Sam, he'd quit."

"Did you talk to Cora?" Penny asked.

"Briefly. She only got back the other day from visiting her mother."

When Penny instructed Diana to cross Route One, Diana was surprised. "You biked to Ursula's with all these crazy turn arounds?"

"You get used to them. I wouldn't want a child to do it, but I'm careful."

"I'm glad you didn't have to bike home. In this rain cars might not see you."

"I could have stayed at Ursula's overnight. I've done it before."

"Did you think it odd that she wasn't interested in the frame I found?"

"No. Why would she be? The frames aren't important, it's those paintings Cora has. They belong to Ursula."

Diana nodded, thinking that the paintings might be the key to Gloria's murder, but had no idea how. "Cora has kept one of the paintings for Grant Cranston. After all he's the heir of the house and its contents. It's a landscape with the Victorian house." She pulled into the Nelson's driveway to a modest, well-maintained house.

"Cora shouldn't have that painting. And she certainly shouldn't have fixed up the house. It should be razed." Penny's voice got louder. "Why can't everyone understand? Its caused nothing but misery for everyone." She unclenched her fists. "Sorry, I didn't mean to carry on. It's not my business. Charlie says it's just a house. But I don't feel that way. It has bad vibes. Sometimes you have to make things right, no matter what."

Penny seemed to be muddled, and Diana didn't know what to say to her. But before the young woman got out of the car, Diana reached out and put a hand on Penny's arm. "One more thing. I know I'm being nosy, but does Charles know about Grant?"

"Of course. Before I married Charlie, I decided he should know about my background and what happened that summer. That's why he could face the city council and not react when Gloria tried to smear my name." She looked at Diana, her eyes glistening with tears. "The child I aborted wasn't Grant's. He helped me, got me a doctor, even helped pay for it."

"Do you blame Grant?"

"For what?" She shook her head. "The doctor was supposed to be reputable, but things went wrong." She sighed. "Bad things happen."

"It seems that way, doesn't it? We make choices then argue with the results."

"Choices. How many wrong ones do we make in a lifetime?" Penny shuddered. "Enough of that. Thanks for the ride and the talk." She got out, fixed the bike's clanking chain and hurried into the garage.

Diana drove away thinking about Ursula's health, the break-in, relationships and secrets.

Chapter 17

Diana's windshield wipers were no match for the downpour. When she pulled into the driveway, she could barely make out Grant's truck. She'd forgotten her umbrella, so she ran to the back door. In the mudroom she hung her damp camel hair coat on a peg, removed her shoes, and put on slippers she'd left under the bench.

In her bedroom she found Grant on his knees, his arm extended into the hole that Sam had made in the wall. "What on earth are you doing?"

He grunted, half-turned, then continued snaking his arm into the hole. "Got something." When he pulled out his arm, he held a package wrapped in gray cellophane. "I thought Sam might have been looking for something." He made a small slit in the paper with his pen knife, dipped the tip of his index finger into the mix and tasted it. "Coke."

"Cocaine?" Diana sat on the bed. "That's what Sam was after?"

"Looks that way. Makes sense from what we know of his background." He left the package on the floor and leaned against the far wall. "Now what do we do?"

"Call the police."

"You trust Detective O'Reilly? Will he believe we didn't plant this? Might even be inclined to arrest us on a drug charge."

"Good lord, he wouldn't do that." She hesitated. "Would he?"

"How do we prove this belongs to Sam and not us?"

"Damn." Swearing was not her usual response, but she'd had it with the events surrounding the house. "When Officer Daniels checked the hole, he didn't find anything. And I antagonized O'Reilly at the police station. Stupid of me. So, you're right. O'Reilly might want to arrest us." She stared at the hole in the wall and the gray package. "We have to report this. We should talk to Police Chief Nelson." She took out her cell, then looked at him. "Did you drop by the station and talk with Nelson?"

He bit his lip. "I got your message and came here first to see what damage had been done." He ran a hand over his jaw. "Okay, call, but ask him to come without O'Reilly."

Diana's conversation with Chief Nelson was one-sided and awkward. She explained Grant Cranston was with her, and they had evidence that Sam Feeney may have been looking for drugs in the house. It took some persuading, but he agreed to come to the house and not involve Detective O'Reilly at this time.

While Grant and Diana waited, he showed her two sealed boxes belonging to Gloria that the lawyer Clayton Morris had given him. "I'd like you to be here when I go through them."

She frowned. "I appreciate your confidence and I'm curious as to their contents, but is that necessary?"

"I need a witness. After finding the cocaine, I think both you and I have to protect ourselves."

She sat in the wingback chair by the fireplace. "Did you find out why Sam thinks the house belongs to him?"

He stopped pacing and sat on the couch. "Gloria had given Sam a letter stating that the house would be his upon her death, but a few months later, she rewrote her will and made me the heir. She told Mr. Morris that she no longer trusted Sam, but didn't say why."

They sat in the living room staring at the boxes as if they contained snakes. Thunder rattled the windows, rain beat on the roof, and the sky turned black. Grant turned on lights in the room and on the porch. "My fingerprints will be on the package of cocaine."

"Naturally, you pulled it out. Why didn't Sam or Officer Daniels find it?"

"If they'd searched deeper, they would have. The cross section between the studs had rotted out allowing the package to slide down to the next cross piece."

Diana looked at her watch. "The Chief should have been here by now."

"He'll come. Just hope he holds to his side of the bargain." He stood. "I'm going to make coffee. Want some?"

"I'd prefer tea."

He nodded and walked to the kitchen. Diana remained seated, rubbing her forehead. There were too many people with too many agendas, and clues led in all directions. She went to her laptop but before she could turn it on, there was a knock on the front door.

She welcomed Police Chief Nelson and Officer Daniels into the living room. Nelson was tall and broad shouldered with a craggy face and wavy dark hair graying at the temples. His brown eyes were serious, but there was a warmth about the man.

"Nice to meet you, Mrs. Bellfore. Penny's told me about you. Since Officer Daniels was the arresting officer in the incident involving Sam Feeney earlier today, it's important that he's here."

Diana nodded to the officer. "Glad you came."

Grant came out of the kitchen with a coffee mug in one hand and a tea cup in the other. After placing them on the table by the couch, he introduced himself to the Chief and Officer Daniels.

Chief Nelson clasped his hand. "I'm glad to finally meet you." The Chief then turned to Diana. "I have questions for both of you, but first show us what you found that might involve Sam."

Diana and Grant led the way to the downstairs bedroom, then stood aside while the Chief and Officer Daniel inspected the package and the hole in the wall. "Did you see this damage earlier?" the Chief asked Officer Daniels.

"Yes sir. I inspected the hole and found nothing, but it was a cursory look. Sam yelled at Mrs. Bellfore about something she'd stolen and said he'd get even."

Diana stepped forward. "I'm not sure he was talking about me. Sam said, 'I'll get even with her.' I was standing right there, so he couldn't have meant me."

"Who then?" the Chief asked.

She shrugged. "I don't know."

"It's cocaine, sir," the officer said after he'd knelt on the floor and tasted it the way Grant had.

Chief Nelson nodded. "Bag the evidence, take photos of the area and log in the evidence at the station. Your shift is over, so after you finish writing your report, go home." He sighed. "It's been a long day."

Chief Nelson motioned for Grant and Diana to follow him back to the living room. The lights glinted off the pale yellow walls, and the heavy drapes muffled the sound of rain.

"Would you like coffee or tea?" Diana asked him.

"Thanks. Coffee, black."

She picked up the mug and cup that Grant had brought in earlier. "I'll freshen these and be back shortly."

When she returned with a laden tray, Grant and the Chief were seated on the couch talking. Officer Daniel had left.

The Chief took his coffee mug. "I will not talk about my officers in front of my men. Why didn't you want me to involve Detective O'Reilly? He's my lead detective."

Grant picked up his mug. "We were afraid he'd arrest us, claiming the cocaine belonged to us."

"He wouldn't do that without cause." The Chief's eyes narrowed. "He's a good police officer. Been with the department even before I arrived. Never had anyone accuse him of mistreatment or false arrest."

"O'Reilly has a history with Sam." Diana sat in her usual chair and picked up her cup of tea. "Ten years ago when Sam was arrested for being involved with a drug operation, O'Reilly vouched for him and helped get him off with probation. Ten kilos of crack cocaine were missing from the original bust. Hetch Feeney, Sam's father, told me that Gloria hired Hetch's company to rewire her house, this house. Hetch assigned Sam to the job. That gave Sam an opportunity to hide the cocaine here."

Chief Nelson frowned, but said nothing.

Diana took a breath and continued. "When I met O'Reilly this morning at the police station, we had words. My fault. I said things I shouldn't have." She turned her cup around and around in its saucer. "O'Reilly was in charge of the investigation into Gloria Feeney's murder. I understand the weapon was never found. O'Reilly said he had Officer Murphy search the attic. Why didn't she find the baby's remains?"

"I spoke with O'Reilly," Nelson said. "He plans to speak with Murphy, but she's retired. It's also possible that the remains were put there after the murder."

"Murphy was the security guard here at the house after the murder," Grant said. "It seems odd."

"She knew the local police, had police training and needed the work. I okayed her hire."

"Who recommended her?"

"O'Reilly. He felt bad about the way the other officers had treated her. Said she was a good police officer."

Grant leaned forward, his forearms on his knees. "O'Reilly hasn't been honest about his history with Sam and has taken a dislike to Mrs. Bellfore and myself."

"I think you're both too sensitive. This is a murder investigation. Police have to ask questions, be suspicious."

"There's one other thing," Diana said. "Why hasn't O'Reilly interviewed Cora about the baby's remains we found? She'd been in charge of repairs to this house."

"I'm sure she's on his to see list. There was vandalism here while the estate was being settled. I doubt she had anything to do with the remains that were found, but O'Reilly will speak to her. After Cora fixed up the house, the lawyer for the estate hired her to rent the house." He looked at Diana. "She didn't have much luck until you signed a lease." He glanced at Grant. "By the way, renting the house was at your request."

Grant nodded, stared at his coffee mug, then looked up. "I spoke with Gloria's lawyer. A few months before her death she rewrote her will and left the house to me."

"Then you're the one to file charges against Sam, not Mrs. Bellfore." After taking a sip of coffee, Nelson said, "Since you found cocaine, we need to search the entire house."

"I don't want the walls torn apart," Grant said.

The Chief smiled. "It won't come to that. I'll get a Narcotic K-9 unit." He stared at Grant. "Do you want me to get a warrant?"

"That won't be necessary. I'll be interested in what they find."

Chief Nelson turned to Diana. "Where did you dig up this information about O'Reilly helping Sam get probation?"

"The Boston Globe and the Providence Journal. I can forward the websites to you and the dates when the stories ran."

He gave her his email address. "If Sam was involved with a drug ring ten years ago why wait until after Gloria's death to get the stuff?"

Diana shook her head. "When you read the newspaper articles, you'll see that a Phil Yukovitch was sent to prison for his part in that drug case. He was released from prison just before Gloria was murdered."

"You think this man killed Gloria?"

"It's a connection. From what I've learned of the time line, the house was vandalized after Gloria's murder. With our recent discovery of cocaine, it seems a given that Sam was after it."

The Chief placed his empty cup on the side table. "I'm hearing poor judgement on Detective O'Reilly's part, but nothing criminal."

Grant nodded. "That might be all there is to it, but O'Reilly hasn't been forthcoming about the relationship."

Nelson held up his hand. "I'll speak with O'Reilly about his connection with Sam."

Grant asked, "Have you learned anything about the baby's remains?"

The Chief glanced from Grant to Diana "I pulled the file on the Feeney murder and the other problems found here at the house. Hetch Feeney's DNA matches the remains of the baby we found. The bones were of a newborn, deformed. I've already talked with Hetch. The couple's first baby was buried properly, so this has to be a more recent one. One he had no knowledge of."

"How did he take it?" Diana asked.

"Surprised, but resigned. Normally, I wouldn't give out this information, but you're due an explanation. If either of you divulge this information to anyone, I will not be lenient."

Grant and Diana nodded, and Nelson continued. "Although Gloria's doctor is retired, he remembered her. She was pregnant but didn't want her husband to know since they were in the middle of a divorce. When she didn't return for her next appointment, the doctor assumed she'd gone to another physician. We haven't found any record of her visiting another doctor or hospital. Of course, she could have gone out of town."

Diana's hand went to her throat. "She had it here. Alone?"

The Chief shook his head. "We don't know that."

"If she did, that would have been horrible for her. The poor thing. Hetch told me their first child was deformed and died. She never got over it and wanted to have another, but he refused." Diana stared at the two men. "Could that be why she became so bitter? Hetch said she gained weight and wore baggy blouses for a while before their divorce was final. She was probably trying to hide her pregnancy."

Grant shook his head. "It might have caused her bitterness, but that happened long before I ever arrived. Why take it out on me and treat Penny the way she did?" He glanced at Nelson. "Sorry, I didn't mean to bring your wife into this discussion."

Nelson sighed. "The past may be mixed up in what's happened in this house. If it helps solve the murder and the drugs you found, I'm willing to open old wounds. And Penny would understand."

Diana wondered if Gloria's anger toward Penny could have been jealousy. Penny aborted an apparently healthy baby, the kind of baby Gloria couldn't have. If Gloria believed Grant was the father, she could want him to suffer. If she felt that way, why leave the house to him? The woman was an enigma.

Chapter 18

The rain continued the following morning, turning the backyard into a sloshy marsh. When Diana heard an engine, she glanced out the kitchen window to see Bert's van pull into the gravel driveway. Marlene got out and hurried to the back door.

"Mrs. Bellfore, it's me, Marlene Schukart," she called from the mudroom.

"Come in and welcome." Diana watched the woman hang her raincoat on a peg.

"I'll be with you in a moment, Mrs. Bellfore. I need to change my shoes. Ach, the weather is schlect."

The German word took Diana back to folks in rural Pennsylvania. Marlene appeared in the kitchen, wearing a short-sleeved blouse and an apron over baggy brown slacks. She was tall, big-boned with short curly brown hair, and sparkling blue eyes. Her square face held a wary expression. When Diana smiled and reached out to shake Marlene's calloused hand, the woman's features relaxed.

"So, you tell me what you want done." Marlene glanced around the kitchen perhaps expecting piles of dishes. "You have breakfast already?"

"Yes. Captain Cranston is an early riser."

Marlene's eyes widened. "He's here?"

"Let's sit, have a cup of coffee, discuss what's going on here today and what we'd like you to do." Diana motioned to the kitchen table.

"We sit together?"

"Do you mind? It'll be easier."

"I get the coffee. You relax." Marlene took two cups from the cupboard and poured coffee from the urn on the counter. "You take cream, sugar?"

"Black, thanks."

As they sat across from each other, the wind increased and the rain slashed against the windows. Marlene folded her rough hands on the table behind her steaming cup, looking expectantly at Diana.

"Some odd things happened here yesterday, and the police are bringing in a narcotic K-9 unit. A dog will be in the house sniffing for drugs." Marlene showed no apprehension only interest. Diana continued, "I hope it won't be too disruptive, but with this rain, a dog will bring in mud."

"I clean up after." Marlene smiled. "I like dogs. When do they come?"

"We don't know, but they said they'd phone beforehand."

"Bert said he helps fix the place with a sergeant who lives here. It's good for Bert to be busy. Is the sergeant still here?"

"Yes, but you see, the sergeant is really Captain Cranston."

Marlene looked baffled, then said, "Ach so. The sergeant is the captain."

"Right." Diana nodded and chuckled. "It's confusing, but Captain Cranston didn't want anyone to know he was home until he'd adjusted to the area. He hadn't been here for many years, and the murder of Gloria made him apprehensive."

"The murder. Ach du liebe Gott, so schlect. So bad, I mean. Excuse me for saying, Mrs. Feeney was not nice lady."

"You didn't like her?"

"No." She hesitated then added, "I work for her. Pay was good. She write notes, never talk to me, then she get mad when I don't do what the note say."

"You couldn't read her writing?"

"Ja." Marlene nodded. "The writing."

"I won't write notes." Diana took a sip of coffee. "I gather the police talked to you after the murder."

"They talk to me, to Bert, to everyone." She looked down at her hands. "I had bad fight with Mrs. Feeney the last day before, you know, the murder."

"Thursday?"

"Yes. Police think I kill her." Her chin came up and her eyes met Diana's. "I tell you what happened. So you understand. Saturday, Bert and I had words about her. I got mad and go out of house not thinking about storm. Mrs. Nelson saw me, and gave me ride to library. We spend time there together. Sunday I go to church, then play cards with friends. Bert meets with his friends that day, too. That's what we always do."

"I didn't mean to imply that you had anything to do with her murder."

"I understand. You should be worried, renting this place. Murder and now drugs. Not good."

Diana smiled. "No, not good. Let's talk about what needs to be cleaned." As she finished her instructions, Grant walked into the kitchen.

"Mrs. Schukart, I'm Grant Cranston. I'm pleased you came despite the weather. I didn't see your car."

Marlene stood. "Bert drive me. I don't drive." She bobbed her head. "I should say welcome home from the war."

"That's kind of you. It's good to be back in the U.S."

"I'm sorry about Mrs. Feeney."

"Thank you." He leaned against the counter. "I gather Mrs. Bellfore has explained the situation to you."

"The dog, the drug and you, sergeant before, now captain."

He grinned. "Well, yes. I guess that covers everything."

"Bert said you don't need him today, right?" Marlene gripped her hands together. "He likes to work with you."

"I'm glad. He's done a good job. When it stops raining, I plan to paint the exterior. I'll need his help."

Marlene wrinkled her nose. "Miss Jacob don't trust him to paint inside. She hired others to do the work. I hope she charge you not too much."

"The estate paid for it," Grant said. "She chose good colors." He started to turn away, then stopped. "There was something odd in the living room. May I show you?"

Marlene and Diana followed him and stood in the middle of the room. Grant pointed to the wall where two paintings had hung. "I understand you worked here for many years."

"Five years, maybe more."

"Do you remember Ursula Von Reiter's paintings hanging here?" he asked.

"I liked them. I work for Miss Von Reiter, over three years now. She gave me a painting."

"Mrs. Feeney had two of Ursula's paintings," Diana said.

Marlene shrugged. "I mean Miss Von Reiter gave to me. I don't know about Mrs. Feeney's. Sometimes my tongue is not so good with English, but Mrs. Nelson say I'm getting better."

"When did you notice the paintings were missing?" Grant asked.

"Missing? They were never missing."

"Could you be specific? We're a little confused about this. Cora Jacob said there was only one painting, and in a crime scene photo there was only one painting, but there was a lighter area indicating that another painting or picture had been hanging on the wall."

Marlene face grew long, her eyes narrowed. "I do not take them."

"No, no, that's not what we mean." Diana was taken aback by Marlene's interpretation of what they were asking. "What the captain is trying to determine is when was the last time you saw both paintings on the wall."

"Ach, so. Thursday before she was killed. I dusted frames. They were there," she pointed to the wall.

"Both paintings?"

"Ja. Ja, both."

"What did they depict?" Diana asked, noted Marlene's frown, and rephrased her question. "What was their subject matter?"

"Ach so." Marlene nodded. "One was the pond in front of the land, and the other had this house with the same landscape. I thought it funny. Two paintings of the same area side by side."

"That's helpful." Grant folded his arms over his chest. "It gives us a time line for when the one went missing. From what I've been able to determine, it's the painting without the house that's missing." He turned to Diana. "We should ask Ursula."

"Did any police officer ask you about the missing painting?" Diana asked Marlene.

"Nothing about paintings."

Diana's cell phone lilted Greensleeves. It was George Crandall, Paul's friend at the university. "Excuse me, I need to take this call." She stepped into her bedroom and closed the door. "George, thanks for returning my call. I've been worried about Paul." She sat on the side of the bed.

"Why?"

"What's going on at the university?"

"I have no idea what you're talking about."

"George, don't play games. You're Paul's best friend. He's in some kind of trouble, and I need to know what it is."

"Have you asked Paul?"

She stood and paced the room with the phone pressed to her ear. "You know how closed-mouthed he is when it comes to his teaching. Normally, I wouldn't interfere, but Paul and I are at a rocky point in our marriage."

She heard him sigh and pressed on. "George, I don't want to lose Paul. When I go home, I don't want to walk into a firestorm." She paused, then added, "I need your help."

"It's complicated. I'm not sure Paul will be happy I told you, but the two of you need to start communicating. I don't want to see your marriage fall apart. At least not over this stupid mess."

"So, tell me."

"A female student accused Paul of improper sexual advances."

"Sexual advances?" She almost yelled into the phone. "What?" She sat, gripped the bedspread and tried to be calm. "Paul's always careful about being alone with female students. Does the dean believe her?"

"He's been difficult about the situation and has started procedures for a hearing. If word gets out or the girl goes to the police and the press gets hold of the story, the dean will have to act."

"So she's only talked to the dean?" She sighed.

"That's my understanding. Paul's so angry and frustrated by the accusation and the dean's behavior that he refuses to respond to the allegation. He'll have his full pension, so I think he's throwing in the towel."

Stunned, Diana's mind raced, jumping from one solution to the next. "Why won't Paul fight it?"

"You know how it is. He said, she said."

"Is there anything I can do?"

"If you were here, you might talk sense into Paul." He hesitated. "On the other hand, he might not want you to interfere or even know about this. Since he wouldn't call to tell you, I didn't think I should."

"Has anyone questioned the girl? I don't mean a chat, but a face to face confrontation to find the weakness in her story."

"Paul asked me to stay out of it. He doesn't want to confront her for fear he'd make matters worse."

"I understand his reluctance. Perhaps a woman could talk to her, whereas a man might get into trouble."

"Can you employ one of the formidable women characters in your novels to go after this student?" He let out a quick, deep ha-ha.

If his news hadn't been so serious, she'd have joined in his laughter. "I do have the resource of a private investigator, but perhaps an angry wife might be a more potent weapon. What do you know about this girl?"

George explained that the accuser was Sally Tuttle, originally from New York, a junior transfer from Brown University.

"When did this so-called inappropriate behavior happen?"

"Last week. Why?"

"The semester started a month ago. Can you find out when she applied for the transfer? And email me her address and anything else that might be pertinent."

"Will do."

"I'll see what I can find out about Sally Tuttle," she said. "There has to be a reason for her to go after Paul. Thanks for letting me know."

After she hung up, she stared out the window at the rain and dour sky, letting depression seep through her. Any allegation of sexual impropriety would taint his character even without proof. He'd never be able to get another teaching job.

Diana went into the living room and was thankful that Marlene had begun working upstairs. She sat at the desk and opened her laptop to begin her search.

Grant came in and stood next to her. "Starting your new novel?"

"I wish. No, this is research concerning an allegation against my husband." She swiveled around to meet his gaze with a steely look in her eyes.

"Can I help?"

"I hate to put my problems on you, but maybe an extra set of eyes and ears would help."

"Tell me." He drew up a chair.

She told him what she'd learned from George about Sally Tuttle and the accusation she'd made against Paul. "The timing's odd. If grades were about to be given, then I could understand a girl playing the age-old game of 'I'll do anything for you if you give me an A' and Paul refusing."

"I hate to ask, but are you sure Paul's innocent?"

She reeled back. "Paul's no angel, but if he's involved with someone, it wouldn't be a student." Was she wrong? She thought of the cute young realtor Paul was listing their house with.

"Okay, I had to ask." He studied her screen. "Try the newspaper sites and then Brown University's. I'll bring my laptop down here."

"If this doesn't work, I'll contact Max, a private detective I've had to do research for my novels." She searched his face. "What? You don't think I'd ever use a PI to find out something about Paul, do you?"

"Ah, no, but not everyone knows a PI they can call." He started to leave, then said, "What about putting your PI to work investigating Phil Yukovitch, Sam, and O'Reilly."

She'd thought of hiring Max earlier, but had decided to wait. Perhaps it was time.

"I'll just be a minute," Grant said. "I'll check on how Marlene's doing upstairs."

"She seems to be efficient and responsible. I like her."

"Yeah. Seems like a good sort." He smiled. "What did you think of her statements about the paintings?"

"As you said, it gives us a time line. Do you think Cora is telling the truth about having only one painting?"

"We'll find out soon enough. Now that I've admitted to being Cranston, she'll have to give it to me." He stared at the wall. "If she doesn't have the other one, what happened to it?"

Chapter 19

Grant returned with his laptop. "We should check to see if this girl has a Facebook page."

"How stupid of me. Of course." As he logged on, she glanced at him. "You're on Facebook?"

"Even though I don't say much on my page, it allows me keep in touch with friends, like Morgan. He was friends with every sergeant in our area, so if I go to Morgan's Facebook page, I'll find Sally's." He put his laptop on the desk next to hers and began to search. He found Sally Tuttle, a junior at Brown University. When he scrolled down her page, Diana understood why Sally went after Paul.

She leaned back, shocked and saddened. "Oh my God. It's about revenge."

"Looks that way. Her brother's death must have unhinged her."

"I wonder if Isabel knows the man who saved her had a sister."

Grant read further. "She's posted that Sergeant Tuttle was awarded the Distinguished Service Cross for his valor in Afghanistan. Apparently he not only saved Isabel but three others as well." He turned to Diana. "Why pick on Paul and not the families of the other three?"

"We don't know if she targeted any of the others. A professor is an easy mark. If you accuse a teacher of sexual advances, it's he said, she said, and a reputation is ruined."

"From what I'm reading on her page," Grant said, "I don't think she transferred out of Brown. This says she's a junior there. Would that make a difference?"

"I doubt it. The fact that she's a young woman would be enough. I'll check to see if Paul's friend is aware that she might not have transferred." She sighed. "That seals it. I've got to go home. Perhaps I can talk to the dean, make him see how absurd her accusations are." When he frowned, she realized she'd been mumbling. "Sorry. I have a habit of talking to myself when I'm upset." She studied Sally's Facebook page. She's a child psychology major and her favorite professor is Dr. Helen Horowitz." She leaned back, lightly rubbing her lips. "I could drive into Providence and talk with her professor tomorrow. I promised to take Ursula to the Brecks on Saturday. Perhaps Penny could take Ursula home after the art exhibit at the Brecks and I could leave for home from there.

"I understand your need to get home. Let me know when you'll return."

She gave him a small smile. "I did rent the house for three months."

"Yeah. I've been meaning to talk to you about that. I'll see that Cora Jacob cancels the lease without imposing a fee and returns your deposit."

"Trying to get rid of me?"

"Hardly. You've been a great help. And I've enjoyed getting to know you."

"What I have to do at home should be done while Paul's away."

"Why when he's gone?"

She smiled. "Would you want a woman running interference for you?"

He shrugged. "It depends on the woman and the situation."

"Knowing Paul's mindset at the moment, I'd rather he not find out I'm interfering." She straightened in her chair. "But I shall return." She laughed. "I sound like MacArthur, don't I?"

"Your family comes first and—"

Marlene's heavy steps alerted them to her presence at the bottom of the stairs. "Excuse please. Police cars coming into drive. It's good they come in back. Get rid of mud."

"They said they'd call first." Grant followed Marlene into the kitchen.

Diana picked up her cell to call Max, who answered on the third ring. He must have recognized her number. "Hey, mystery writer, it's been a long time. Got another book going?"

"Hi Max." Diana walked out onto the front porch to be alone and got right to the point. "This time it's a real life situation. Could you meet me tomorrow in Providence at Brown University?"

"I'll be on Long Island. I can take the ferry across. Where exactly on the campus?"

"The best choice is J.D. Rockefeller Library on Prospect Street."

"Usual fee plus expenses, okay?"

"Yes. How about two o'clock?"

"One would be better."

"This case might mean you need to spend a few days in Rhode Island."

"I'll pack. With the fall colors in New England, Rhode Island, could be first prize in a travel contest." His bellowing laugh made her hold the phone away from her ear. "Okay. See you then."

She hung up, returned to the living room and heard a commotion in the kitchen. She walked in on a discussion about the upcoming search between two uniformed police officers and Grant. Marlene stood at the counter washing out a rag.

Grant made the introductions. Colton was the dog-handler from the Narcotic K-9 unit and the other man was Officer Donaldson. Colton glanced down at his dog. "This is Prince, a border collie lab mix we got from a shelter." The dog wagged his tail. "She's friendly and trained to sniff out narcotics." Colton beamed like a proud parent, then turned to Grant. "We'll start in the attic and make our way to the basement."

Diana glanced at Marlene. "The upstairs has just been cleaned."

"We'll be careful, but if Prince indicates there are drugs, we'll cut into the walls." He studied Grant. "I was told you understood this."

"Yes, but I'll accompany you during your inspection."

Colton nodded. "I have orders to allow you to do that, but please keep out of our way." He nodded to Diana and Marlene. "I'd appreciate it if the two of you would stay here."

The others left the room and Diana turned to Marlene. "We might as well relax while we're waiting."

"I fix more coffee or you like tea?"

"Tea, please."

"I saw cookies, but no cake. Mr. Grant needs a homecoming cake. I can bake tomorrow and bring."

"I'm sure he'd love it." Diana sat at the table, thinking about what might be happening upstairs.

"I see boxes in living room that I packed," Marlene said.

"You packed?" Diana asked.

"Ja. After police make lists, I help Miss Jacob sort clothes for thrift store and pack up other things for the captain."

"Grant hasn't opened them yet. I think he's a little nervous about what they might contain."

Marlene turned with a cup in her hand. "Only jewelry, books, papers and snaps."

"Snaps?"

"Ja. Photos." Marlene put sugar and cream on the table.

When they heard the sound of an electric saw, they looked at each other. Diana hadn't believed there were any drugs remaining in the house. "They found something."

Marlene nodded. The two of them sat frozen to their chairs, listening. The sound continued, then voices, then silence until the tread of footsteps echoed on the stairs. Later they heard Colton giving commands to Prince and thumping on walls in the living room. Despite her curiosity, Diana remained seated. Grant pushed open the kitchen door with the men and the dog trooping behind him.

"They found cocaine in the upstairs back bedroom's wall. Nothing in the attic," Grant said.

He might have continued, but Bert stormed through the mudroom, screaming, "Marlene, Marlene." He skidded to a stop, glaring at the police. "You can't arrest her. She didn't do it. I did—"

"Ach, Egbert. Pass auf! My floor," she yelled, stood, and pushed him back into the mudroom. "Mud everywhere." Her hands were on her wide hips.

A flushed Bert tried to look over her shoulder. "What's going on? I saw the two police cars. I thought—"

"What did you think?" Grant stepped forward.

Before Bert could speak, Marlene said to her husband, "Off with your shoes."

He bent, untied his shoes and put them by the bench while his wife stood over him. Muttering to herself, Marlene grabbed a mop and cleaned the floor. No one moved from the kitchen while the scene between the Schukarts played out. Bert wiped his long face with the sleeve of his jacket and in stocking feet edged into the kitchen.

"I'm sorry," Bert mumbled, looking down. "I thought Marlene was in trouble."

"Why would you think that?" Grant asked.

The group looked expectantly at the thin man. Marlene moved to his side. "He worries all the time. My accent and poor English. People think I'm not legal."

Bert nodded. "Yes, yes, that's it. We're married. She has a green card."

"We aren't from immigration, sir," Colton said. "We're a Narcotic K-9 unit."

"Nice dog." Marlene nodded. "Border collie lab mix," she continued as though reciting her catechisms.

Colton turned to Grant. "We'll check the basement, then the mudroom and leave by the back door." He smiled at Marlene. "Help keep the floor clean."

"Ja. Thank you."

Instead of following the officers, Grant stayed behind, walked over and poured himself a cup of coffee. "Anyone else?"

Bert seemed to be glued to the spot with Marlene glaring at him. Their faces showed confusion mixed with a quiet understanding.

Grant sipped his coffee, then said, "The two of you have some explaining to do."

Marlene shook her head. "No. We have nothing to say."

Grant motioned to the kitchen door. "Let's go into the living room. All four of us. We'll wait until the police have finished their search. Then we'll have a pow-wow."

Marlene frowned and glanced at Bert. "What is this pow-wow?"

Bert explained and then with their heads bowed, the couple followed Diana and Grant into the living room. Despite Marlene and Bert's reluctance to sit on the couch, they agreed at Grant's insistence.

Marlene turned to her husband. "Did you know the sergeant is the captain?"

"What are you talking about?"

As Grant explained, Bert's chin came up, and his hands coiled into fists. "You lied to me. I thought you were too friendly. What do you want from me?"

"The truth?"

Bert lowered his head and grabbed Marlene's hand.

The foursome sat in silence until Officer Donaldson came in to announce they had found nothing more and would leave. Grant saw them out and returned with two steins filled with beer. He handed one to Bert and held the other out to Marlene.

With a heavy sigh, she took the stein. "Ja. Good idea."

Grant turned to Diana. "How about you?"

"Might as well join the group."

After a short time Grant returned, handed Diana her beer and sat in a chair opposite the couch. He raised his stein. "To the truth."

Bert gulped a quarter of his beer and wiped his mouth with the back of his hand. Grant took a sip. "Before we begin, I want you to know that I don't believe either of you killed Gloria Feeney. But you're hiding something, and I want to know what it is."

Bert stole a glance at Marlene. Diana, unsure of what Grant was up to decided to explain what she knew. "On Saturday the weekend of the murder, Penelope Nelson gave Marlene a ride to the library, where they remained for the rest of the afternoon."

Bert stared at his wife. "That's what you said, but you never go to the library. It didn't make sense. You were so angry, I thought you went to Mrs. Feeney's and…and I was afraid of what you might have done."

"Ach, ja. I was mad at you, at her, at everyone. Mrs. Nelson picked me up on the road. She understood why I was mad at Mrs. Feeney for always writing notes and not talking to me."

Diana leaned forward. "You don't read English very well, do you?"

Marlene shook her head. "German, ja. English, no. Night school was hard after working all day."

"I'm sorry Mrs. Feeney didn't understand your difficultly," Diana said.

Grant turned to Bert. "So you thought Marlene had been here?"

"I…I'll go to jail."

"It depends," Grant said. "What did you do?"

"I'm glad you didn't do it, Schatzie." Bert held his wife's hand. "I thought you did. I know your temper."

"Ach, Egbert, dummkopf. I can't even kill a chicken."

"I'm sorry." Bert looked at Grant, his shoulders slumped. "I drove over here Saturday. It was raining, but not too much. I found Mrs. Feeney in the backyard, face down, dead. I thought I could make it look like she fell and hit her head. You know, an accident. I wrapped her head in a towel, picked her up and carried her into the house."

"And like a well-trained husband you were neat. Left your boots in the mudroom and laid her on the floor in the living room." Grant pointed to the spot.

"How do you know that's what I did?" Bert asked.

"I wasn't exactly sure, but I had a good idea of what happened."

"How?" Diana asked.

"Things began to add up. Bert's obsessive about shedding his shoes before entering the house. You let the backyard go wild, changed the stone pathway. Artistic, you said. Not your style. The load of topsoil was delivered on Monday, and you spread it over the area in the rain. That wasn't like you either. I gather you were trying to hide the blood. According to the local deliveryman, you usually waited a few days and never spread it until rain abated. The storm didn't pass until Wednesday. When you charged through the door this afternoon, yelling for the police not to arrest Marlene, I was certain you'd done something you shouldn't have."

"Ach, Schatzie, you didn't?" Marlene moved closer to her husband.

He put his head on her shoulder. "I'm sorry. I did it for you."

"Was there a weapon around?" Grant asked.

"A shovel. I threw it into the bushes. You're right about the blood. There was so much."

"The police searched the grounds," Diana said. "They didn't find the shovel or a bloody towel."

Bert's long face grew sadder, his eyes full of tears. "I came back Monday and buried the shovel deep under the new topsoil toward the back of the property. I changed the stone path layout to cover up the bloody spot. I took the towel with me and threw it in a trash bin in the next town. "

"You'll have to tell the police exactly what you did," Grant said.

Bert nodded. "I don't care what happens to me as long as Marlene is safe." His lower lip trembled.

"What will happen to him?" Marlene's blue eyes held fear.

"I don't know," Grant said. "He didn't commit murder, but he tampered with the crime scene. He'll need a good lawyer."

Diana shook her head. "If Bert didn't kill Gloria, who did?"

Chapter 20

By Friday morning the storm had drifted north, leaving scattered clouds on the horizon. Diana and Grant had just finished breakfast when the police arrived with Bert, who had been taken into custody upon confessing that he tampered with the crime scene.

Diana remained indoors, preparing to leave for Providence. She'd been able to schedule a meeting for eleven-thirty with Sally Tuttle's advisor, Professor Helen Horowitz. Once someone knew Diana was a mystery writer, they assumed she wanted information for a novel and that's what Diana had implied. At the interview she'd be honest about her reason for the meeting. She hoped the professor wouldn't be upset by her subterfuge.

While she ruminated about her appointments, Grant stuck his head in the doorway to her bedroom. "The police plan to charge Bert with murder, not just the coverup."

"That's so wrong. Why?" She gripped her purse, feeling the clasp dig into her palm.

"He showed them where he hid the murder weapon and where he found her body. He had motive and opportunity. That's enough for O'Reilly." He sighed. "I feel bad. I know he didn't do it, but convincing a jury might be difficult."

"We had no choice once we learned what he'd done. If we'd kept quiet, we'd have been guilty of aiding and abetting."

"I know, but it doesn't make me feel any better."

"He needs a good lawyer." She looked at him expectantly.

He shook his head. "I only know Clayton Morris, the lawyer for Gloria's estate."

"I know a few in Pennsylvania, but he should hire a Rhode Island attorney. I'll ask Max today. He's sure to know a good criminal attorney."

"The Schukarts don't have much money."

"That's the least of their problems right now. Will they let Bert out on bail?"

"Don't know. They kept him overnight. Now they'll add the murder charge. Bert said Penny took Marlene to her job at Ursula's this morning."

"What a mess. The real killer is out there. It's obvious Bert didn't do it."

"We may think that, but the evidence against him is overwhelming. I didn't think it through. My fault."

"Oh, stop. You know damn well it isn't." She picked up her coat. "I've got to leave, but I'll be back around four or five."

As she walked past him, he put his hand on her arm. "There are added complications. They discovered a kitchen knife near where Bert says he found the body."

Diana stopped and frowned. "Gloria wasn't stabbed, was she?"

"No, but it adds to the puzzle. They also found a piece of canvas about the size of Ursula's missing painting with a piece torn off. They sent it to a lab, but not sure they'll learn much since it was in a bad state of decay."

"Where did they find these things?"

"After Bert spread the topsoil, he moved the slate stones to cover up the blood. He seemed surprised the knife and the canvas were there."

"Do you believe him? About being surprised, I mean."

"I do, but O'Reilly doesn't."

She went into the living room. "Would Ursula be able to identify the canvas?"

"The police plan to ask her."

"I'd stay, but I'm not sure what I can do to help." She checked her watch. "I'll just have time to make my meetings." By the time she walked to her car, the police had left. After the chaos, the silence was eerie.

On her drive she thought about Bert's reasons for tampering with the crime scene. The real murderer might have been apprehended if Bert and Marlene had confided in each other.

Communication between people was key. She thumped her palm against the steering wheel. "Hypocrite, thou art." Communication was sorely lacking between Paul and herself. She tried to remember the last time they'd been honest and open with each other. But it takes two and Paul had clammed up and climbed into a shell. But much of the guilt rested on her shoulders. She'd allowed her mother to interfere. Diana wasn't sure she could stand up to Beatrice. But she must, even if the confrontation caused a complete breakdown in their relationship. Sometimes a meat cleaver was better than a Band-Aid.

She needed to return home. Solving other people's problems seemed to be easier than dealing with her own. Her worry about what others might think and say about Jeffrey's lifestyle had caused Diana to withdraw from him. Stupid. Her fear for Isabel's safety had driven a wedge between them. Could that divide be healed? Isabel had yet to respond to Diana's attempt to make amends.

In her reverie she almost collided with a stalled truck. She swerved, caught her breath, and put her attention back on the road. The highway was still slick from the rain, causing traffic to slow. By the time she found a parking place on a side street near the Center for Human Development, she had only a few minutes to find the professor's office. With frayed nerves she grabbed her purse and hurried to Waterman Street.

Professor Helen Horowitz, a large bosomed woman with a pale face framed by a mass of dark red hair, greeted Diana warmly. The small office was decorated in outdated furniture. "How can I help with your research?"

"I hope you'll forgive me when I explain the reason for requesting this meeting." While Diana recited what had happened regarding Sally Tuttle and her accusations against Paul, the woman listened without interrupting.

The professor sat back with a scowl darkening her features. "Sally was devastated by her brother's death. He was the only family she had. She's been my TA for Psychology 101, but I gave her a month off to deal with her grief. I didn't know she went to Philadelphia. She's hardworking and cares deeply about her career. I can't fathom why she would act against your husband, but grief does strange things to people. What do you want from me?"

"I'd like to talk with her."

The professor stared at her desk and pursed her lips.

Diana hurried on. "Not in an adversarial way, but to find out why she'd want revenge against my family. My daughter was an interpreter in her brother's unit. He not only saved her, but three others. I wonder if she has the same animosity toward the other families as she does toward us."

The professor gave her a benign smile. "Have you talked with your daughter?"

"Not yet. She was wounded and sent to Jordan. I haven't been able to reach her since I found out about this incident."

"I'm not sure I can help. Sally needs to talk to a psychologist about her anger. That's why I gave her time off. I wasn't sure how she'd deal with her feelings." The professor shuffled papers on her desk. "She's due back Wednesday. I'd prefer you meet her here in my office in case she needs an intermediary."

"That might be too late. The dean at my husband's college has a disciplinary hearing scheduled for Tuesday."

"Is Sally to testify?"

"I don't know."

The professor rubbed the side of her face. "I realize this is difficult for you and your husband, but if you present all the details perhaps the outcome won't be bad."

Diana caught herself from sneering. "You and I know that once such a hearing is held the outcome will be negative for my husband, no matter what the facts are. No one knows what happened except the two of them. Once the word gets out, and it will, the newspapers will have a field day."

"You want to discredit Sally?"

"No. She's suffering, but I want the truth." Diana leaned forward. "Do you have a cell number, email, a friend of Sally's I could talk to?"

"I understand your dilemma, but I also need to protect Sally." She hesitated, then said, "You might want to talk to her friend, Maude Groggin." The professor flipped through a Rolodex, wrote information on a sheet of paper and handed it to Diana. "I wish the best for all of you. Sally needs help, not condemnation. Please remember that."

Before Diana walked to the Rockefeller Library, she phoned Maude and left a message. Across the street, Max Templer, an unassuming man of five foot eight with brown hair and brown eyes, waited on the steps.

As she walked up to him, he said, "You look perplexed."

"Very." She gave a curt nod.

"I saw a restaurant two blocks over. Shall we?" He smiled and took her elbow. "Your treat, of course."

"Of course."

The restaurant was quiet, not too expensive and had good pasta dishes. Over lunch Diana laid out the case she wanted Max to investigate, explaining Sam Feeney's relationship to the earlier drug busts, the Yukovitch brothers, Joe O'Reilly, and how years later drugs were found in Gloria Feeney's house. Max listened and took notes.

"I've got a few contacts that might give me a handle on the situation," Max said.

"I think O'Reilly's investigation into the Feeney murder and the drugs at the house may have been compromised by his past relationship with Sam." She took a sip of her iced tea before continuing. "Captain Cranston and I have spoken about our feelings to Police Chief Nelson, but I'm not sure he'll question his lead detective."

"Nelson's probably playing it safe. That's normal. No need to cause trouble for O'Reilly if there's nothing to your assumptions."

Diana twisted her napkin in her lap. "What I need is information about the drug bust that occurred ten years ago. Where Phil Yukovitch is and if he's still involved with drugs and still in touch with Sam."

"You also mentioned Gloria Feeney's unsolved murder. You want me to dig into that?"

"Yes. It's a cold case and the arrest of Bert Schukart for the crime makes O'Reilly look good despite his earlier, shall we say, poor police work."

Max pushed his empty plate away and wiped his mouth with his napkin. "You have it in for O'Reilly."

"I don't trust him."

The waitress asked if they wanted dessert. Max patted his waistline and declined.

Diana folded her napkin and put it on the table. "Just the check, thank you."

"Not sure how long this will take. I'll call you when I find something definite."

"Something else I need to ask." She paused after the waitress brought the bill. "Bert Schukart needs a good criminal lawyer. Know anyone?"

He nodded, wrote down a name and handed the slip of paper to her. "She'll cost you."

"I understand."

"You're picking up that bill?"

"If I have to. Hope I don't." Her phone lilted Greensleeves and she held up her hand to Max. "I need to take this."

"Go for it." He stood and shook her hand. "I'll be in touch."

He walked out and she answered her phone. "Miss Groggin, this is Mrs. Bellfore. I got your number from Professor Horowitz. I'm trying to get in touch with Sally Tuttle. Can you help me?"

The girl was hesitant until Diana assured her that Professor Horowitz felt it was in Sally's best interest that Diana speak with her. Diana soon had Sally's address and phone number in Philadelphia and hoped she could meet the girl face to face.

Her thoughts turned to the missing painting. How soon would the police talk to Ursula? Would O'Reilly investigate Bert's involvement in Gloria's murder thoroughly? She hated to leave Quamscutt in the middle of so many unknowns.

Chapter 21

When Diana arrived back at the Victorian, Grant was painting the storm window frames.

He waved. "Hi. How'd it go?"

"As well as could be expected. I got the name of a lawyer for Bert. Anything new happen while I was gone?"

He put down his brush. "I went to Ursula's to talk to Marlene, but she'd been in such a state that Penny had taken her home, so I went to the Schukart's house. Unfortunately Penny was still there."

"You had to meet her sooner or later. How did she react?"

He rubbed the back of his neck. "I'm not sure. Kind of aloof, formal, like she didn't know how to deal with me."

"Sounds like a normal reaction to the situation."

"I suppose. She stayed in the background while I talked with Marlene."

"We've both had a long day. Let's go out to dinner. I heard the Matunuck Oyster Bar is a great restaurant. It's on the other side of Potters Pond on Succotash Road."

"Good idea. I'll finish up here. In an hour, okay?"

Diana went inside, collapsed on her bed and thought of her problems at home. She had stopped by the post office but there was nothing from Paul. Any delay to sign documents might allow her to discuss the issue with him before they committed to selling the house. If his hearing before the dean went awry, she'd be willing to sell and move on. But where to?

She must have dozed off, for she awakened to Grant calling her from the living room. "You ready?"

She sat up and checked the clock. An hour had slipped by. "Sorry, I'll be with you in a minute."

Since she'd been on the road most of the day, he offered to drive her car. Being chauffeured allowed her to enjoy the lush fall colors. They pulled into the busy gravel parking area at sundown. They both wore warm jackets and asked to be seated outside where they had a clear view of the pond. After they ordered, he handed her a piece of paper with the security guard's phone and address.

She glanced at him. "So you want me to do the honors and question Angie Murphy?"

He shrugged and cocked his head. "A woman's touch might get more info than the heavy hand of the law."

"Back to our lack of faith in O'Reilly." She sighed. "Okay, I'll see what I can do. Do you know if Angie works during the day?"

"No idea. That address is near Port Judith, not too far from here."

She wasn't looking forward to knocking on the woman's door unannounced, but calling first might make Angie wary and uncooperative. She could read the papers like everyone else and would know about the discovery of the baby's remains.

He studied her. "Are you okay with going to see her?"

"I can think of more pleasant ways to spend the day, but I'd just as soon get it over with."

"Okay then, thanks." He leaned back.

Diana fingered the paper with the address, touched the Google maps app on her cell phone and pulled up the directions. "Okay. It's not too far away. I'll try to see her tomorrow morning." She viewed the calm waters of the pond and the meadow beyond. The light of dusk twinkled on the water. The tranquility was at odds with the events at Grant's house. "Do you know anything about the history of your house? I mean, before you lived there with Gloria."

"Not much. I was a teenager. What did I care about the history of a place I came to hate? I do know that early on there were wool and grist mills in the area. Most of the Potters Pond area was farmland."

"What about Ursula Von Reiter's house? Do you know when it was built?"

"I think she came here in the seventies and built it. She'd already left for New York when I lived here. When I stayed with Mrs. Feeney, I don't remember any paintings on the wall, but what teenage boy would?"

"Speaking of paintings, have you gotten the paintings back from Cora?"

"Not yet." The waiter brought their clam chowder. "Looks good."

She tasted it. "It's superb. Not floury like some chowders."

They continued to enjoy their meal of salad, mussels and oysters discussing generalities and avoiding what was uppermost in their minds. Grant stopped in mid-sentence, nodding toward the entrance to the restaurant. Diana looked over to see Penny and her husband, Police Chief Nelson, waiting to be seated. As the couple passed their table, Penny hesitated and smiled. Grant stood. "Penny, Chief, good to see you."

Charles shook his hand and nodded to Diana. "I'm looking into your concerns."

"What about Bert Schukart?" Grant asked.

"Sorry, I can't comment."

Grant started to argue, but Diana interrupted him. "I understand you and Penny will be going to the Brecks tomorrow afternoon for the show of Ursula's work. Although I'm taking her, I'm hoping you can bring her back. I have urgent business in Philadelphia and need to be there Sunday morning. The sooner I leave, the less time I'll spend driving at night."

Penny turned to her husband. "Would that be all right?"

"Glad to help." He glanced at Grant. "Will you be at the Brecks, too?"

"No. I'm in the midst of painting the house and I'd like to get it done before another storm hits."

"We've been lucky this year," Penny said. "Every time a hurricane brews in the Caribbean, I worry."

"You're planning to return to Quamscutt, I presume," the Chief said to Diana.

"Yes."

"Even so, please leave the address and a phone number where you can be reached with my office." Charles nudged Penny and nodded toward the maitre d' who waited to seat them. "See you at the Brecks," he said, before they moved on.

Grant watched them, then looked at Diana. "It's a long drive to Philly. Are you sure you can't wait and leave on Monday?"

"I need to get home. I know where Sally Tuttle is staying and hope to talk to her before the hearing on Tuesday."

"Have you told your husband your plans?"

She shook her head. "He's in Chicago. Some things are best done surreptitiously."

"Are you sure about that?"

She gave a hollow laugh. "I'm no longer sure of anything."

They finished dinner and left, feeling pleasantly sated. Back at the house, Diana stood in the living room and pointed to the boxes sitting next to the couch. "When are you going to open them?"

"I'm not looking forward to going through the stuff."

"Marlene said there were only books, jewelry and snaps."

"Snaps?"

"Photos."

He shrugged. "Okay, I can't put it off forever." After shoving the boxes toward the couch with his foot, he leaned over and tore off the tape, then looked at Diana. "Well, you promised to be by my side when I opened them, didn't you? Come sit down and we'll go through them together."

She chuckled. "Men can be such wimps."

He removed old books about the history of Rhode Island and set them aside before he took out several files. He flipped through them, grunted, and passed them to her, while he continued to look at the rest of the contents.

"Interesting," Diana said, looking through a file. "These are letters to the Feeneys from Ursula, dating back before this house was built." She glanced at another letter. "The language gets nasty." She handed it to him.

After a quick read, he said, "Wow. She was not a happy camper. I'll go through all of this more thoroughly tomorrow."

"From the tone of the letters, Ursula was at war with the Feeneys over the land. What about the photos, or snaps, as Marlene calls them?"

He opened the second carton and found a lacquered box containing jewelry and an envelope of old photos. He laughed and sat back. "And to think I was worried about what I'd find." He held up a pearl necklace. "Do you think these are real?"

"No idea. The pieces appear to be old. You'll have to get a jeweler or an antique dealer to tell you." She thought for a moment. "Wouldn't the lawyer have given you a list of Gloria's things?"

"You'd think so. He said the boxes held miscellaneous stuff of little value. He was glad to get rid of them."

"Not very professional of him."

"Yeah, well, who knows how Gloria found him?" He glanced at her. "Speaking of lawyers, are you going to contact the lawyer Max recommended or should I?"

"Since it looks like I might have to pick up the bill, I'll call her tomorrow morning."

"Wish I could help, but my paycheck doesn't leave much to put away for the future. Unless I sell this place, which I might, after I fix it up."

"I thought you'd keep it as home base."

"I don't think so. Too many memories. Besides, I have no idea where I'll be stationed."

"You have until the end of the year to decide."

"Yeah, or wait until we get to the bottom of what's been going on here."

She glanced at the envelope in his hand. "Let's take a look at the photos."

"Pictures of land and…hey, these are of different stages of this house being built." He leaned closer. "Look at this one."

She took the picture. "Oh my. This might be important."

He touched the photo, smiling. "Those must be photos of Ursula's two paintings. One of the land before the house was built and the other afterward."

"The photos have faded, but you can see how lovely the area was. The house changed everything. I can understand why Ursula wanted the land. The view from her house must have been glorious and now she looks over at this Victorian."

"I wonder just how unhappy she was," he said. "Could she have…?"

"What you're implying is outrageous." She stared at him, then checked the back of the pictures and shook her head. "These were taken in the seventies. Ursula moved to New York and came back occasionally. That's a long time to carry a grudge."

"When you see her tomorrow, you can ask how passionate she felt about the land."

"She's a tiny old lady, for heaven sakes, and successful, too."

"You told me that her paintings were like children to her."

"You're way off base." She held up her hands. "But to make you happy, I'll quiz her. Gently." She stood. "I'm for bed. I have a long day tomorrow and I'm exhausted. Enjoy your new acquisitions."

"Sleep well." He didn't look up as he inspected more photos.

Chapter 22

The following morning Diana packed a few things before going into the kitchen. As usual the coffee was brewing, and Grant was cleaning up after his breakfast.

"You're up early." He glanced at his watch.

"Going to pay Angie Murphy a visit before I take Ursula to the exhibit."

"Before you leave—" His cell phone rang. "Hello. Oh." He glanced up at Diana while he listened and then said, "Thanks for letting us know. I'll tell her." He hung up.

"That was abrupt."

"It was Penny. Sam was released on his own recognizance."

"And Bert?"

"He's being held and will be arraigned on Monday for interfering with a crime scene. He hasn't been officially charged with murder, yet."

"I'm surprised she'd call you with the information."

"After our conversation at the restaurant last night, I think the Chief asked her to do the honors."

"Time for me to call the lawyer Max recommended." While she stood in the kitchen with Grant, she phoned Attorney Lorraine Brodsky, but she wasn't in. Her secretary took Diana's phone number and information and said Mrs. Brodsky would return her call on Monday. When Diana made it clear that might be too late, Mrs. Brodsky's assistant, Glen Barnard, came on the line. After the retainer fee was established, he agreed to look into

Bert's situation and act as his lawyer until other arrangements could be made.

Diana felt as though she was doing a high wire act. Meeting with Angie Murphy might be important, but so was returning home to straighten out problems in her own life.

It was nine o'clock when she pulled her car to the curb outside Angie's small house a block from the ocean. There was a pickup truck in the driveway. As she mounted the weathered wood steps to the front door, the pungent smell of the sea and the nearby fishing docks filled her senses. She rang the bell and waited. Not a sound came from inside. She turned to leave just as a woman dressed in jeans and carrying a plastic bag, stopped on the sidewalk in front of the house.

Diana waved and walked toward the short, stocky woman. "I'm looking for Angie Murphy."

The woman's eyes narrowed. "I don't talk to the press."

"Neither do I."

"What do you want?"

"I'm Diana Bellfore," Diana said with a smile.

"Oh yeah, the mystery writer who found the baby in the Feeney's attic."

"You're Angie?"

"Duh. Who else?" Angie walked past Diana up the steps to the front door, then turned to look back at Diana who had remained on the sidewalk. "Well, you comin' in or standin' there with your mouth open?"

Although taken aback, Diana followed Angie into the house.

"Wait here," Angie said. "I gotta stow this fish in the fridge."

Diana nodded and remained standing in the small neat living room. There were a few doodads on the fireplace mantel and a picture of three smiling people in police uniforms. One was Angie, one man was older, the other much younger.

Angie came back into the room wiping her hands on a towel. "That's my old man and my brother." She went to the mantel and picked up the frame. "Both are gone. Just me." She let out a long sigh. "So what can I do for you?"

"You already know I'm staying at the Feeney house and found the remains. I'm interested in Gloria Feeney's murder. Detective O'Reilly said you were one of the officers on-scene with him. He said you searched the attic."

"So?"

"I'm trying to determine if the remains were there then or if they were put there after the murder."

She folded her arms in front of her ample chest. "Let me give you the straight scoop. O'Reilly didn't give me shit about being a woman, but I often got the thankless tasks, like checking the attic. When the murder happened, I was due to retire in two months, full pension. I didn't want to screw up. Yeah, I went up to the attic. The floor was covered in dust, not a footprint to be seen. Highly unlikely the murderer, or anyone else for that matter, had been up there in years. There were a few small suitcases but I didn't walk over to open them. Hell, in looking back, I goofed. I should have tramped through the dust and opened up every Goddamn one of those cases, but I didn't."

"Were other officers on-scene besides you and O'Reilly?"

Angie grinned. "It was a police convention. We didn't get many murders and every officer on duty wanted to be in on it. O'Reilly had a hell of a time keeping the number of officers to a minimum. It was chaos until Chief Nelson arrived. He scattered the officers back to their routes. Didn't win any points doing it either."

"I appreciate your candidness."

"Hell, I'm retired. What can they do to me?"

"Has O'Reilly talked to you yet?"

"Nope. Only the press boys pushed their mugs into my business."

"I had a run-in with them, too. I find them overbearing."

Angie laughed. "Overbearing. God, you're polite." She moved toward the door, as if to suggest the interview was over, but she hesitated. "You gonna make a novel of this?"

"I write fiction, not true crime."

Angie grinned. "I get it. But if you do write about this, let me know. I'll be glad to help you with details." She dropped her hand off the doorknob. "Did they ever find out what happened to the painting?"

Diana tried to hide her delight at the question. "You noticed it?"

"Sure. After I came back from the attic, I told O'Reilly a painting was missing. The place was bedlam, and I thought he made a note of it." She shrugged. "Not sure what he did."

"Anything else you remember about that day or the crime scene? Did anyone ask or say anything interesting?"

Angie laughed. "A lot of black humor. When I saw the body, I knew it had been placed there, but we never found the kill zone. Besides going up to the attic, the next shitty job I got was to search the backyard and the shed. It was raining hard and the ground was mucky. I tramped all over that area. Other than the crazy stone path to the shed, I didn't notice anything out of the ordinary. The shed was full of junk. I mean, stuffed. Hard to figure if anything new had been added to the pile."

"Did you happen to see an old picture frame?"

Angie remained standing by the front door. "Nope. I was looking for a murder weapon, not a frame."

Diana handed one of her business cards to Angie. "If you think of anything else give me a call. And if O'Reilly questions you, would you let me know if he's developed any new leads?"

Angie swung the door open. "Not sure. I'll think about it. It depends how O'Reilly acts. He's still miffed I made a remark about Sam." She shrugged. "I'm not the most tactful person."

"You knew Sam Feeney?"

"Sure. He got the contract for the electrical maintenance of city hall. I told O'Reilly that his friend Sam must know the right people. O'Reilly thought I was claiming he'd gotten Sam the contract. I wasn't. Although when I thought about it later, I wondered if O'Reilly had something to do with it." Angie motioned for Diana to leave. "Sorry to toss you out, but I need to get going."

"I appreciate your talking with me." Diana went down the steps and got in her car. Before she drove off, she reflected on what Angie had said. It might have little bearing on the murder but it added pieces to a growing puzzle.

In the afternoon Diana drove to Ursula's. The woman opened the door before she could knock. "Glad you're prompt." As Ursula stepped into the car, she pulled her long maroon coat around her. "Do you know the way?"

"Penny gave me the directions. You look lovely."

"You don't think it's too vivid for the occasion? Haven't worn this outfit in a long time." Ursula played with the fuchsia-colored scarf at her throat.

"You're noted for vibrant colors, so I'd say it's appropriate." Diana turned onto the main highway. "You've heard about Bert Schukart."

"Yes. What a mess." Ursula looked down at her scarlet nails. "Men do the craziest things when they try to protect their women. Why couldn't he mind his own business?"

"Marlene is his business, and he's hers."

Ursula sighed. "I know. Poor Marlene, she's out of her mind with worry."

"She might be in for a very difficult time if they indict him for the murder as well as mucking up the crime scene."

"Impossible. He didn't do it."

"I don't think he did either, but Detective O'Reilly has a different opinion." Diana glanced at Ursula. "Why are you so sure he didn't do it?"

"Not his nature." The woman looked out her side window. "Does Bert have a lawyer?"

"I retained one this morning."

"Thank God. Is he any good?"

"She comes highly recommended." Silence followed until Diana said, "Grant found some photos and letters dating back to when you and the Feeneys argued about the land they bought." Ursula pursed her lips, but said nothing. "Two photos were of your paintings. One before they built their house and one afterward. You certainly had a magnificent view."

"Until they ruined it by building that monstrosity. Now that Cranston fellow owns it. Maybe he'll tear it down."

"I don't know what he plans to do."

"I saw all those police cars around the house. What's going on? Penny has been mum about it. Not like her."

Ignoring Ursula's questions, Diana asked, "Would you like the photos of your paintings?"

"Why? Gloria had the originals."

"Cora took the one painting down when she had the house repainted. It's in her house. There seems to be a mystery about where the other one is."

"Not my problem." Ursula trembling hands fiddled with the button on her coat.

Diana asked, "How many paintings will be in this exhibit?"

"I gave my New York agent carte blanche as to which ones he'd send. I have the list, but haven't bothered to read it. Lately my life has become complicated."

"You aren't well?"

"Physically I'm as good as one can be at eighty-five, but mentally I'm in the sink." She sighed. "Penny worries too much about me. Everyone my age is on some type of medication. The heart can only last so long and mine is on its last journey."

Diana gave a slight nod.

"Penny gets upset if I gasp or feel bad. It's depressing not to have energy to do the slightest thing."

Diana's grip on the steering wheel tightened. "I'm sorry. Penny idolizes you."

"I know, but I've become an obsession with her and that's bad. She seems so fragile these days. I'm not sure what's going on in her head. There hasn't been an opportunity to have a serious talk with her." Ursula stared out the window. "I'm no saint. My hope is that I'll be remembered for my art." She chuckled. "Not much of a legacy."

"You sound depressed and fatalistic."

"I am." As they drove over the Newport Bridge, Ursula turned to view Narragansett Bay. "Lovely day, the air's crisp and clean." Then, unrelated to their conversation, she blurted out, "I like opera. The marvelous convoluted plots and the tragic endings. Past deeds haunt the characters. Opera is like real life, because not everyone lives happily ever after."

Chapter 23

Diana followed Penny's directions and five blocks after passing the oldest synagogue in America, she turned right and followed a maze of streets until she found the address. A long driveway led to a large house made of gray granite that had all the earmarks of old wealth. After the valet took her car, she helped Ursula up the steps to the double door entrance where a maid in a black dress with a white apron took their coats and ushered them down a hall that opened to a vast high-ceilinged living room.

"Aah," Ursula let out the sound when she viewed her paintings on the walls. People milled around chatting, drinking and looking at the art work unaware that the artist stood in the arched entryway.

A tall woman with streaks of gray in her auburn hair, wearing a bejeweled dark green dress with a low bodice, hurried forward. "Ursula Von Reiter," she gushed in a loud voice. After bending down to give a gentle hug to Ursula, she turned to her guests, asked for quiet, and announced, "Please welcome our celebrity artist Ursula Von Reiter. Her landscapes of the local area have graced many museums and galleries as well as the walls of Newport's oldest and finest families."

Ursula smiled and nodded her head in acknowledgement of the light applause.

The woman continued, "Ursula will be available to sign autographs as well as tell you about any paintings you wish to purchase." She flung out her hand. "Continue to enjoy her lovely paintings."

Ursula turned to Diana, "This is Judith Breck, benefactor of the arts."

Judith acknowledged the introduction with a quick nod. "Do read the pamphlet dear, it will edify you about the artist." She thrust one into Diana's hand, took hold of Ursula's arm, and led her away. Before the crowd swallowed Ursula, Diana said, "Remember, Penny is taking you home."

Ursula nodded, then turned back to her hostess who was already grabbing people to be introduced to the celebrity artist. Diana scanned the pamphlet. Von Reiter was born in Munich, Germany, and came to the United States in 1968. She lived in Rhode Island until moving to New York in the late 70s. Her paintings hang in the Whitney, the National Museum of Women in Art and the DC Moore Gallery in New York, to name a few. She tucked the brochure into her purse and walked through the living room to view the paintings. Most were landscapes, but two portraits intrigued her. One was a self-portrait with Ursula's face masked by shadows of trees and in the background the sky was dark with heavy clouds. Anger spilled from the painting. The other portrait was of Evelyn Stein, the woman who had been Ursula's partner. This painting was full of light, the woman's face was hypnotic, with probing eyes and flushed skin as if she'd just risen from a bath. An obscured face watched from behind a white billowy curtain, giving the work a haunting quality.

A stocky man who stood next to Diana said, "I think it's one of her best. And the most expensive."

"It's extraordinary," she said.

"When I gave her the list of paintings I'd have in the show, I was afraid she'd phone me in a fit of anger."

"You're her agent?"

He bowed slightly. "Franklin Harper, owner of Marcel Gallery in Manhattan. I saw you come in with her."

"Diana Bellfore, a new acquaintance of Ursula's."

Behind his horn-rimmed glasses, his blue eyes sparked. "Glad she's meeting people again. After Evelyn died, she holed up and went into a funk."

"When I met her, she was painting in the area around Potters Pond."

"I was afraid she'd never paint again, but soon after she returned to her Rhode Island home, she painted at a frenetic pace, as if her life depended upon her output." He touched Diana's elbow. "Let me show you some of her work from her last show."

"I don't want to take you away from promoting her work to others who might be interested in buying."

He grinned. "Look around you. How many knowledgable buyers do you see? Oh, they'll buy. Judith Breck will see to that. She's a shark at closing a deal during events like this, not like me or her husband. We're only the presenters." He leaned closer. "And let me tell you, Ursula's recent bad reviews of her last show have stimulated Judith's killer instinct. She likes difficult causes."

"Ursula's work is good. The paintings should sell themselves."

"Only a few pictures from her recent show are here in the other room." He walked ahead making a path between the art patrons who gawked, sipped champagne, and nibbled on caviar canapés.

"What about her very early work?" Diana asked as they strolled across the marble floor. "I mean paintings from when she first arrived in Rhode Island."

"Most were sold long ago. I visited her home on Potters Pond a little over a year ago. She asked me up to see two oil paintings that hung in a neighbor's house. It was an odd experience." He shook his head. "The paintings were good, but the woman who owned them had let them deteriorate. I suggested she hang them in another spot to prevent further sun exposure, but she got defensive."

"Do you remember the woman's name?"

"Oh yes. Gloria Feeney. Nasty experiences are memorable, aren't they? Ursula and that woman had their claws out. No love lost between those two. Ursula is difficult at times, but that woman was impossible. I was glad to leave before a cat fight broke out."

"Did you know Gloria was murdered about a year ago?"

He frowned. "No, I hadn't heard. She wasn't very friendly, so perhaps she had enemies. But murder? That's a bit over the top."

"The murder was never solved."

"Didn't figure Ursula's little town could have such excitement."

"Would those paintings have been worth a great deal?" she asked.

"Possibly, but I think Ursula set greater store by her early paintings than perhaps they merited." He cocked his head. "Of course, I'm not certain of that. The market for her work has fluctuated." They walked on side by side.

"She said her paintings are like children to her," Diana said.

He ignored her statement and stopped in front of a jarring painting of a lake and trees behind a prism of shattered glass. "What do you think?"

"I'm not an art critic."

"But you know what you like. Right now I want to hear your reaction, and don't be shy."

Diana studied the painting. It bothered her, gave her a sense of disorientation and yet there was something mystical about it. "Eerie, yet it draws you in. I don't know what she was trying to express, but it feels disjointed. Even the colors clash."

"I think that's how she felt after Evelyn died. Disjointed is a good word for it."

"It definitely makes you react emotionally to it."

He grinned and looked at her. "Ah, you see. You get it. Her critics didn't, but then Marshal Duvell is homophobic. He's never liked Ursula and therefore doesn't like her work."

"He's just one man with an opinion."

"True, but some critics mail in their critiques and follow the master, Duvell. However, I'm showing more of these in January at my gallery in New York." He turned to a couple behind them. "What do you think?"

Diana smiled and said, "Peter and Corrine O'Reilly, this is Franklin Harper, Ursula's agent." From their blank expression, she realized they didn't remember her. "We met when I was having brunch with Ursula. I'm Diana Bellfore."

"Oh, of course," Corrine O'Reilly said with the warmth of a toad. Her husband nodded gravely as if meeting the opposition's lawyer. Perhaps their son had told them about his disagreements with her.

Franklin barged on, either ignoring or refusing to acknowledge the couple's icy demeanor. "Have you seen Von Reiter's work before?"

"Oh yes." Corrine turned her full attention to him. "We have two lovely landscapes hanging in our home."

Franklin gestured to the paintings in front of them. "How do you respond to this one?"

"Interesting," Corrine said, "I wouldn't want it in my house. Much too dramatic, too stark. I don't see why she went in that direction. Not at all marketable."

Franklin turned away, winked to Diana, studied the painting and said, "We'll see about that. Some are more discerning art critics."

"Duvell didn't like them," Peter O'Reilly said. "And that's good enough for me."

A chubby woman came up to the O'Reillys. "Corrine, Peter, I haven't seen you in ages. How are you?" The woman didn't wait for a response, but barreled on. "How is that nice detective son of yours? He must be very busy. I hear he may not stay in Quamscutt much longer because of his lack of success in solving crimes. Such a shame."

Corrine's chin rose and she took her husband's arm. "He's very well. We said we'd talk to Ursula before we leave." Without acknowledging the woman, Franklin, or Diana, they moved off into the crowd.

"Well, I never," the woman said, and exhaled in a large puff. "No manners. I used to think they were so pleasant."

"Perhaps speaking that way about their son wasn't tactful," Diana said.

"I didn't mean to be rude, just repeating what others are saying. Small talk, you know." She wore a wounded expression her round face. "I'm sure they know I meant no harm?"

"Speaking of children's faults can be hurtful," Diana said.

The woman's shoulders slumped and she walked off to chat with other people.

Diana turned toward Franklin. "You've been generous with your time and knowledge, thank you."

"I enjoyed talking with you. Do you have a business card? I'll send you an invitation to the exhibition in January."

She dug in her purse and gave him her card. He read it and grinned. "I thought your name was familiar."

"Don't tell me you're a mystery fan?"

"Oh yes. A dreadful pastime, which I enjoy immensely." He handed his business card to her. "Please come to Manhattan for the show. I'll even promote your latest book."

She laughed. "I'll look forward to hearing from you." She glanced at her watch. "I have to leave."

"But you haven't tasted the incredible food."

"I'm driving to Philadelphia and need to get going. Penny and Charles Nelson are driving Ursula home, so she'll be in good hands."

Diana searched for Judith Breck to thank her, but felt relieved that the woman was in a deep discussion with a couple. From the woman's posture, the shark was sealing a deal.

At the best of times, it was over a four hour drive to Philly from the Brecks. The party had given her some useful information and although she wanted to pass it on to Max, she decided to wait until tomorrow. Questions spun through her mind. Could she be wrong about O'Reilly? Maybe he believed everyone was a suspect. Was that why he had her in his crosshairs? But then why not question Cora, Ursula, Angie and all the others close to the case?

When the traffic slowed to a crawl, her attention was brought back to driving. Between road repairs and an accident, hours slipped by. When it started to rain, she slowed down, letting braver and more daring drivers pass her. She struggled with what she knew about Sam. If he had stowed the drugs from the heist in Gloria's walls, why had he waited almost ten years to get them?

She pulled off the highway and stopped at a cafe she knew. With the hood of her parka over her head, she ran for the entrance. Inside the smell of coffee and baked goods roused her senses. After removing her parka, she sat in a booth and ordered soup, half a turkey sandwich and coffee. The meal would hold her until she got home.

When her cell emitted its ringtone, she retrieved it from her purse. It was Max. "Hello. Glad you called."

"After what I've just learned, I want you to be careful. The Yukovitch brothers were tied to the mob operating out of Boston. When Robert Yukovitch was released from prison he got in a shootout with the Providence police."

"I told you that."

"Yeah, but you didn't tell me the cop involved was Joe O'Reilly." While she absorbed the news, he continued in his raspy voice, "The report omitted the names of the cops involved and it was filed away, actually buried."

"The police were involved with the mob?"

"Not necessarily. Protecting their fellow officers from being targeted is a more likely scenario. Joe was the one who'd learned about a drug deal going on, and that's why the cops were there. Afterward Joe was promoted to sergeant."

"Could Sam have been the one who tipped off Joe?" Diana looked up as the waitress brought her food. "Max, wait a sec. I'm in a restaurant on my way home." The waitress left and Diana continued, "Okay. What do you think about what I said?"

"You could be right. If that's the case, then Sam is on the outs with the mob. Phil Yukovitch got out of stir a year ago and might be after Sam's drug stash. Good thing you aren't at that rental."

"Grant Cranston is there. I told him about you. Would you call him and tell him about what you and I have discussed?"

"Give me his phone number."

She did and then said, "I told you that Bert Schukart had been arrested for tampering with the crime scene of Gloria Feeney's murder, but O'Reilly wants to pin the murder charge on him as well. I got the lawyer you recommended."

"Okay. Anything more on your problems with Miss Sex and her accusations?"

"I have her address in Philadelphia and hope to speak with her before she meets with the dean. I'll keep you posted."

"Right. I'll do the same. Keep your eyes open and watch your back."

After hanging up, she stared at her food. She was no longer hungry, but knew she had to eat to maintain her energy for the drive.

When she got back on the road, her thoughts dwelled on her conversation with Max. Eventually she stopped thinking about what had happened in Rhode Island and thought about what might happen in Philadelphia. She almost fell asleep at the wheel several times and had to open the window, sing, and turn the radio to full volume. With the snarled traffic and the rain, it had taken her nearly six hours to get home.

She turned into the driveway of her colonial house, dark in contrast to the street lights. Thank God there was no For Sale sign planted on the lawn. Dragging her small suitcase out of the trunk, she inserted her key into the front door's lock, went inside, and flipped on the hall light. She gazed at the familiar furniture and pictures on the wall. At least neither Paul nor his real estate agent had denuded the house of its family's history.

The creak of a door and footsteps upstairs gave her pause. Paul? No. Who? She backed up feeling the wall behind her. She fingered her cell phone, ready to call 911. A robed figure stood at the top the dimly lit stairway.

Was she dreaming?

"Mom?"

"Isabel?"

Chapter 24

Diana ran up the stairs, drew Isabel into her arms and received a warm hug in return. They stood wrapped in each other's arms, tears flowing. Diana kept repeating her daughter's name as if she might disappear.

At last they separated and even in the dim light, Diana could see Isabel's flushed face. She felt her forehead. "You've got a fever."

"A little."

"Should you see a doctor?" She placed her hand on the side of Isabel's cheek.

"Mom, I'm going to be okay."

"You look a little shaky. Go into my bedroom and get into your dad's side of the bed while I bring up my suitcase, then we'll talk." She nudged her daughter, then hurried back down the stairs. By the time she fetched her bag and went into her bedroom, she had her emotions somewhat under control, but her heart pounded with joy and trepidation.

She's home, she's safe. God, thank you.

Diana sat on the bed next to Isabel. "When did you get here? How did you get in? Does your father know you're home?"

Isabel had the covers drawn up to her chin, looking thin and waif-like. "This evening about seven. Found the key in the usual spot under the back mat and no, he doesn't."

"You're ill?"

"I'll be okay. I'm on antibiotics for an infection from my wound. I report to the hospital in Maryland in a month. After they assess my condition, I'll get reassigned."

"Are you in pain?"

"The shoulder's sore, but I'll be fine. It was a long flight and my fever spiked, that's all. Don't worry."

"Worry is what I do best when it comes to my family." She hesitated. "Did you get my email or my letter?"

Isabel smiled. "Both. Thanks, I needed to have you tell me that."

Diana clutched her daughter's hand. "I've been such an idiot. I plan to do better."

"I know. We can all do better." Isabel massaged Diana's hand with her thumb. "You look tired."

Diana nodded. "Like you. Had a long drive with a lot on my mind."

"I thought you were going to stay in Rhode Island. Why did you come home?"

"That's a long, painful story. Let me shower first." She stood and studied her daughter. "It's been two years. We have a lot of catching up."

After Diana came out of the bathroom in her nightgown, she slipped under the covers on her side of the kingsized bed. "I haven't snuggled with you since you were a youngster."

Isabel grinned. "I remember. It was the night after my first kiss. A lifetime ago. You came into my room and asked if I was okay, and I talked nonstop. You listened."

Diana chuckled. "You were so happy." She turned on her side toward Isabel. "We had some good moments, didn't we? Until...until Grandpa died, and I let Beatrice take control of my life." She sighed. "Let's not go there tonight." Diana hesitated. "Does Beatrice know you're back in town?"

"No. How could she? I didn't tell anyone."

"Good. It'll be easier for you and me. I hope I can do what has to be done and leave before she knows I was here."

"Coward."

"You bet." She rose on one elbow and faced her daughter. "Now tell me all that's happened to you."

Isabel laughed. "All? I'll give you a short version or we'll be up all night." As Isabel talked, it brought Diana into her daughter's world of military life, her ordeal through boot camp, a run down of officers training school and some of her experiences in Afghanistan. Isabel seemed reluctant to share much of her life when she was in Central Asia. "I was promoted to First Lieutenant a few months ago."

"You deserved it after all you've been through and all you've done. I'm so proud of you."

Isabel turned to face Diana. "Okay, I'm talked out, now tell me why you're here and how I can help."

Diana snapped out the bedside light, and in the darkened room, she explained about Sally Tuttle's accusations against Paul. Isabel didn't interrupt, and after a time, Diana thought she might have fallen asleep and stopped talking.

Isabel had not only stayed awake, but asked what Diana had hoped she wouldn't. "Does Dad know you're doing this?"

"No. And I'm not sure he'd like me interfering."

"You know he wouldn't."

"I have to try. George told me that Paul decided not to fight the allegation." Diana took a deep breath before adding, "And your father wants to sell the house. He's already hired a real estate agent, that young Janie Newcomb."

"I can hear it in your voice." Isabel laughed. "You're jealous."

"No, I'm not." She let the silence hang, before saying, "Okay, I am."

Isabel leaned over and turned on her bedside lamp. "I'm glad you're coming to Dad's defense and I might be able to help when you talk to Sally. I want to tell her about her brother. Benny was a tough, but considerate sergeant and a hero." She stopped, stared at the ceiling then turned to face Diana again. "And...I think you should sell the house. I'm not comfortable living here any more, and Jeffy won't come back no matter what happens to his partner."

Although Diana knew Isabel was correct, the idea of selling was difficult to accept. Years of memories were in this house.

Isabel continued, "Haven't you noticed how discouraged Dad's felt about teaching? He's got enough years in for his pension, doesn't he?"

"Yes, but that's not the point. I..."

"Maybe this is a good time for him to stop teaching and finish that book he's been working on."

"If he wants to quit teaching, fine, but I don't want him to go out with his reputation smeared."

"I understand and agree with you. So tomorrow we tackle Sally Tuttle and the dean."

"Thank you. I appreciate your willingness to help."

"The least I can do. And it might help me deal with some of my guilt."

"Guilt? About what?"

Isabel closed her eyes. "I'd rather not discuss it now, okay?"

Diana nodded and said, "Let's get some sleep." After Isabel turned off the light, Diana lay awake, listening to her daughter's gentle breathing until sleep overcame her, too. During the night she awoke to Isabel's loud moaning and gibberish talk. What was she saying? Diana recognized a word or two and realized she was speaking Arabic. She put her arms around her daughter and drew her into an embrace.

"Sorry," Isabel murmured. Her moaning was supplanted by soft sobs.

Diana thought of Grant and his nightmares. How would Isabel deal with her demons? Diana wished her daughter would never have to go back to a war zone, but knew there was nothing she could do about it.

Early morning sunlight streamed through the curtains and the sight of Isabel peacefully curled up next to her brought tears to Diana's eyes. Her daughter's lean and muscled body seemed healthy despite the infection, but after listening to her moaning and sobbing during the night, Diana was concerned about her emotional health. She crept out of bed and went to the window. The sun sparkled on the garden with its fall plumage. Through the years she had labored over it and now she would move on, leaving someone else to care for it. Change. It was difficult to face.

By the time she finished dressing and left the bedroom, Isabel had begun to stir. In the kitchen Diana checked the contents of the fridge and was delighted that Paul had left enough supplies for breakfast. She hummed as she put on the coffee, set the table in the alcove and began to mix the ingredients for crepes, Isabel's favorite. If only Paul and Jeffrey were here. She wondered if she should call Paul or wait to hear the results of Dave's surgery. She checked the kitchen clock—too early to disturb them. She turned on the small radio by the breakfast table, tuned to a classical music station, sat and sipped her coffee.

Isabel, dressed in her fatigues, came into the kitchen. "Coffee smells wonderful."

Diana smiled. "You look very military, trim and heroic, First Lieutenant Bellfore." She pointed to the Purple Heart pinned next to several other ribbons. "I know that one, but what are the other ribbons for?"

"Oh, things like overseas duty, good conduct, the usual crap."

"I wouldn't put it like that." She caught herself from admonishing her daughter's language. "I'm very proud of you." She went to the burners where a pan sat ready for the crepes. "Sit down, enjoy your juice and coffee while I make your favorite."

Isabel ate two crepes without saying a word until she'd finished the last bite. "That was divine. Exactly how I remember Sunday mornings at home."

"I'm glad you remember the good times. I guarantee a home-cooked meal every time you visit me, and I hope that's often."

They were discussing how they would approach Sally Tuttle, when they heard a car drive up. Diana walked to the living room, looked through the bay window, and felt a knot in her stomach. She returned to the kitchen. "It's your grandmother. What's she doing here? She couldn't know I came home. She probably drove by to snoop. What'll I do?"

"Maybe she'll be delighted to see us and be pleasant."

Diana made a sour face. "I wish, but doubt it. We've been at war for months."

"More like years," Isabel said.

"I don't need her interference. Stay in here. Maybe you'll be able to avoid her." When the doorbell rang, she squared her shoulders and went to answer it.

Beatrice stood on the threshold, her dyed blonde hair coifed to lacquered perfection, a scowl on her powdered face. "I drove by on the way to church and saw your car. What's going on? Why didn't you tell me you were coming home?" She strode past Diana into the living room. "You could have stayed with me instead of being here all alone. You poor dear, it must be terrible for you." She wagged her finger at Diana. "But you left and men will play."

Diana waited, hoping her mother would wind down if she didn't react.

"I heard Paul plans to sell the house. Good idea. You should get a good price and it will make the divorce simpler."

"What are you babbling about?" Anger rose, bile stuck in her throat, and she trembled with annoyance and anger. "We are not getting a divorce. Paul is not playing around, and I came back because I have business in town."

For a moment, Beatrice was speechless, then dismissed Diana's words with a wave her hand. "You don't have to pretend with me. Everyone knows that young woman Janie has been here all hours of the day and night. I'll use the nice word, 'flirtations.'" She sneered. "Of course everyone knows what must have been going on."

"You love the gossip vines, don't you? You're the biggest rumormonger of them all. For your information Paul hired Janie as our real estate agent. That's why she's been here."

"Where will you live?" Beatrice's chin came up, and she almost snorted. "I knew it. Your moving to Rhode Island was to get away from all the ugly rumors."

"You love to make up things and spread them about."

"I never gossip. As your mother, I have your best interest at heart." She reached out to pat Diana's arm. "You know that, dear, don't you?"

Diana took a step back. "No. What I know is that you have your own agenda."

"Don't be rude. I'm your mother."

"Then act like it. Stop treating me like your puppet. I've had it with your interference. Do you realize you've been an absolute horror to me and my family ever since Dad committed suicide?"

"Don't you throw his sin at me. I withstood enough talk from everyone after what he did. How could he do that to me?" She moved forward and plopped her heavy purse on a chair, making her action feel like an exclamation point.

"To you? He did it to get away from you. You drove him to it."

"That's a lie. Don't you dare talk to me that way."

"Hello Grandmother." Isabel stood in the kitchen doorway.

"Isabel? You're home. How wonderful." Beatrice went to Isabel and gave her a perfunctory hug. "Your mother is a little unstable right now, saying things she shouldn't. You can help your mother through all the sordid details of her divorce." She stepped back, hesitated, then looked Isabel up and down. "You don't have to wear that awful camouflaged baggy uniform when you're home, do you? It makes me sick to look at it. We have no business sending women to war especially to those barbaric regions. They treat women like cattle. The war has nothing to do with us."

Diana was about to interrupt and throw her mother out of the house, but Isabel handled the situation.

"Grandmother, I wear this uniform proudly. Men and women have died so you can keep your foolish ideas and lifestyle. You can say what you want about our government's policies, but don't ever deride the men and women in uniform in my presence. And for your information, these camouflaged uniforms are called BDUs. Short for Battle Dress Uniform."

"Oh. Well, I still don't like them." Beatrice dug a handkerchief out of her purse. "Why are you both so mean to me? I only want what's best for you."

"No, you don't," Diana said. "You want what you want. And what you want is not in my or my family's best interest. From now on you will be civil in my house and keep your rumors and innuendoes to yourself."

Beatrice blinked. "I'm seventy-four. I'm the head of the family. I don't deserve to be treated like…like…. You'll be sorry you were so nasty."

"Nasty? You're the one who's been nasty and unfeeling. For years I've let you get away with it, because I felt sorry for you after Dad's suicide. No more." Diana opened the door and pointed for her mother to leave. "When you come to my house, you will be civil and kind and if that's not possible, you won't be welcome."

"You can't do this. I have no one else." She sobbed. "Why are you doing this to me?"

"I'm not. You've done it to yourself. If you ever want to see me or my family again, then you need to make a major adjustment in your attitude toward Paul, Isabel, Jeffrey and me, and Jeffrey's partner, too. You don't have to accept what we do, but you will hold your tongue." She stood erect by the open door. "Good bye, Beatrice."

In the silence that followed Beatrice's exit, Diana and Isabel stood mute, looking at each other. Finally, Isabel said, "I'm impressed."

"I'm exhausted," Diana said and they fell into each other's arms laughing.

Chapter 25

It was eleven o'clock when they drove to the house where Sally Tuttle rented a room. They'd decided not to call ahead, worried she might refuse to see them or worse yet, flee the area. It was a twenty minute drive without the weekday traffic. As they drove through unfamiliar streets, Isabel guided them by using her phone's GPS.

"I'd like to go back to Rhode Island with you," Isabel said.

"Dad might need you and will be overjoyed to be with you."

"I'll have time to come back and visit with him. I don't want to be here alone for even one day." She glanced at Diana. "I no longer feel I belong here."

"I understand, but Rhode Island might not be safe."

"Safe? What are you talking about?"

Diana sighed and shook her head. "I seemed to have stepped into an old murder investigation. Recently, drugs were found in the house I'm renting, stored there for the past year. So you see it isn't a good situation."

"Wow. I hadn't heard all that." Isabel laughed. "You're a kick. I've been in a war zone, been shot at, wounded, and you think I'd be scared of an old murder and drugs?"

"The mob might be involved."

"Mom, that's all the more reason I should be with you. You shouldn't be alone there."

Diana squirmed. "I'm not exactly alone."

Isabel lifted the seat belt away from her sore shoulder. "Who's there with you?"

"Captain Grant Cranston owns the house. He wasn't there when I rented it, but there was a mixup and he came back and well, we reached an amicable agreement."

"Oh? That's interesting."

"Don't make something of it. He's more your age than mine."

"I can't wait to meet him," she said with a mysterious smile playing across her face.

"He's a nice young man. I think you'll like him."

"I can't wait."

Diana felt there was something else Isabel wanted to say, but they were nearing Sally Tuttle's boarding house. After she turned off the engine, she looked at Isabel. "I want you with me, but it's a difficult situation. I'm not sure how this is going to turn out."

"Right. So we'll do it together."

"You're an impossible child." Diana grinned. "Come on."

They got out of the car, mounted the stairs leading to the door of a two story wood frame house and rang the bell. The door was opened by a middle-aged woman dressed in a plaid skirt and lavender wool sweater. "Yes? May I help you?"

"We'd like to speak to Sally Tuttle, please," Diana said and nodded to Isabel. "My daughter knew her brother."

"Oh, I'm so glad. The poor girl has been in such a state. She told me about her brother being killed in Afghanistan. Such a tragedy." She stepped back. "I'm Mrs. Barker. Please, come in. Sally's in the garden. That's where she spends most of her time, reading and studying, she says. But I think she just sits and mopes."

"Perhaps we can help," Diana said.

"Go through that door there," she pointed down the hall. "I'll bring some hot tea. It's a little chilly in the garden."

"That's kind of you," Diana said and walked through to the garden with Isabel behind her.

Sally sat on a bench in the sun, a book on her lap, her hands clenched. Isabel put her hand on Diana's arm. "Let me start the conversation."

When their shadows fell over Sally, she looked up, frowning. She stared at Isabel's uniform then studied her face. "You're Isabel Bellfore."

"Yes. I just got back and wanted to talk to you about Benny. May I?"

"Who's she?" Sally nodded toward Diana.

"My mother, Diana Bellfore."

"I don't want to talk to her."

"All right." Isabel motioned with her head for Diana to move away. "May I sit and tell you about Benny?" Without receiving an answer, Isabel sat.

"Benny was a tough sergeant, but fair. The men liked him and so did I. He saved the squad and the girls at the school."

"Girls?"

"Yes. Our mission was to talk to the local villagers about the troubles they were having with the Taliban. I was there as an interpreter."

"If you hadn't been there, he wouldn't be dead."

"If I hadn't gone, there would have been another interpreter, but they needed a woman to talk to the village women. There had been threats against them for sending their daughters to school. Our job was to learn how credible the threat was. The Taliban attacked while we were there."

Sally said nothing and Isabel waited. "Do you want to hear this?"

Sally nodded. "How did Benny die?"

Isabel looked down at her hands before she said, "Benny had deployed the squad around the perimeter of the school. It was a small building surrounded on three sides by stone walls. I was in the yard talking to the teacher when something slammed into my shoulder and I was driven backward. Ended up flat on my back. I heard firing. The girls screamed. The teacher was dead, shot in the head. I yelled for the girls to stay inside. There were eight of them, ages nine to fifteen."

As Diana listened from a few yards away, she was shocked to hear Isabel's story.

"I crawled over to Benny. I outranked him, but he was an old hand at fighting. The Taliban had us pinned down and outnumbered. We radioed for help, but knew it wouldn't come in time. There was one chance. I pointed to a spot to our right. It was high ground. If we could get two men up there, we'd have them in a crossfire, but we had to cross open space to get there. I told him I'd take Corporal Mantera with me. He was the fastest guy in the squad. Benny argued. Said I wouldn't make it, cuz I was shot." Isabel's words came slow. "That's when I realized blood was dripping down my arm. Benny said, 'No way, lieutenant. You can't make it. Your eyes are already getting dull. You'll just get yourself killed and that won't help any of us one damn bit. You anchor this spot. I'll make the run with Mantera.'"

Isabel stopped and gazed at Sally. "They made it and got the enemy in a crossfire. We'd only taken light casualties until then, but another group came over the rise, firing. Benny got hit. Mantera dragged him back behind the wall where I was. Blood spewed out of his chest. Charlie, our medic, did his best to stop the hemorrhaging. Benny remained conscious. He said, 'Izzy, get the squad and the girls out of here.' He and I both knew someone had to stay and protect our withdrawal. I got the squad organized and asked Charlie to carry Benny. I figured I'd stay behind to cover them." Isabel started to cry. Wiped her eyes and continued, "Sorry, I get upset when I think about this. Benny said, 'No way. The girls won't leave unless you talk to them and go with them. No one but you can do that.' His actual words were, 'You fuckin' well aren't staying behind. Go, lieutenant. Now.'"

Isabel took Sally's hand. "I yelled back, 'I outrank you, sergeant, I'm staying, you're going.' He smiled and shook his head. 'Not if you want to get the girls to safety.'" Isabel waited to catch her breath, then continued. "Mantera and Benny stayed behind. We got out, saved the girls and most of the squad, all because Benny stayed and covered our backs. Mantera made it back. Benny didn't. Later they recovered the bodies of Benny and a young private."

There was a long silence. Diana's breath quickened, her eyes misted. The breeze ruffled the maple trees. Leaves fell in a lazy downward spiral.

"In a way, I am to blame for Benny's death. I didn't think either of us had a choice. He was very brave. We all got out and saved the girls because of him."

Sally pulled a piece of paper out of her jacket pocket. "This was Benny's last letter to me. He always wrote about you, said you were tough as nails and sweet as candy, you were smart and kind and he thought I'd like you." She sniffed. "Benny was the only family I had. You had a family. I don't have anyone any more. I found out where your father worked. I wanted someone to pay for Benny's death, but after I started the rumors, I felt awful. I didn't know how to stop them. Benny would be mad if he knew what I've done." She sobbed. "I'm scared."

Isabel put her right arm around her. "You're no longer alone. You have me."

Diana stepped forward. "It'll be all right, Sally. I'm sure I can convince Dean Crowley to meet with you, so you can tell him the truth."

Sally shook her head. "No. I'll go to jail." She sobbed.

"Nobody's going to jail," Diana said. "Paul won't press charges. Professor Horowitz is expecting you back Wednesday."

"I can't go back after what I've done."

"You can undo what you've done," Diana said. "Just tell your story to the dean."

Isabel took Sally's hand in both of hers. "I'll go with you if you like."

Sally nodded, her lips trembling.

Isabel looked at Diana, then said to Sally, "Benny saved my life. I'd like you to be my friend. It might be too early for you to accept my offer, but it's genuine and forever."

Sally clung to Isabel. "Please, thank you, be my friend."

Mrs. Barker came out with a tray. "Is everything all right?" She set the tray down on the wrought iron table.

"Everything's fine," Diana said. "I'm driving back to Rhode Island tomorrow and Sally is coming with me. All right, Sally?"

"Will you be coming, too, Isabel?" the girl asked.

"Absolutely." She winked at her mother.

Chapter 26

Getting Dean Crowley to meet with Sally Tuttle before the hearing on Tuesday took a great deal of persuasion. He insisted that two other members of the committee be present, and Diana concurred. Talking Sally into the arrangement was another matter. Finally at four-thirty that same Sunday Diana drove up to the dean's home with Sally and Isabel.

As they exited the car, Sally clung to Isabel's hand as if it were a lifeline to safety, and perhaps it was. Mrs. Crowley, the dean's wife, answered the door and Diana made the introductions. Diana had always liked the woman and felt comfortable in her presence. Dean Harry Crowley, on the other hand, was serious, conservative and too proper. She'd always thought of him as a cold fish.

Mrs. Crowley said, "The committee is waiting in the study."

Diana introduced Isabel and Sally to the dean, Professor Bob Warner and Professor Margaret Logan. "I won't stay during Sally's explanation, but Isabel will. If you have any questions later, I'll answer them." She turned, gave an encouraging smile to Sally, and closed the door behind her.

Mrs. Crowley offered her coffee, but she declined. Her stomach was doing flip flops. "I'm sorry to take up the dean's time on Sunday."

"Don't apologize. If Miss Tuttle can settle this matter, everyone will be relieved." Mrs. Crowley fiddled with the buttons on her sweater. "I understand you're in Rhode Island for a while."

"Yes. Doing research for a book. It's taking longer than I expected."

"What's the book about?"

Diana clasped her hands together and reeled off the explanation. "An old murder investigation leads to an artist and an old drug bust." She hesitated, then added, "And missing oil paintings are involved, too." Why had she added that? Totally unnecessary, but Franklin Harper's comments about the animosity between Gloria and Ursula had Diana thinking about motives for murder. Was Grant right in his musing over Ursula as a suspect in Gloria's murder? She had motive. Well, kind of a motive, if anger over a blocked vista was a motive.

"I don't see how you come up with your plots," Mrs. Crowley said. "They seem so real."

"That's the idea." Diana swallowed and took a deep breath. "Do you mind if I go outside? I'm nervous about this meeting and need some fresh air."

"Of course, I understand. This must be very trying for you and Paul." She walked to the front door with Diana. "Ring when you want to come back in or I'll come get you when they've finished."

Once outside, Diana called Paul. He answered on the third ring. "Diana, I should have called earlier, but Jeff and I were up all night and I just woke up. Dave's going to be all right."

"Thank God. How's Jeffrey?"

"Much better now that Dave's out of the woods. I plan to stay here until he's released from the hospital. My TA will continue to handle my classes."

That surprised Diana, knowing that the committee had expected him to be present at the Tuesday meeting, and no one had said it was canceled. At least not yet. Since she wasn't supposed to know about the meeting, she couldn't say anything. "I didn't get the real estate papers, so I came home." She took a deep breath. "Isabel is here."

"She's home? Why didn't she let me know? Is she all right?"

"She didn't tell anyone. She had a slight fever from an infection, but seems fine today. Her trip home was exhausting and might have brought it on."

"How long will she be home?"

"She has to report in a month and then will be reassigned. She's coming back to Rhode Island with me."

"But I want to see her."

"And she wants to see you and will visit you later." She hesitated, then said, "She doesn't want to stay here alone, and I can't blame her. Beatrice came by the house, and we had words. I told her she had to stop interfering and trying to control me and my family or she wasn't welcome."

"You told her that?"

"Yes, I finally did." She could hear his relief from his sigh. "I'll have Isabel call you in about an hour. Is that all right?"

"Perfect."

"And Paul, if you want to sell the house, I'll understand. Perhaps it's time for us to downsize, but please, in the future, don't leave me out of decisions that affect both of us."

"I've had a lot on my mind. I was too abrupt. I"m sorry about that." The line went silent for a moment until he said, "Diana, I'm glad you and Isabel are together."

"Me too. She's amazing. Take care and give my love to Jeffrey and my best to Dave, and my love to you, too."

"Take care of yourself." He hung up.

No sign-off of "love," but she had hope. During the call, she'd walked down the block and now turned back toward the Crowley's house.

Isabel stood on the steps. "There you are," she said. "Wondered where you'd gone off to. The committee wants to talk to you."

"Where's Sally?"

"Wiping away tears in the powder room."

Diana walked up the steps and stood next to Isabel. "How did it go?"

"Good, I think." She shook her head. "It was tough on Sally though."

"We knew it would be. You and I will have to do what we can to help her." She started for the door, turned and said, "I just talked to your dad. Dave's going to be okay, but Paul plans to stay with Jeffrey until Dave's released from the hospital."

"Did you tell him that we were meeting with the dean and his committee?"

"Couldn't. Paul doesn't know I know and I left it that way. When you talk to him, avoid the subject, okay?"

"He wasn't going to come back for the Tuesday meeting, was he?"

Diana nodded. "That's what I surmised."

When she entered the house, the dean was talking to his wife. He turned toward Diana. "Would you come into the study for a moment, please. We have a few questions."

The two professors were standing by the fireplace talking. When they smiled, Diana took it as a good sign. The dean walked behind his desk, sat, then thumbed the end of a stack of papers.

"I'm sorry you and Paul have been put through this ordeal. Miss Tuttle rescinded her accusations toward Paul. Her story is sad, but you must understand we had to look into it." He glanced at his colleagues, as if looking for support. "Your daughter claims that you have no intention of suing for defamation of character or taking any legal action against Miss Tuttle, the university or me. Is that correct?"

This question surprised Diana, but she realized he, the university and Sally were all liable. "I have no intention of doing so."

The dean smiled and started to stand, but she added, "However," she stood more erect, "when my husband gets back from Chicago, you'll have to ask him. I'm sure you understand that I can't speak for him on this matter."

The dean blustered and looked to the professors for help. "I'm sure Paul will be reasonable."

"He's always been reasonable, but you jumped to the conclusion that he was guilty. You never investigated Miss Tuttle's claims or talked to any of the students she'd spoken to. You didn't even know she wasn't a registered student here."

"We were in the process of investigating," the dean said.

"Wouldn't it have been better to investigate first before bringing Paul before the ethics committee?"

"Well, you see, we have a reputation—"

"So does my husband." Although her hands remained at her side, they were now fists. "You will find some way to repair my husband's reputation without destroying Miss Tuttle's. If not...." She stopped, letting them draw their own conclusions. "That's all I have to say, good day." She walked out of the room, closed the door firmly but quietly, nodded to Mrs. Crowley, and left the house.

Isabel and Sally sat in the car, waiting for her. She climbed into the driver's side and let out a long sigh. "Well, girls, let's go to dinner."

In a small voice, Sally asked from the backseat, "Is it over?"

"It is for you," Diana said. "However, Dean Crowley must deal with the fallout and I hope he does a good job, otherwise there might be repercussions, not from me, but from the faculty. What happened to Paul could happen to any of them if the administration doesn't do a better job of investigating allegations before it starts a witch hunt."

"Mom, you've become a warrior," Isabel said. "Where's all the fighting spirit been for the past years?"

"Asleep, I guess."

"I talked to Dad, but didn't say anything about today's meeting, although I did tell him about your confrontation with Grandmother. He sounded impressed."

Diana wondered if Paul was impressed enough to forgive her. Did he still love her? "I'll call George tonight and explain about Sally Tuttle and today's meeting. Perhaps he'll tell your father what's happened."

"Why don't I tell him?"

"Isabel, I got you into this mess, but it's not your problem."

"Oh, yes it is. You're my parents. He's my dad and I was involved with this mess."

"It wasn't your fault."

"I know that, but let me tell him about Sally. I can explain how she felt and why she did what she did."

Diana gave her a weak smile. "All right, but don't be surprised if he doesn't appreciate my interference."

After dinner, they dropped Sally off at her rooming house and told her they'd pick her up the next day about eleven. On the way home, Isabel said, "Tell me a little more about the old house you're renting."

Diana went through all that had happened since she'd arrived in Quamscutt. When she finished, Isabel sat mute until they drove into their driveway.

"I'm looking forward to seeing the place and meeting the people."

"There's a cast of characters, and I'm not sure who is bad and who is good, but I'm beginning to think there are shades of gray." She shrugged. "At any rate, I'm glad you're coming and there shouldn't be a problem of you being my guest. I haven't been reimbursed yet, so technically I'm renting, but I doubt if Grant would mind you staying with me for a few days."

"I hope not." She smiled at her mother. "You like him, don't you?"

"Yes, I do. What I don't understand is why, after the incident with Penelope, Gloria made Grant her heir, yet had treated him miserably years earlier." Diana pulled into her driveway.

"Maybe she felt guilty about the way she treated him. After all, you said, she took him in after his parents died. How did they die?"

"Automobile accident. A hit and run driver. Never caught." Diana turned off the engine.

"Oh, I wondered." Isabel unbuckled her seatbelt, but continued to sit in the car. "Have you ever wondered why there are so many loose ends to the crimes involving that house?"

"Of course. It's gotten very complicated."

"You always told me that all loose ends come together in a pattern. You have an unsolved murder, questions about the drugs stashed in the house, a missing painting, and an unsolved hit and run case. Doesn't it make you think they might all be tied together?"

"I'd never thought about the hit and run being tied to the murder. It seems far fetched. Fiction is not like real life."

Isabel said, "You're the mystery writer. How would you plot it?"

How indeed?

Chapter 27

The following morning Isabel came downstairs dressed in a stunning outfit—a jade green A-line skirt with a cream-colored top and a pair of red pumps. Diana smiled at her daughter. "You look beautiful, but you realize we'll be in the car all day."

"I know." Isabel blushed and twirled around. "It's fun to dress up after wearing fatigues and uniforms. Besides, I need to make an impression on your landlord." She laughed. "I think Beatrice would approve, don't you?"

"Oh yes, but she'd probably tell you to buy a pair of green suede pumps."

"Mother, are you teasing me or are you acting like Grandmother?"

Diana was taken aback, realizing how she might have sounded to Isabel. "Definitely teasing, not nagging. Now let's eat breakfast and get going."

After stopping for Sally, they enjoyed a sunny drive to Rhode Island with Isabel and Sally chatting like old friends. Diana remembered Isabel's slumber parties and the carpools during her children's early years. Today Isabel skillfully helped Sally reminisce about her brother Benny. The hours skated by with a stop for lunch and gas, and in the late afternoon they arrived in Providence.

On the outskirts of Brown University, they dropped Sally off at the house where she rented a room. The girl stood on the sidewalk with a mournful expression, her suitcase by her side. Diana stood next to her. "Thanksgiving is coming soon. I'm not sure where Isabel will be." She hesitated. "And I'm not sure if my husband and I will be here or in Philadelphia, but wherever we are, we'd love to have you spend the holiday with us. Our son and his partner might be home then, too." Of course having Jeffrey home was too much to hope for, but she wanted Sally to look forward to being included in a family.

Sally's thin face lit up. "Oh, that would be super." She leaned down and glanced at Isabel who sat in the passenger seat. "Maybe you'll be posted stateside."

"I have no idea, but I'll keep in touch and let you know. You have my email address, so write me."

It was almost six o'clock when Diana pulled into the Victorian's driveway behind Grant's pickup. The kitchen light was on. While she retrieved her suitcase from the trunk, Isabel hauled out her canvas bag and stared at the house.

"Is something wrong?" Diana asked.

"Ah, no. Just taking it all in. Maybe we should have called ahead. I'm a little worried Grant will be too surprised." She brushed at the wrinkles in her skirt with a nervous gesture.

Diana frowned. "There's nothing to be concerned about, really."

"Oh, ah, sure." She gave a nervous laugh.

They dropped their suitcases in the mudroom and entered the kitchen. Grant turned from the stove to face them. "Hi, I…" He gaped.

"I brought Isabel with me. She's home on leave."

"Hello, Captain Cranston." A broad smile graced Isabel's face. "You look different in civvies." She looked down at her skirt and heels. "I guess I do too."

He grinned. "You look fabulous." He stepped toward Isabel and they embraced. "You're safe and I'm damn glad to see you." His words tumbled out before they kissed.

Diana stood, her mouth agape. Deep in their emotional reunion, they ignored her presence. She didn't know whether to be angry or happy. After some time the couple parted, but kept an arm around each other's waists.

Diana sagged into a chair. "Would someone tell me what's going on."

"I'm sorry, Mom, there didn't seem to be a good time to explain, about Grant and me."

"When I talked about Grant, you could have told me then. And Grant, I can't believe you didn't tell me. You had ample opportunity." Diana wagged her finger at him. "You pretended not to know Isabel."

He held up his hand. "Forgive me. With everything that was happening, I didn't want to make things more complicated. I thought you wouldn't understand or approve of our engagement."

"Engaged?" She shook her head. "Am I the last to know?"

"We haven't told anyone else." Isabel laughed. "Our assignments were too iffy to make plans much less an announcement. I couldn't shake the infection, kept going to the doctor, and unexpectedly got leave."

Diana stood. "The least you can do is give me a hug. Both of you." Diana held Isabel in her arms then reached for Grant. Then, she took a step back and took a deep breath. "Isabel, you're going to have your hands full with this charming fellow." She looked at their smiling faces. "I approve, but now that I know, shouldn't you tell your dad?"

"After dinner. I'm starved." Isabel gave Grant a nudge in the side. "Mom says you're a good cook."

"Easy when you have a choice of food and ingredients." He turned off the burner. "I'll help you with your gear, and while you unpack, I'll cook up more pasta and there's plenty of Alfredo sauce."

While Grant carried Isabel's duffle bag upstairs, Diana rolled her small suitcase into her bedroom. She didn't ask where Isabel would be sleeping. Understanding that Grant and Isabel needed time alone, she took her time unpacking. Although she had a million questions, they could wait.

Later, over pasta, salad, and red wine, Diana plied them for information. "You fell for each other rather fast, didn't you?" Their sidelong glances told her they'd expected that reaction. "I'm not judging, mind you," she added hastily, "only stating the obvious." She took a bite of salad during the silence that followed. "Okay, let's have the story of how this all happened."

Grant leaned back and gave Isabel a loving smile. "She was a raw second lieutenant and a pain in the butt when I first met her. She needed to learn the ropes."

Isabel punched his arm. "You were no angel with all your gruff instructions. You were harder on me than on any of the others."

"Hey, my job was to keep everybody in the platoon, including you, safe." He held her hand. "When you're together in difficult circumstances, you get to know each other fast. Falling in love was the last thing I expected when I deployed."

"Danger can accelerate emotions." Diana remained worried about the speed of their romance.

"We've talked about that," Grant said. "You want to grab and hold on to any joy you can when you're not sure if you'll make it through the next day."

Isabel glanced at Grant and back to her mother. "We felt this was right for us."

Diana nodded. "You're both old enough, so I won't say any more. Meeting the right person at the right time isn't easy. I'm glad you found each other." She surveyed the young couple. "Isabel, were you with Grant when he was wounded?"

She shook her head. "I was at camp acting as an interpreter for the captured prisoners." She took a sip of wine. "When they brought Grant in, I almost lost it. I was scared he wouldn't make it. After he was stabilized, they were taking him out on a chopper to the main hospital along with a prisoner. Sergeant Tuttle knew about us and insisted I go along to interpret for the prisoner. At the hospital, I had to dodge the brass and make excuses to stay."

"You never said a word to Dad or your brother," Diana said.

"It was all too new, too wonderful, and after he was wounded, too stressful. I had to wait and pray he'd recover."

"What do you expect to happen now? How can you be together? You're supposed to report for duty in a month, and Grant's on leave till the end of the year."

Isabel smiled and hugged Grant's arm. "It'll work out somehow."

"She's an unapologetic optimist." Grant's eyes sparkled. "I—" His cell's ringtone interrupted him. "Sorry, I have to get this." He stood and walked to the far side of the kitchen. "Miss Jacob. I know I said I'd come get the painting tonight, but something's come up." He listened, frowned, then said, "I understand. I'll come by within the hour." He clicked off and shook his head. "Damn woman. She isn't around for a long time then orders me to come by this evening because she plans to leave early tomorrow morning." His shoulders slumped. "I'm sorry, Isabel."

"I can pick up the painting." Although tired, Diana was pleased to help out, knowing they'd been separated for so long. Besides, she had a few questions for Cora. A half hour later, Grant and Isabel were happily doing the dishes. As she went out the door, Diana said, "Don't wait up."

They laughed.

She stopped for gas before following the directions to Cora's house. Clouds skittered across the face of the moon, making shadows come and go. There were no lights in the rural area. She turned onto a street, thinking it was Clampton Road, but it was Clampton Circle and she had to double back. She thought of calling Cora to tell her she'd be late, but decided the woman could damn well wait. She'd taken her own sweet time to contact Grant and now she'd ordered him to get it immediately.

Fifteen minutes later she found the correct street. Slowing to a crawl, she checked the numbers on the mailboxes. The high beams from an approaching car blinded her, zooming by going at least sixty. After it passed, she put on her high beams and eventually found Cora's mailbox hidden beneath drooping pine boughs. She turned into a long gravel driveway and pulled up to a small older home, isolated from neighboring houses. The front porch light was on, but the house was dark. Perhaps Cora was in the back or was watching TV, but the silence felt eerie. Unbuckling her seat belt, she got out, walked up the stone walkway and rang the bell. No answer. She knocked hard and called out, "Cora. It's Diana Bellfore. I've come for the painting."

The wind stirred the trees. A car was parked in the back. The woman had to be home. She walked around the side of the house and peered in a low window, but couldn't see anything. In the back she went up the concrete steps and banged on the door. It creaked open.

"Cora. Cora," she yelled. She heard a shriek and was about to flee when she realized it was coming from a tea kettle. Fumbling her way into the house, she bumped her knee on a table, found a light switch and flipped it on. Blinking at the sudden brightness, she stepped into the kitchen. The sink was full of dishes, the water faucet was running and a gas burner remained lit under a pan with remnants of food. A dish towel lay on the floor.

She turned off the burner and the water, then stood in the middle of the kitchen pondering her next move. "Cora," she called out. Taking a deep breath, she walked into the living room. Shafts of moonlight streamed through a window, sparkling off broken glass on the carpet.

Death had a certain smell.

Chapter 28

    Cora lay sprawled against the pale blue wainscoting. Her head tilted to one side at an odd angle. A large knife protruded from her stomach. Blood seeped from the wound, leaving a pool of red on the beige carpet. Cora's eyes, dulled by death, stared at the room she could no longer see.
    "Oh, God." Diana's gasped words echoed in the room. She stumbled, grabbed the back of an upholstered chair and retraced her steps into the kitchen, her heart thudding. Her cell phone was in the car. She reached for the telephone on the counter by the door, but stopped. Fingerprints. She mustn't contaminate the crime scene. A business card next to the phone caught her eye: Hetch Electrical Company. A three by four foot package leaned against a cabinet with brown wrapping paper hanging in shreds from it. The painting? She pushed aside the paper exposing Ursula's oil landscape of the Feeney's Victorian house—slashed. The canvas sagged like a discarded rag.
    She stood mesmerized, her mind a jumble of discordant feelings. Horror. Sadness. The backdoor creaked open, then slammed against the jamb with a soft bang. She stifled a yell. Her stomach lurched. She fled to her car, opened the door,
    paused, and studied the dark for any sign of movement, but saw only the waving shadows of the pines. She got in, and locked the car doors.
    Taking deep breaths, she rummaged in her purse for her cell phone and with trembling fingers punched in the phone number of the local

police. She explained to the dispatcher who she was and that she'd found Cora Jacob's body in her home on Clampton Road. "Tell them I'm parked in the driveway with my headlights on. Please notify Police Chief Nelson." Despite the dispatcher's request to stay on the line, she hung up.

Diana thought of calling Grant, but decided that the young couple didn't need to be disturbed. There was nothing he could do. She shivered, eyeing the surrounding woods, then put in a call to Max. When he didn't answer, she left a message.

She pulled her coat tighter and crossed her arms. Why would anyone kill Cora? Had she been involved with the drugs? Every time Diana thought she had a handle on what was going on, new events threw her a curve.

Sirens stabbed the night and flashing red lights lit up the woods. She got out of her car, wishing she'd worn warmer clothes. When an officer strode up to her, she explained what she'd found and gave a statement to another officer. Detective O'Reilly arrived, gave her a brusque nod, and went into the house. While she paced by her car, minutes ticked by. When O'Reilly came out, he motioned to her to follow him. She refused and he came up to her. "I need you to come to the police station."

"Why? I gave my statement to the officer."

"Mrs. Bellfore, you claim to have found Cora's body, and I need to know the details." The flashing police lights threw shadows across O'Reilly's narrow face, distorting his features into an abstract painting.

"It's late. Can't it wait till tomorrow?"

"No. A murder has been committed, and you claim to have found her."

"Claimed? I found her and called it in. I explained that to the officer."

"Getting every detail of what you saw and did is important."

When Chief Nelson drove up, O'Reilly walked over to confer with his boss, then they both strode toward Diana.

"Good evening, Mrs. Bellfore," the chief said. "You certainly have a knack for being at crime scenes."

Diana gulped, wondering if he would accuse her of the crime as O'Reilly seemed to believe. "I found Cora, called it in immediately and gave my statement to the officer. I had nothing to do with her murder."

"Never entered my mind." He turned to O'Reilly. "It's late and she's given the officer her statement. If we need more information, we know where she lives, right?"

"Yes, sir." O'Reilly's mouth drooped in disappointment, but he opened Diana's car door, letting the interior light spill onto the gravel driveway. "You're free to go."

Before she got into her car, Chief Nelson said, "I thought you went to Philadelphia."

"I did. I got back this evening. When Cora called Grant to come get his painting, I offered to get it for him."

He frowned. "Why didn't Grant come?"

"He...ah...was in the middle of a project."

Nelson looked askance. "Did you give the officer the time of Cora's call to Grant?"

"Ah, no." Her grip on her car door tightened.

"Do you know when it was?"

"About seven, maybe a few minutes before."

O'Reilly stepped closer. "Your call came in at eight fifty-two. If you were at Captain Cranston's house why did it take you so long to get here? It's not more than a fifteen minute drive."

Diana felt both men's eyes on her. "We were in the midst of dinner, and I didn't leave right away, and then I went to the gas station." She dug into her purse for the receipt. "Here." She thrust it at O'Reilly. "After that I got lost. I've never been here before and turned onto Clampton Circle instead of this street."

"What time do you think you got here?" Nelson asked.

"I'm not sure." She hesitated. "I was only in the house a few minutes, saw the body, and came out to my car to get my cell phone."

"You didn't touch anything inside?" Nelson asked.

"I don't think so. Well, the backdoor jamb, the kitchen light switch and the burner knob. You see the tea kettle was whistling and the water was running. Oh, and I grabbed the back of a leather chair for balance."

Nelson nodded. "Okay. We'll check with Grant tomorrow. Have you let him know what happened here?"

"No, not yet."

"I'd have thought you'd call him right away." O'Reilly leaned back, his expression grim. "After all, you and he are...close."

"I don't like what you're insinuating, Detective." In her anger, she almost spit out the words. "My calling or not calling Grant has nothing to do with this murder."

"We'll see. It's important we get all the details and learn the truth," O'Reilly said.

"I'm not sure truth is what you're after." She got in her car and slammed the door shut, then lowered the window. "I'm going home if you have nothing else to ask."

O'Reilly's face was an unreadable mask, but Diana felt his anger and was sure he felt hers. She backed out of the driveway and drove home, gripping the steering wheel as if she would strangle it.

Chapter 29

Diana arrived home to a dark house, save for the back porch light and a lamp shining in the corner of the living room. Although the house was warm, she was freezing and ached from exhaustion, anger and shock. Having a strong drink came to mind, but she settled for a hot shower and fell into bed.

She heard Isabel calling, "Mom, Mom, wake up." Why was she waking her up in the middle of the night? Her arm was jostled. She opened her eyes, then closed them, startled by the daylight streaming in through the window.

"What?" she managed to ask.

"Chief Nelson is here. He told us about last night. Why didn't you call?"

Diana sat up, rubbing her eyes. "What time is it?"

"Almost nine thirty." Isabel sat on the side of the bed. "I'm so sorry. You must have had a terrible experience. I should have been there with you."

Diana patted her hand. "Nonsense. Better that you're not involved. The Chief will have to wait while I get dressed."

"I'll bring you a cup of coffee," Isabel said and left the room.

Diana groaned, got up, and went into the bathroom. The mirror showed a woman in her fifties who needed a weekend at a spa and a couple of hours at a hair salon. God, she felt old. She brushed her hair, noticing the gray was more than just a strand or two. When she went back into her room, a mug of black coffee was on the bedside table. She sat on the edge of the bed and sipped, reveling in the warmth and taste. After dressing in gray wool slacks and a black turtleneck, she was ready, but prayed facing O'Reilly would not be part of the day. Just thinking about his attitude infuriated her. She was not the criminal, but he might be. Chief Nelson's questions last night hadn't helped.

In the kitchen she found the police chief sitting at the table talking with Grant. They stood and Nelson said, "Sorry to barge in again so soon after last night, but I needed to talk to you."

"I don't mind as long as you don't claim that I killed Cora."

"What?" Isabel moved to her side. "Mom, if that's the case then don't say a thing until you get a lawyer."

Chief Nelson put up his hands. "I have no intention of claiming or believing that Diana had anything to do with Cora's murder." His look included all three of them. "I will not suspend Detective O'Reilly unless I hear evidence of his being involved in criminal activity. He's my lead detective and believes everyone is a suspect until proven otherwise. I will agree that he has not been as tactful as he should have been."

That was an understatement as far as Diana was concerned. O'Reilly hadn't been as thorough in his investigation as he should be. "It's a little crowded in here," she said. "Let's go into the living room." She hesitated. "Unless you want to speak with me alone."

"I'd like Grant to be present and since your daughter is staying here, she might as well sit in on the conversation."

Diana poured more coffee into her mug. "Anyone else?" There were no takers, so she took her mug and followed them into the other room. Grant and Isabel sat on the couch, while the chief took a chair next to it and Diana sat by the hearth.

Nelson looked at Diana. "Grant told me you have new information from your detective, Max Templer."

Diana glanced at Grant. She'd hoped to keep Max's involvement private. "If I was going to help Bert, I had no choice but to hire Max."

Chief Nelson nodded. "Bert posted bail yesterday."

"Who came up with the bail?" Diana asked.

"Ursula Von Reiter."

"I'm glad. I know what Bert did was illegal, but he thought he was protecting Marlene."

"Good intentions don't absolve his actions. He committed a crime." The chief must have seen Diana's frown, for he added, "He's never been in trouble with the police before, so he might get probation with no prison time."

"Bert doesn't belong in jail," Diana said.

"That's not for me to decide." He took out his notebook. "I have the time of Grant getting Cora's phone call and your call to 911. You told the officer on-scene that you neither saw nor heard anyone else around the house."

"That's right, but a car did pass me traveling fast in the opposite direction. A sedan I think, but he had his high beams on, and I can't give you a better description than that. I told your officer that there was a Hetch Electrical Company business card near the phone."

"Half the homes in Quamscutt have that card." He put the notebook on his lap. "There were tread marks in the mud beside the gravel driveway. They weren't from your car, so we're checking on tire matches."

"What about Sam?" Diana asked. "He made that threat about 'getting her' for taking the cocaine. I wasn't sure who the 'her' was at the time, but he could have meant Cora. She had plenty of opportunity to take any hidden drugs out of the house."

"We've questioned Sam and we're checking his car's tires. He said he was at the movies, but no one can support his alibi, and he didn't keep his ticket stub."

Diana said. "From Gloria's murder to the vandalism and drugs here at the house, O'Reilly has been protective of Sam."

His jaw tightened, his eyes narrowed. "Sam has admitted he was involved with the drug heist ten years ago in Providence and hid the drugs in this house when he rewired it. He claims he didn't know what else to do. He will face charges on those crimes."

"Why didn't he go to the police?" Grant asked.

"Afraid of going to jail, afraid of the mob. He was a nineteen-year-old scared kid."

"He could have gone to the police, then none of this would have happened," Grant said.

"Phil Yukovitch was sent to jail for his part in that drug deal." Diana thought that Nelson didn't understand what she was trying to get at, or he didn't want to see the connection. "The timing of Phil's release from prison and Sam's recovery of the cocaine is too coincidental. Could Yukovitch have threatened Sam, forcing him to retrieve the stash?"

"Maybe if he's scared of Yukovitch."

"How does this relate to Cora's murder?" Isabel asked. "I know I'm late to the party, but I don't see the connection."

Grant turned to her. "Cora was hired by Clayton Morris, Gloria's estate lawyer, to take care of the house until the estate went through probate."

"I was involved with that," Nelson said. "I got tired of sending my officers over here to deal with the vandalism. Cora had the qualifications to do the job."

"Could Cora have realized what Sam had hidden here?" Diana asked. "If she found cocaine, she may have tried to sell it."

"We'll be contacting the FBI and DEA and have them check on Phil Yukovitch. In the meantime, we're looking into Cora's credit cards and finances."

"Are you any closer to arresting someone for Gloria's murder?" Diana asked.

"Unfortunately, no. Do you have some insight?"

"Just speculation and I don't want to smear anyone's reputation if I'm wrong."

Chief Nelson nodded. "Fair enough. You and Grant have talked about missing paintings. Do you know anything about the painting at the crime scene?"

"I went to Cora's house to get an oil painting by Ursula that belonged to Gloria. It hung on the wall in Gloria's living room and rightfully should be Grant's."

"Cora said she kept it for safety reasons when the house interior was painted," Grant said. "I'd like it back."

Diana turned to Grant. "I haven't had a chance to tell you. It was slashed. Destroyed."

He frowned. "Why? Who would do something like that?"

"I have no idea."

Chief Nelson looked from one to the other. "Could you describe the painting?"

Grant glanced at Diana. "I have a faded photo from when it hung in the living room." He pointed to the wall. "We don't know what happened to the other one. Cora claimed there was only one, but Marlene said there were two when she cleaned the week before Gloria's murder." Grant hesitated to mention the crime scene photos he had that showed the dark outline of a missing picture. "Ursula could identify it."

"I met Ursula's agent, Franklin Harper, at the Brecks. When he came up from New York he was asked to appraise the two paintings Gloria had in her house. That was a few weeks before she was murdered. Harper was under the impression that the women were angry with each other."

"I'd like to speak with Mr. Harper," the chief said. "And I'll check with Ursula."

"I have his card in my purse." Diana went to her bedroom and when she returned the three of them were discussing the hit and run accident that killed Grant's parents.

Chief Nelson nodded as Diana handed him the card, then said to Grant, "Since the crime happened eighteen years ago, and occurred on the highway and not within Quamscutt's jurisdiction, it would be in the state or county archives under unsolved cases." He opened his notebook and made notes. "No one likes to have an unsolved case on the books. I'll have one of my officers get the police report and let you know." He closed his notebook and stood. "That's it for now. I'll be in touch." He smiled at Diana. "Mrs. Bellfore, I understand why Grant's project came first." He nodded to Isabel, shook hands with Grant and left by the back door.

"What did he mean by that?" Isabel asked.

"Last night I explained that Grant was in the middle of a project so I went to Cora's to collect the painting."

"Mother." Isabel shook her head and laughed. "You have a devious side."

Diana grinned. "I'm hungry. How about you?"

"We've eaten," Grant said. "We thought we'd take a walk on the beach."

"Sounds like a good idea. I need time to think and collect myself." After they left hand in hand, she made herself two fried eggs and toast and sat at the table. The day was clear and cool, but her thoughts bounced from Paul to Cora in a crazy mixed pattern. "Get a grip," she scolded out loud. Logic was needed, not helter-skelter ideas.

She went into her bedroom and called Max. This time he answered. "Hi, Diana. Sorry I didn't get back to you about Cora Jacob. Anything more on that?"

Diana explained all that had happened, then added, "The police are finally investigating the Sam Feeney - Joe O'Reilly connection, so there's not much else you can do on that front. What have you learned?"

"According to my sources, your boy Yukovitch has kept his nose clean, but he's got a brand new condo in Providence, paid for in cash. That sent up flares to me. But he's had no contact with anyone in the drug business or his old gang as far as the police or I can determine."

"They found tread marks at the crime scene. Can you find out what kind of car Phil drives and the tires it has?"

"Sure, I might be able to find that out sooner than the police since they have to play by the rules." He laughed. "I'll be sending you a bill. Hope you're selling a lot of books."

"Ursula Von Reiter came up with Bert's bail, so I didn't have to deal with that."

"Interesting that she'd do that. Do you know why?"

"I presume she wanted to help Marlene."

"Now, Mrs. Mystery Writer, are you getting lazy? When did you start presuming and believing what you're told?"

She gripped her phone tighter. Of course he was right, she had accepted much of what people had said about many things that involved the various crimes. "Max, I appreciate the critique."

"Any time. I'll call when I have something to report on Yukovitch."

Diana hung up, went into the living room and sat at the desk, staring at her laptop and thinking about what Max had said. All the crimes involved this old house. She looked at the floor where the body had been found. The boxes that Grant had gotten from Gloria's lawyer stood in the corner. She walked over and studied the contents that were now in disarray: old books, papers, and a photo album. An old leather bound book caught her eye. Curious, she pulled out a family Bible, walked back to the desk with the heavy tome and examined it. The leather spine was cracked and brittle, the pages brown and stained. As she leafed through it, she found several pages glued together at the sides creating an envelope with something tucked inside. Gently, she tugged on the papers and removed them. Newspaper clippings.

She read, gasped and rubbed her brow, trying to absorb what she'd learned. Solutions to mysteries can sometimes be difficult to accept. How would Grant react? The implication could solve a crime or cause anguish. She went out on the porch and sat in one of the Adirondack chairs. The autumn air was cool and calming. So many tangents, so many deceptions. How soon would the rest of the puzzle be solved?

Across the pond, Ursula's home glistened in the morning sun. If Diana could see that no one was at home, then Ursula could see this porch. Was

Ursula complicit in Gloria's murder? The two had argued, disliked each other. Ursula was a small woman, but hitting someone on the head with a shovel didn't take strength, only leverage. Could she have done that in anger? And if she had, could Diana prove it? Was the reason for Ursula putting up Bert's bail, guilt or compassion?

And then there was Cora. Either Sam or Phil might have had a motive to kill her. Did Sam have the courage? She thought of him more as a confused and angry man, rather than one who would stab someone face to face. Maybe Hetch would have some insight into his son's behavior.

While she ruminated about the various crimes, Grant and Isabel came around the bend of the pond, their arms around each other. Where would their love take them? It wasn't going to be easy with both of them in the military. When they reached the porch, Diana said, "I have something important to show you."

They followed her into the house, where she pointed to the desk. "The newspaper clippings may answer your questions about the past."

He frowned, took them and went to the couch with Isabel sitting next to him. "This is crazy." He shook his head. "It's about the hit and run." He continued to read the articles. "Jesus!"

Isabel put her arm across his shoulder, while he read out loud. "During a heavy rain storm, a hit and run on Route One killed a New Jersey couple. Witnesses reported that a Chevy Impala with a Rhode Island license plate was seen leaving the accident. The police are checking all registered Impalas.

"This next article is four days later," Grant said and continued to read. "Mrs. Gloria Feeney reported that her Chevy Impala had been stolen from her driveway. She claimed she'd come home from shopping, hurried into the house, and left her keys in the ignition. She didn't notice the car was gone until the following morning. The police believe there is a strong probability that her car caused the accident and have put out an area-wide search for the stolen car."

Grant put the newspaper down. "I found pictures of her and different cars." He stood and rummaged through the boxes until he found an envelope, threw several photos on the floor, and held up two others. "This is her with a Chevy Impala, and this one is her with a new Ford Mustang." He went to the window and stared out at the pond. "They never found the Impala. Why? And why would she keep these clippings and photos?"

He turned to face them. "I need to see the complete police report or...." He went to Diana's laptop and turned it on.

Diana motioned to Isabel, and they slipped into the kitchen while he browsed through newspaper sites.

"Are you thinking what I'm thinking?" Isabel asked her mother.

Diana nodded. "If Gloria was the driver, then that's why she stepped forward to be Grant's guardian. She had the right to do so, because years before Mr. and Mrs. Cranston had named the Feeneys as Grant's guardians in case anything happened to them."

"I wonder what happened to the car," Isabel said.

Grant stormed into the kitchen. "I think I know. Gloria was paranoid about my going near the pond. I'll bet she drove her Impala into the pond. That's why it was never found."

Isabel frowned. "Grant, you're accusing her of killing your parents. That's a despicable thing for her to have done."

"We're jumping to conclusions. The police would have found tire marks leading into the pond," Diana said.

"Not necessarily," Grant said. "I found out that the worst rain storms hit this area during that time. She waited a whole day to notify the police. The pond rises with the tides. By the time the police arrived, all marks could have been obliterated. They had no cause to search for the car in the pond."

"It could still be there," Isabel said.

"Right. I've got to get some scuba diving equipment." He checked his watch. "There's a dive shop in Providence. I can be there before they close and dive tomorrow morning."

"The pond is full of algae, sludge and catkins. It's not safe," Diana said. "Besides, if it's there, it will still be there in the future."

"I've waited too many years for answers. I've had training in scuba diving."

"So have I," Isabel said. "You'll need a dive buddy and that will be me."

"Now wait a minute," Diana said. "There's no need to hurry. We need to bring in the police." She hesitated. "What if you're wrong?"

"More reason for me to look first before calling the police. Who knows how long it will take the police to decide to investigate? I'm not waiting." Grant ran upstairs and came down fast with the keys to his truck in his hand. He looked at Isabel. "Coming?"

Chapter 30

After they left, Diana decided to visit Hetch. On the drive she stopped at Pete's Pet Store for a squeaky toy for Shelly and at the Sweet Bar for a box of fudge for Hetch.

When she arrived, it was after one, so he'd have had lunch. The woman at the front desk said Hetch was out on the grounds walking Shelly. "He's a changed man since he got that dog. He talks with people now and has made a number of friends."

"Does he have many visitors?"

"Not many, although that good looking blond Detective O'Reilly has been here several times. Hetch doesn't seem as bitter about his son not visiting. I think the dog helps."

Diana went out into the park-like grounds and spotted Hetch throwing a ball and Shelly racing after it. When she drew near, she said, "You've got a powerful pitching arm, Hetch."

He looked up. "Well, Mrs. Nosy Writer. Didn't expect you."

"I'll take that title as a compliment."

"Just stating the truth." He winked and gave a husky laugh.

She nodded and held out her gifts. "Brought a toy for Shelly and something for your sweet tooth."

He grinned. "A little bribe for information?"

"Of course not." She laughed at his expression of doubt. "Okay, a small bribe for some conversation."

"I'd have talked with you anyway." Shelly came bounding up with the wet tennis ball in her mouth. Hetch took it and threw it again. "Two more throws and we can go to my apartment. In this brisk air, I get cold unless I'm throwing the ball or wheeling like mad to give Shelly a romp."

Diana watched Shelly chase the ball and nodded to several people who greeted Hetch. After a few more tosses, they made their way back to the building with Shelly trotting by Hetch's left wheel, her tongue lolling out. Once in the apartment, Diana placed her gifts on the coffee table, took off her coat, and sat across from Hetch. Shelly curled up on a throw rug in the corner with a contented sigh.

"Looks like you and the pup are happy together."

"You know it." He picked up the box of candy and opened it. "Hey, I love fudge. Glad I still have my own teeth." He took a piece, then smacked his lips together. "This won't last long." He held the box out to her. "Have one."

She declined and enjoyed the contented look on his face while he devoured a large piece of fudge. She took the two photos of Gloria with her Chevy Impala and the Mustang out of her purse and handed them to him. "Do you recognize these?"

He frowned and fanned the air with the photo of the Impala. "This one was taken when she first got the car. She sent it to me to prove that she could pay for it. She always complained she didn't get enough alimony from the divorce, but when her parents died, she had enough money to buy whatever she wanted. This photo was a 'see I don't need you' kind of thing. Made my wife, Lilly, furious."

"What about this other one?"

He shook his head. "Never seen it, but that's a 1995 Mustang. I guess she got it after her Chevy was stolen."

"You knew about that?"

"Hell, everyone in Quamscutt knew it. It was in the newspapers. She got her fifteen minutes of fame." He looked at Diana with a raised eyebrow. "There's more to this than showing me an old photo of Gloria with these two cars."

"I'm afraid so."

He laughed. "You are too much! I hope you stay around a long time. Gives me something to chew on other than this fudge."

"Do you remember anything else about her car being stolen?"

"The police thought it was used in a hit and run. That was in the papers."

"They never found the car or the driver," Diana said.

"Yeah. The story faded." He poked around in the candy box, then looked at her. "Now I know why you're on this. The Cranstons were killed in that crash and that's when their son went to live with Gloria. My wife and I had Sam and didn't want to deal with another kid."

Diana nodded. "Grant seems to think Gloria pushed her Impala into Potters Pond."

Hetch's jaw sagged. "Whoa. That's a new one."

"Do you think Gloria would have been capable of such a thing? I mean, if the car is in the pond, then that means she may have been driving the car that hit the Cranstons."

"I get the implication. Could she do such a thing? Lord, I don't know." He let out a deep sigh. "Still, Gloria in 1996 was not the woman I married. She changed, became vindictive, turned on old friends. When the boy came to live with her, she was better, but after a few years, she was full of anger again. Even gave the boy a hard time. I tried to stay away, but she'd call about every month to rant. Finally, I told her never to call again, or I'd file a complaint for harassment. So, to answer your question, yeah anything would have been possible in her state of mind."

"If she did kill them, do you think it was accidental?"

"You mean she may have deliberately run into their car. That's a heavy load of presumption. Why would she?"

"It seems far fetched to believe it was an accident. Why were the Cranstons in the area? Were they coming to visit her or just passing through? They had been friends with you and Gloria, wouldn't it have been natural for them to call her or you."

Hetch held his head in his hands. "Oh God, I'd forgotten until just now. I got a call from the Cranstons saying they were in town, but I was busy and couldn't see them."

"So they might have called Gloria, too."

He nodded, his eyes sad, his mouth sagged.

"I'm not a psychologist, but from everything I've learned, Gloria verged on being a functional insane person. She had a still born baby, born about the same year as Grant. She could have believed that Grant should be hers. After all the Cranstons had given her the right to care for him in case something happened to them. In her state of mind, she could have believed he rightfully belonged to her."

"I hope like hell you're wrong, but it makes sense." He studied her. "But only if you can prove she actually drove the car that killed them."

"Grant plans to search the pond. He's gone to Providence to rent scuba gear."

"Well, then you'll know soon enough." He put down the box of candy. "I'd like to wet my whistle with something strong right now, but coffee will have to suffice. Would you like a cup?"

"That would be great. Can I make it?"

"It's instant." He pointed to the kitchenette. Diana got up, took out two cups, added the instant mixture and turned on the electric burner. "How do you take yours?"

"Sugar."

She put the bowl on the table and while they waited for the water to boil, she asked, "Can you tell me anything about Gloria's relationship with Ursula Von Reiter?"

"You sure like to dredge up old shit, don't you?"

"The past can uncover present day truths."

"Maybe."

When the water boiled, she made the coffee, took a cup to Hetch, then sat holding hers. "Grant inherited Gloria's estate and there seems to be some confusion about two older oil paintings by Ursula. One is missing and Cora had the other one at her house."

"That woman, Ursula. What a fire-breathing dragon. When Gloria's parents deeded the land to us to build our house, I had no idea Ursula would be so cantankerous. She loved the view from her house, even wrote an article for the paper about the land. Gloria found Ursula's landscape in a local gallery and bought it."

"Weren't other houses already blocking her view?"

"Not back then. The Perry family owned a farm in the hills, but the land we ended up with wasn't good for farming. Too salty. See, the ponds around here are salt marshes, open to the ocean and subject to the tides. The farmland was higher and slopes toward the pond."

"There are houses on the hills now."

"When the older Perrys died, the grandkids sold the land. The building boom started in the eighties, but a few farm parcels remained until the nineties. That's when that big brick house on the hill got built." He laughed. "Now if Ursula had still been a full-time resident here, she'd have been up in arms over the building boom."

"Penelope told me Ursula and her partner came back for a few weeks every summer. Did she paint landscapes of this area then?"

"No idea. I was long gone."

"I see. What about earlier when you lived in the house with Gloria?"

"Gloria wanted to build a Victorian. Hell, I didn't care what it looked like, I just wanted a nice place. Ursula was furious our house stood so tall even though I did try to hunker it down between the two hillocks. Didn't win any points with either woman for that. After we built, I commissioned Ursula to paint the same view but with our house in it." He shook his head. "That woman must have needed the money, otherwise I doubt if she'd have agreed. But she did, and we ended up with two of her paintings hanging in our living room. Gloria got them in the divorce settlement. What did I want with them?"

"When the police found Gloria's body, one of those paintings that hung on the wall was missing. The one with the Victorian is at Cora's. But that's now a crime scene." She thought he'd be surprised, but he only grimaced. "You know, don't you?"

"Yeah. I thought you'd want to talk about that."

"Did Detective O'Reilly tell you?"

"He was here early this morning." He studied her while taking a sip of coffee. "He doesn't like you."

Her lips twitched. "The feeling's mutual."

"Well, I like you both." He popped a small piece of fudge into his mouth.

"O'Reilly has tried to cover up your son's crimes."

Hetch finished chewing before he said, "I told you Sam and I owe Joe a lot. When we lived in Providence, Joe got Sam back on the side of the law. Mentored him, you might say." He leaned back, then pointed to the squeaky toy. "I'll give that to Shelly tomorrow. Otherwise, she'll drive me nuts until she's disemboweled it." He looked at his dog asleep in the corner and smiled. "Dogs are like two-year-olds that never grow up."

He turned his attention back to Diana. "Lilly and I kept wondering where we'd gone wrong in raising Sam. When he got in trouble as a teenager, we thought he'd grow out of it, let him go his own way. Shouldn't have. Should have been more strict with him."

"I'd think that you and Sam would get on well with each other."

"No, and not sure why. As I told you last time, he doesn't talk to me much. O'Reilly keeps me informed." He shrugged. "I think it goes back to when I recommended Joe for the job in Quamscutt. I had a little political pull back then. I owed Joe. If he got the detective job here in Quamscutt, he might be able to keep Sam from getting into any more trouble. Sam figured out what I'd done and hasn't forgiven me. Claims I didn't trust him, which of course I didn't then. Now it's different. Sam would like to sell the business and move somewhere else."

"Would that bother you?"

"For a while I was angry when he talked about letting the business go. Then I thought, what the hell. Life is full of change, and you gotta roll with it. Hetch Electric won't exist forever anyway."

"The police are questioning Sam about Cora's murder."

He nodded. "He's done stupid things, but he didn't kill her."

"I don't think he did either, nor do I think he killed Gloria. Can you tell me anything that might lead to the real killer?"

He shook his head. "Joe and I have gone over everything, but nothing fits."

"What about Phil Yukovitch? He got out of prison about the time of Gloria's murder and that's when Sam started removing the drugs from the Victorian."

"If Sam admits he gave those drugs to Phil, he could go to prison."

"Better that than being convicted of murder. Besides, he's already admitted to the police that he stashed them in the house, and it's obvious he took them out. What did he do with them?" She put her coffee cup down. "Did he sell or give the drugs to Phil?"

"How the hell should I know? The drug case was ten years ago. Isn't there a statute of limitations on that?" He frowned. "Look, Sam wanted to go straight and didn't know what to do with the drugs. He was scared of the mob."

"He told you that?"

"No, Joe did."

"O'Reilly knew about the drug stash and the removal?"

Hetch shrugged. "He was trying to help Sam. There's no law against that."

"Actually there is."

Hetch's expression hardened. "I have no idea if Sam told Joe what he did with the drugs." He shook his head. "Look, Joe said Sam was making things right after he'd screwed Phil by testifying against him at the trial."

"So, O'Reilly must have known where the drugs were and that Sam was removing them."

He wagged his finger at her. "Now don't go getting Joe into trouble about this."

"If O'Reilly withheld evidence, he can be prosecuted."

He shook his head. "He wanted to help Sam. What was the harm in Sam hiding those drugs? He kept them away from the mob and off the streets."

"But they didn't stay hidden." She repeated what Chief Nelson had said about Bert's tampering with the evidence relating to Gloria's murder. "Good intentions don't absolve you of a crime."

"I shouldn't have told you." He leaned forward. "Promise you won't say anything. I don't want to get Joe in trouble. I'll deny I told you."

"You could, but I don't think you will. It's not your nature. You're a straight talker. I understand your dilemma, but if I keep quiet, then I'm complicit, too."

"It's not fair. Please, implicating Joe won't solve anything."

"I'll make you a deal," she said. "I won't say anything until you talk to O'Reilly. That will give him time to tell Chief Nelson on his own terms what he knew and when."

"I don't like the deal."

"Take it or leave it."

"I'm not sure I like you after all."

"I can't help that," she said. "Look, Hetch, I don't have a choice in this matter."

"Yes, you do."

"I'm sorry, but I don't." She stood to leave. "Tell O'Reilly he has a week." As she went out the door, a shiver ran through her. She'd placed herself in O'Reilly's crosshairs. When she got to her car, she shrugged at her sense of foreboding. After all, what could he do to her?

Chapter 31

When Diana got back to the house, Isabel and Grant had not returned. The day had been clear, but clouds had begun to gather. She hoped the weather would hold for tomorrow. Searching the pond might prove difficult, and she worried about Grant and Isabel's safety.

She ached to talk to someone about her conversation with Hetch, but she'd promised to give him and O'Reilly a week. How would O'Reilly handle the situation? It could mean the end of his law enforcement career, but that was his problem, not hers. She didn't relish the role of informer, but saw no alternative.

She heated up a can of lentil soup and toasted a muffin. While sitting at the breakfast table enjoying the hot meal, she jotted down her thoughts in a small spiral notebook.

Gloria's murder: *The missing painting, parts of a shredded old canvas under the stone at the murder scene with a knife, the frame hidden in the shed, ill will between Ursula and Gloria, Hetch's story about the paintings, Franklin Harper's view of the women's animosity to each other, Ursula's possessive feelings about her work and her anger over a lost view. Who would want to destroy the remaining oil painting? Ursula wouldn't have had the strength to stab Cora and wouldn't destroy her own work.*

If Ursula killed Gloria, how could she prove it?

The hit and run case: *Gloria's involvement, the car photos, taking in Grant after his parents were killed, her paranoia about Grant going near the pond, her reason for leaving her estate to Grant. Had Gloria driven the car that killed Grant's parents? And if so, had she done it intentionally? Had she hidden her crime by driving the Impala into the pond? How would any of that have led to her murder?*

She wasn't sure she wanted Grant to find the car in the pond. The result might settle an old crime, but would it help him deal with the past? Was it better for it to remain a mystery? Even as she thought this, she knew that mysteries needed to be solved. People needed closure, no matter what the truth revealed.

<u>Cora's murder:</u> *Did the drugs have anything to do with Cora's murder? Did Sam give or sell the drugs to Phil Yukovitch? How much did O'Reilly know and when did he know it? Did Phil kill Cora or have her killed by someone else? Why? If Cora sold some of the drugs, how did she know to whom to sell them?*

Questions with no answers. Cora had not seemed like a woman who had mob connections. For over five years, she'd led a comfortable life in Quamscutt, a well-liked and reasonably prosperous realtor. Why would she jeopardize her lifestyle?

She shoved the notebook aside, washed her dishes and went out onto the porch. After looking at the pond and the path leading away from the ocean, she went back inside, grabbed her coat and cell phone. Once outside, she studied the flat terrain from the driveway to the pond. Even if Gloria had somehow held down the accelerator, Diana doubted the car could have been driven far enough into the pond to be hidden from view when the tide went out.

She walked north, looking at the houses near the pond. Hetch's description of the land giving way to rolling hills was accurate. Eventually a large brick colonial at the top of a hill with the land sloping down to the pond came into view. Now at high tide, water lapped the edges of the path and stirred the reeds. If Gloria had wanted to send her car into the pond, then this would have been the most reasonable place, but the stone wall across the entire front of the property would have prevented that.

An elderly couple walked toward her. When they came near, Diana said, "Excuse me, I'm new in town and I was wondering if you knew anything about the homes on the hills that abut Potters Pond."

"You interested in buying?" the man asked.

"I'm renting the Feeney house." She noticed their look and nodded. "I know about that house; it's these others I'm curious about."

"The Feeney house is the only one with bad vibes," the woman said. "We live in the smaller clapboard back there." She pointed where they had come from. "We walk to the beach every day."

"Now, Maude, not every day." He smiled at Diana. "When it storms, we stay home."

"That's a given, Marvin."

"How long has this beautiful colonial been here?" Diana asked.

"It's the newest," she looked at her husband. "It was awhile back. The late nineties, wasn't it?"

"Early twenties I think," he said. "New Yorkers. They got money. Don't use the house much. Mostly summers."

"Do you know what the land looked like before the house was built?"

Marvin nodded. "Mostly farmland."

"Was there a path or a lane from up above down to the pond?"

He frowned. "Yep. Why?"

"Curious, that's all. The house has a stone wall around it, and I wondered if it had always been there."

"The new owners said they wanted the wall to keep the old farm look." Maude gazed at the wall. "They managed to do that, but the wall made some of the locals think they wanted to shut the world out. Like they thought they were better than us."

"Come on." Marvin tugged at his wife's arm. "If we don't get going, it'll be dark before we get home." He nodded to Diana, and they walked off hand in hand.

Diana took one more look at the colonial and the slope, and began to retrace her steps when her cell rang.

"Hello, Grant?"

"No, Mom, Isabel. We wanted to let you know we won't be home tonight."

"You couldn't get the scuba gear?"

"Ah, we plan to get it in the morning. We'll get back by noon. The weather should be okay tomorrow." Isabel hesitated, then added, "I talked to Dad."

"I'm glad. Was he surprised?"

Isabel laughed. "Oh, yeah. He said he'd fly into Providence Friday night. Grant and I will pick him up. He'll stay at the house, okay? Isn't that super?"

"Yes, wonderful news." Totally unexpected, Diana thought. "How's Dave?"

"Doing very well. Jeffy is blown away with my news, too, but he can't make it."

"It would have been nice to have the entire family together. It's been a long time."

"Ah, the reason Dad's coming is that while Grant and I were near city hall, we got our marriage license. Grant called Penny, and she's set it up with a local pastor for us to say our wedding vows in church at four on Saturday."

Diana stared into space. Wedding? Why hadn't she seen this coming?

"Mom? You still there?"

"Yes. I'm…I'm just surprised." That was an understatement. She was stunned.

"Oh, and don't tell Grandmother. I have to go now. We're going shopping for a wedding outfit for me and a suit for Grant. I'll see you tomorrow." Isabel clicked off.

Dumbfounded, Diana walked over to the stone wall and sat, trying to absorb the news. If Paul was coming, she needed to get her hair cut, her nails done. A wedding. What should she wear? There needed to be a reception after the ceremony. Where? There was so little time. Tomorrow was Wednesday. She had no idea how she'd manage everything, until she thought of Penny. She got up and hurried back to the house.

Her daughter was getting married. All other thoughts flew out of her mind. When she got Penny on the phone, Diana said, "You've heard the news." Without waiting for an answer she asked for the names of a salon, a florist, and a women's clothing store where she could buy an outfit for the wedding.

After giving Diana suggestions, Penny asked, "Where do you plan to hold the reception?"

"I haven't thought that far ahead yet. I'd rather not hold it at the church. Something more elaborate, perhaps."

"You don't want to have it at Grant's place, not with all that's happened there."

"You're right. What about the inn where I took Ursula for brunch?"

"I already checked, and they're booked with a big anniversary party. I'm at Ursula's right now. What about having it here? I think Ursula would be delighted."

Diana had no idea how to answer. Her daughter's reception at the home of a possible killer?

"Hello, are you still there?"

"Yes, I'm thinking."

"The caterer would handle everything, so there'd be no work for Ursula." Before Diana could say anything, Penny said, "Let me ask her. She's right here."

Diana heard the conversation and had no idea how to stop what seemed inevitable.

"Ursula would be thrilled to have it here. I'm so glad you called me and that Grant and Isabel confided in me." Penny gushed on and on. "He's a great guy, and I can't wait to meet your daughter. She must be very special. I can call the caterer for you. How many people are we talking about? Besides Charlie and myself, there's you and your husband, Ursula and of course, the wedding couple. Anyone else?"

"Yes. There's a friend of Isabel's who goes to Brown University. I think she'd like to be included. I'll have to check with Grant and Isabel, but I think that's it."

"Great. Think about what you want to have, and how much you want to spend. I'll talk to the caterer and see what she recommends and get back to you. Did I tell you the caterer is a friend of mine? I do her taxes."

Diana cut the conversation short, saying she had to make more calls. Afterward she thought of how Penny's enthusiasm had roped Diana into agreeing to have the reception at Ursula's. She let out her breath and reprimanded herself for acquiescing. Her assumption about Ursula's guilt could be wrong. It might work out all right, but she felt uneasy.

She continued to stew. Should she call Paul? Why? Damn, she felt out of sorts. After making an appointment for Friday morning at the beauty salon, she drove to the Warwick dress shop Penny had recommended. When her cell sang its melody, she was just turning into the shopping center. Parking, she answered. "Max, if you already have the info I asked for, you're quick."

"It was easy. Your guy, Phil, didn't kill Cora Jacob. Doesn't drive. It would be a long shot for him to have forced Sam to remove the cocaine from the Cranston house."

"How can you be sure?"

"The guy's almost blind. Macular degeneration. I talked to him at his upscale condo. He's got a caregiver and is through with crime."

"Wow, that's a surprise." Diana thought a second and asked, "How's he paying for that lifestyle?"

"Even criminals inherit money. In his case, he says an aunt left him the money. Except for his blindness, he's relatively happy and living well."

"If he's telling the truth about the aunt then that puts the onus back on Sam."

"Looks like it, but I'll check Phil's story about the inheritance."

"Would it be possible for you to dig deeper into O'Reilly and Sam's past?"

"What are you fishing for?"

"I'm not sure. Financial trouble maybe. If Sam decided to remove the cocaine after ten years, then he must have had a reason. O'Reilly may have been in on it."

"I'll see what I can find out, but the police would be the ones to get financial records."

"True, but O'Reilly's a cop. Not sure if Chief Nelson would or could investigate one of his own to that extent. For now, he's on O'Reilly's side. I'd have to give him facts to change his mind and I don't have any." She thought of Hetch's revelation that O'Reilly knew about the drugs at Cranston's house, but she'd promised to wait a week before divulging what she knew.

"I'll see what I can dig up. Let me know if the police are checking on Sam's finances."

"They might not tell me, but I'll see what I can learn. Call if you have any news." She hesitated, then said, "I'll be busy this weekend. My daughter is marrying Grant Cranston, and my husband is flying in for the wedding."

"Hey, congratulations. I thought she was overseas."

"Home on leave. The marriage is unexpected." She laughed. "Well, it was to me, anyway."

After she hung up, she went into the store. On a Tuesday afternoon it wasn't crowded. The lone saleswoman looked up from behind the counter. "May I help you?"

Diana explained what she was looking for and was shown a selection in her size. It didn't take long to find an outfit she adored. A bit pricey, but how often does your only daughter get married? The coral jersey dress with a scooped neck and a matching coat was perfect. She hoped Isabel wouldn't think the color too bold.

The saleswoman smiled. "You've got good taste, and I'm not saying that since it's a sale. How about a black belt to go with it?"

"Hum." Diana placed it on the dress that lay on the counter. "Just the right touch. Thanks. I'll take it."

As the woman wrote up the receipt and boxed the dress, Diana told her that Penelope Nelson had recommended the store.

"She does my taxes. I don't know what I'd do without her."

"You're the owner?"

"Sole proprietor and financially responsible." She smiled. "By the way, I'm Maxine."

"Penny has many friends."

"You bet. How do you know her?"

"I'm renting a home in Quamscutt and met her through Ursula Von Reiter."

"You must know Cora Jacob then. She's a realtor there."

"Ah, yes. You haven't heard about Cora?"

Maxine frowned. "What? Is she okay?"

"Why do you ask?"

"She was in here the other day. She was nervous, on edge, not like her. She picked out a sweater for Penny. I didn't think much of it at the time because it was a color Penny would like. Still." She shrugged. "Cora stuck a note in the box and asked me to hold it for her till tomorrow, which seemed strange since she didn't have other things to carry. When she left, some guy confronted her and they argued."

"What did he look like?"

"Big, brown hair, broad-shouldered. In his late twenties. What's this all about?"

"Cora's dead, murdered last night."

Maxine leaned against the wall and put her hands to her chest. "Oh my God, no. It can't be. Who did it?"

"They don't know."

"I can't believe she's dead. Who would do such a thing? Robbery?"

"I haven't heard."

Maude finished boxing the outfit and handed it to Diana. "Hey, what am I going to do with the package Cora left for Penny?"

"I can take it to Penny. We're meeting to discuss the wedding reception." Diana hesitated. "Do you know why Cora bought a present for Penny?"

"She said it was Penny's birthday. I didn't say anything, after all a sale is a sale, but Penny's a Gemini." She fussed with the ribbon on the box. "We discussed astrological signs once."

By the time Diana left the store, not only had she improved Maxine's bottom line, but she had information that might have a bearing on Cora's murder. The man Maxine saw arguing with Cora sounded like Sam.

On the way home Diana stopped for dinner, and by the time she drove into Quamscutt's city limits, it was eight o'clock. When she got to the house, she called Penny's home phone, got the answering machine, and left a message about Cora's package.

She hung up her new outfit, put on a robe and slippers and poured herself a glass of wine. Sorting through her CDs, she chose a collection of Mozart and Schubert, sat next to the lit fireplace and reflected on the day's events. Her head felt heavy, her eyes blurred, and she nodded off to sleep.

Knocking at the front door awoke her. The porch light was off. She checked her watch. It was a few minutes after ten. Through the window she could see a silhouette of a tall figure.

"It's Police Chief Nelson," came his deep voice.

She flipped on the outside light and opened the door. "Is anything wrong?"

The overhead light beam shadowed his face. "Sorry to disturb you. When I got home, I picked up your message about a package from Cora to Penny. She left a note saying she might spend the night at Ursula's. I thought I'd pick it up."

Diana stepped back and motioned him inside. "I would have dropped it off at your house, but it's been a long day."

"I was curious. Since Cora was murdered, I didn't want to wait till tomorrow."

"I'll get the package." He looked tired and cold. "Would you like a cup of coffee or tea?"

"Don't want to bother you, but coffee would be great."

She walked to the kitchen with him at her heels and made a fresh pot. "I'll be back in a second with the package."

She got the box from the chair in her bedroom and returned with the parcel. Chief Nelson was stooped over her notes about the murders. "Those are private." She placed the parcel on the breakfast table with a thump and held out her hand for the notebook.

"Interesting and provocative ideas." He continued to study the notebook.

She pulled it toward her and closed it. "Ideas, not facts." She clasped the notebook, set it next to her on the counter, and then took out two mugs. "The coffee's ready."

He sat at the table. "You and I need to talk."

"How do you take your coffee?"

"Cream or milk. Whichever you have."

She took a pint of half and half from the fridge and placed it on the table along with his coffee. She sat across from him, nudged the parcel aside and placed the notebook next to it. "All right, perhaps we need to clarify things."

He nodded to the notebook. "Let's take it from the top. Your notes start with Gloria's murder. Your ideas about Ursula's involvement make sense, but they're circumstantial. Hard to prove."

"Exactly. That's why I haven't said anything."

He nodded. "Okay. With your speculations in mind, I need to question her."

"Having gotten to know her, I doubt if she'd let anything slip. She might be old, but she's tough and smart."

"Give me some credit. I've been in this business a long time."

"I didn't mean to insult your competence."

He nodded and shifted in his chair. "Other than Bert Schukart there are no other suspects for Gloria's murder. He destroyed evidence, and a jury is likely to take a dim view of that."

"He didn't kill her. I'm sure of that." She leaned forward. "Can't you put in a good word with the district attorney?"

"You know better than to ask me that." He took a sip of coffee, then set it down with deliberate care. "Let's talk about your ideas on the hit and run that caused the death of Mr. and Mrs. Cranston. It was reported that the vehicle was Gloria's car. She didn't deny it, but claimed it had been stolen. After reading your notes, I think a search of the pond is a good idea."

"Grant and my daughter are renting scuba gear and plan to dive tomorrow."

"Searching the pond is a police matter and not something Grant and your daughter should undertake."

"Although I agree with you, I don't think you can prevent them from searching. Legally, I mean." She fingered the side of her cheek. "Wouldn't the media be alerted by your department conducting such a search? What if nothing was found?"

"Mrs. Bellfore, you're a clever negotiator." He smiled. "I see your point. It would also take time, resources, and money. My budget is tight. My men will be on-hand in case they find something." He rubbed his eyes. "It's late, but I need to talk to you about Cora's murder. The tread marks in the mud by her house match the tires of Sam's BMW. We have him in custody. He claims he went to see her after they had a confrontation in town. When he went in, she was already dead. He ran out and didn't report it since he figured we'd believe he did it. Which we do."

"Did he say what their argument was about?"

He shook his head. "He's lawyered up."

"Max reported that Phil Yukovitch couldn't have been involved with Cora's death, at least not personally. He's blind from macular degeneration. Has a caregiver."

"Your PI is good. We questioned Yukovitch and checked on his story of how he got the money to by the condo. There's no record of an aunt, but money has been funneled into his bank account on a monthly basis. Cash. Amounts small enough to be under the IRS radar. It's been coming in ever since Phil got out of prison and corresponds to the time that Sam started extracting the drug cache."

She nodded. "So the time line might indicate that Sam is connected with Phil, but there's no proof that Sam sold the drugs or gave them to Phil. If he did, the question is why. Was Sam indebted to Phil or scared of him? Why would Sam jeopardize all he's accomplished?" She thought of Hetch's remark about how O'Reilly had said Sam was trying to right a past wrong.

"We haven't found any financial problems with Sam's business accounts. No large amounts of cash or checks have gone through his personal account. His company's contracts with the city are legal."

"Could he have given the drugs to someone else to sell? It seems odd that he'd risk his reputation after he'd turned his life around." She leaned back and appraised him. "What about Detective O'Reilly's involvement?"

"I'm not at liberty to discuss that." He rubbed his face, then ran his hands through his graying hair. "Other than what I've read in your notes, is there anything else you can tell me about what you've learned or suspect?"

Should she break her promise to Hetch? She sighed. "Talk to Hetch Feeney."

"That's on my to-do list." He rubbed his face. "I sometimes wish I was back in the big city. It's easier to deal with crimes of people I don't know personally." He pulled Cora's gift toward him and began to unwrap it.

"Cora bought that for Penny. Are you sure you should open it?"

"Normally I wouldn't, but Cora's been murdered and if this can explain anything about that crime, I'm sure Penny would understand." He lifted off the top of the box and peered inside at a lime green sweater. "It's definitely Penny's color." As he lifted it out, tissue paper floated to the floor and a folded note skidded across the linoleum. Diana leaned over to retrieve it and stared at the scrawled message.

Dear Penny, this is a small gift to heal our recent squabble over the painting. I'm sure you realize now that I couldn't possibly give it to you since it isn't mine to give. We have been friends for a long time, and I don't want to have bad feelings over a silly painting. Perhaps after I return it to Captain Cranston, you can get it from him. You said you wanted to give it to Ursula, but she denied wanting it. I hope this sweater makes you feel happy and forgiving. Yours, Cora.

Chief Nelson took the note then frowned. "Why would Penny want the painting?" He shook his head. "I'll have to ask her."

"What about O'Reilly's involvement? It may all tie back to when O'Reilly was on the police force in Providence and mentored Sam. Hetch may give you the answer to some of it." She studied the note. "Do you know where O'Reilly was at the time of Cora's murder?"

"You're letting your dislike for the man mislead you."

She shrugged. "Maybe. It's another angle to be investigated."

He started to put the sweater back in the box in a haphazard fashion, but Diana stopped him. "I'll take care of this." She took the sweater, folded it neatly within the tissue paper, put in the note and put the top back on. After retying the ribbon, she handed the package to him. "When you give Penny the package, you can ask her about the note."

He stood transfixed, staring at the parcel. "Why would Penny be involved with any of this?" He rubbed his palm over his jaw. "I know her past with this house, Mrs. Feeney and Grant, but why would that play into what's been happening now? All that's transpired at this house lately has gotten Penny riled up. Did she and Grant have an argument?"

"Not to my knowledge."

"I haven't been home much, so she spends more time with Ursula. Do you think Penny's unhappy?"

"You'll have to ask her. There might be a simple explanation for her anxiety."

He put his hand on top of Diana's notebook. "When do you expect Grant and Isabel to return?"

"I'm not sure, probably late tomorrow morning. They're getting married this weekend. Didn't Penny tell you?"

"I've been too busy to talk to her."

"You're invited. Penny has made all the arrangements. The reception will be at Ursula's."

"If Ursula was involved with Gloria's murder, my wife will be devastated."

"Putting someone on a pedestal is never a good idea." She wanted to retract her statement, but instead stood mute.

"Penny had no family. She needed a grandmother and Ursula filled that void." He sighed. "I don't want to be the one to destroy that relationship. And I sure as hell can't and won't interrogate my own wife."

"Maybe you won't have to. I could be wrong. It wouldn't be the first time my mystery writer mind led me astray."

"When I put all the information together, your ideas make sense. Ursula might have killed Gloria in a fit of anger. Hell, it's as good a supposition as anything else. But Cora? That doesn't tie in to anyone on our radar."

Chief Nelson walked to the front door with Diana following him. With his hand on the doorknob, he said, "Call me when Grant and your daughter plan to dive. I'll have two of my officers on standby."

After he left, Diana went back to the kitchen to wash the cups, then sat and stared at her notes. She scribbled a name to her list: *Penny*. She shook her head. Improbable. The girl would be devastated if Ursula was the murderer. She doubted if Ursula would admit to the crime. Unless…unless she thought Bert would be convicted for the murder.

Chapter 32

Thursday morning Diana sat on the front porch overlooking the pond. A slight breeze skimmed its waters and ruffled the reeds. Ursula's house across the way added to the charm. She couldn't say the same of the Victorian. Even though Grant intended to spruce up the exterior with cheerful yellow paint, it would remain an eyesore. Penny's comments about wanting the house razed came to mind. Before she could dwell further on that idea, she heard the crunch on the gravel driveway.

She hurried to the side of the porch and leaned over the rail to look out at the driveway. When Isabel and Grant emerged from his truck, she waved. "Hello. Glad you're back."

Isabel hurried around the side of the porch, up the steps, and ran into Diana's open arms. "I'm so pleased for you," Diana said. "I wish you both tons of happiness."

Grant came up the steps with a smile on his face that matched Isabel's.

Diana looked from Isabel to Grant. "You two continue to surprise me. Your marriage plans seem rushed, but under the circumstances, I understand. Or I should say, I'm trying to."

"It's right for us." Isabel took Grant's hand. "We found what each of us wanted to wear." Excitement glowed from her face. "Penny said you and she talked and everything is set. Thanks. Imagine Ursula letting us have our reception at her house. It's perfect."

"Ah, yes." Diana looked at the Cape Cod. "It would seem so."

Grant went down the steps. "While you two chat, I'll unload the scuba gear."

"I'll help," Isabel said.

"When do you plan to make the dive?" Diana asked, following them to the truck.

"After we bring everything in." Grant was half way down the drive when he added over his shoulder, "I don't want to waste time." He jogged to his truck with Isabel and Diana trailing behind.

"Before you dive, we need to talk," Diana said. "It's important."

"What do you mean?" He took out the bags, walked to the backdoor with them, put them down, and returned to stand next to Isabel and Diana.

"I've studied the land," Diana said. "Gloria couldn't have driven the car into the pond from here."

Grant frowned and studied the gravel driveway. "If she had enough speed, and the tide was in, it could've worked."

Diana shook her head and pointed up the road. "There's a brick house on a hill. The hill slants at a steep angle. Back when the car incident occurred, there was no house or wall to stop the roll. That's where she could have accomplished it."

Grant stood by the tailgate. "I know the area you're talking about. Sounds logical. She'd have been clever enough to do that." He nodded and looked at Isabel. "If we enter the water here in front of the house and make our way along the shoreline, we'd stir up the bottom. If we start farther up as Diana suggested, we can back track. That way we'd be going with the tide."

"I promised Chief Nelson I'd let him know when you'd dive so his men can be on hand."

"Oh, Mom." Isabel scowled. "Why did you have to bring them into this?"

Grant put his hand on Isabel's arm. "That might not be a bad idea. If or when we find the car, the police need to know." He took out two large duffles from the back, but left the tanks. "I'll take these upstairs, then we'll suit up."

Isabel looked at her mother. "You'll have to wait to ooh and aah over my dress. The search first." She draped a dress bag over her arm and ran after Grant.

Two hours later Diana stood on the path below the colonial's brick wall while two officers stood near the shore. Her eyes were focused on the trail of bubbles erupting from below the water. Unable to stand the tension, Diana walked down to Officer Daniels. "They've been under a long time, don't you think?"

He glanced at his watch and shook his head. "They have a metal detector, but even with it, this is a long shot. The detector they rented is a Tesoro Sand Shark. It might be good for depth, but I'm not sure it's powerful enough for this job. We could have gotten a police unit in here that would use a JW Fisher Pulse Induction Metal Detector."

"How long would that have taken?" Diana asked.

"Depends if it was in use elsewhere."

"That's the problem," she said. "Grant didn't want to wait days or weeks."

"If they're successful, we've got a tow truck on standby." He thrust his hand toward the pond. "Years under all that muck with the tide coming in and out, the salt water, it'll be a rust bucket of bolts and the—"

"They popped the marker," the other officer called out.

"I'll call the Chief," Officer Daniels said.

Grant and Isabel waded ashore and removed their masks and fins. Grant handed one end of a rope to the officer. "At the other end of this is the fender of a car. When your tow truck gets here, I'll trace it back to the car and attach a chain to the undercarriage." He smiled at Diana. "Nice detective work. It would have taken us several days to come this far up the pond."

"We didn't have several days." Isabel looked at Grant. "I will not be stood up at the altar over an old car."

Grant's face flushed. "I wouldn't have done that."

"Not then." She grinned. "But after the ceremony, you'd have gone back to the scuba hunt, right?"

"Ah, well, I'd have waited until after the reception." He helped her off with her tank and then shed his.

"My romantic husband-to-be." She hugged him.

Chief Nelson arrived, followed by a city tow truck. He came over to where they were all standing. "Tow truck shouldn't interest the media."

Grant's eyes narrowed. "I don't think you won that round." He nodded at the two men standing behind the old brick wall. One had a camera.

"Crap," Nelson muttered, then turned to Daniels. "How did Glenn learn we were out here towing a car out of the pond?"

Daniels bit his lip. "I didn't think this assignment was a secret, sir."

"Who did you tell?" Nelson glowered at his officer.

Daniels looked down. "My wife."

"Right." Nelson walked toward the newspaper men, spoke with them for several minutes then returned to the huddled group. "He knows we're searching for Gloria Feeney's Impala. Now how the hell did he learn that?" He looked pointedly at Daniels. "He's not giving up his source. He'd like an interview with you, Diana."

"Why me? I'm an outsider."

"He knows Isabel is your daughter, that Grant lived with Gloria when he was a teenager and that Isabel and Grant plan to get married on Saturday."

"Shit." Grant said in an undertone. "How the hell did he dig all that up?"

"It's a small town." Daniels shrugged. "People talk."

"I can keep him back from this area, but he's going to search for more info and will probably be in your face for some time." Nelson sighed. "I can give an official statement, but that's not going to stop him from snooping into your lives." His eyes roamed from Diana to Grant to Isabel.

"Grant, I'll play it anyway you like," Diana said.

"As long as he doesn't interfere with our wedding, I don't care." Isabel put her arm through Grant's and gazed at his scowling face. "It's up to you."

"What the hell," he said. "Maybe putting the entire sordid story before the public will open some mouths that have been closed for too long."

"It could jeopardize Bert or Sam from getting a fair trial," Diana said. "It will definitely hurt Hetch emotionally."

Nelson rubbed his jaw. "It depends how much you tell. Detective O'Reilly and the police department could be in for some bad publicity or worse."

"They already know about Sam's involvement with the drugs at the house, and the baby's remains," Daniels said. "They got that from the public records."

Grant turned to Nelson. "I'll meet with them."

"You're sure?" Nelson asked.

Grant nodded. "Tell that newspaperman, Glenn, to be at the house this evening about eight. I'll give him facts, but no cameraman. Pictures of me, Diana or Isabel are off limits." He looked at Diana. "Are you game?"

"It depends how intrusive or belligerent he is. But I think you're smart to meet with him. Better to tell your side than having him write rumors."

Nelson nodded. "Officer Daniels, inform Glenn of the arrangement."

After Daniels left, Nelson turned to Grant. "Let's see what you've dredged up."

Grant retrieved his scuba tank, took the chain from the tow truck in one hand and followed his rope down into the water. It was several minutes before he reemerged and gave a thumbs up to the tow driver. He swam off to the right and clambered ashore to watch the cranking chain draw its prize out of the water.

Like a strange monster, the trunk of a car emerged from the pond. Reeds and seaweed entangled the hulk of rusted metal. When it was on land, the group circled the car. Isabel put her arm around Grant's shoulders. He gulped and stared at the relic's bashed front grillwork. He had his answer to a long held secret.

Accidentally or intentionally, Gloria Feeney had killed his parents.

Chapter 33

Late that afternoon Diana sat on the bed in the upstairs bedroom while Isabel pulled out her wedding dress. It came out of the plastic bag with a whoosh. Cream-colored, three-quarter sleeves, a knee length A-line skirt and a lacy scalloped neckline.

"It's perfect," Diana said with a broad smile and looked at the high-heeled shoes to match. "Good thing Grant's tall or you'd tower over him in those."

"I doubt if he'd care," Isabel said. "He's amazingly unconcerned about looks." After all he found me attractive in my BDUs."

"Don't be so sure about that. He's sprucing up this old house to be the gem of the neighborhood. Do you think he'll sell it?"

Isabel held the dress up to her and looked in the mirror. "He hasn't said. I don't think he knows what he's going to do." She put the dress on the bed and stared at it. "Penny has a thing about this house."

"It's no wonder after all the things that have happened here. It might be difficult to sell. Who would want it?"

"That's what Penny says. She'd like to see it burn to the ground." Diana rose from the bed. "Has Grant spoken about her?"

"We promised no secrets between us. So the answer is yes." She eyed her mother. "Including the letters."

"Good. Have you met Penny?"

"Not yet. Only talked to her. She asked if you and I would come to Ursula's tomorrow about eleven to talk about the reception arrangements. I said yes."

Diana nodded. "That's fine. Now, would you like to see what I plan to wear to your wedding?"

"You bet." Isabel hung her dress in the closet and followed her mother downstairs to Diana's room. Isabel stopped at the doorway. "Dad's staying here. Will the two of you share this room? I'm overstepping my bounds, but the two of you have been estranged, haven't you?" She studied her mother. "Of course, there are other rooms upstairs."

Diana frowned not sure if she should be angry, but Isabel had only voiced her own thoughts. She stopped in front of the closet, then turned to Isabel. "To be frank, I don't know. He and I will figure it out when he arrives." She opened the closet and pulled out the hanger with her coral-colored outfit. "What do you think? It's not too bold, is it?"

"It's super." She went to Diana and put her arms around her. "I'm so glad you're my mom."

As she hugged her daughter, tears of happiness spilled from Diana's eyes.

"Where is everyone?" Grant shouted from the living room.

"In here," Isabel called out and the two women separated.

Grant burst in and stopped at the threshold. "Are you okay? Tears?"

"Of joy." Diana was quick to point out.

Relief flooded his face. "Wonderful. We need more of that around here since I've got bad news about Bert. On top of being indicted for destroying a crime scene, the district attorney added a murder charge."

Diana's heart sank. If Ursula was guilty of the crime, would this news pressure her to confess. "Poor Bert. Is he back in jail?"

"Yeah, with a high bail." He slumped against the door jamb. "I'm sure he didn't do it, but who did?"

Isabel went to his side and looked at her mother. "Any ideas, Mom?"

Diana hung her dress back in the closet. "Maybe, but it's a long shot. If I'm wrong, I don't want to ruin a career and a life."

They went into the living room and milled about as if waiting for a patient to revive. Grant looked at his watch. "The two of you should take a walk."

"What are you up to?" Isabel asked laughing.

"That reporter, Glenn, is coming over soon. It's better if neither of you are here."

"He'll expect me. You sure you don't want me to stay?" Diana asked.

"Do you want to?"

"Not really. Tell him I'll give him an interview about my writing career after the wedding."

Grant smiled. "I think he'll get the message from that statement."

"It's cold outside and windy down by the ocean," Isabel said. "I'll get my parka. She turned and jogged upstairs.

"You're a good man, Grant. I'm glad my daughter found you. You'll be good for one another."

"Thanks. You and I had a rough start, and I'm sorry about that."

"The more I've thought about the so-called coincidence of my renting this house, the more I realize that Isabel must have had something to do with my being here."

"She knew I was coming here," Grant said.

"And she told her father to recommend this town, but how would she know that I'd rent this particular house?"

"Because I told Dad if you chose to rent in Quamscutt, you had to use Cora Jacob. I emailed her about this house." Isabel stood at the bottom of the stairs, smiling. "Sorry, guys. I don't believe in fate unless you push it."

"You little minx." Grant's eyes twinkled.

Diana shook her head. "And I thought I was the clever one. How did you know Cora?" She sighed and nodded. "You checked the internet."

"Well, I thought it was a brilliant idea. I didn't know about the murder." She turned to Grant. "Sorry about that."

"You didn't know. I never told you the history of the place. It's turned out okay. I've learned who killed my parents, but we may never know who killed Gloria."

Diana stared across the pond. "Let's go, Isabel." She grabbed her jacket and scarf and went out to the porch. Arm in arm they walked around the pond until Diana stopped where the path branched to the ocean. "We could pay an impromptu visit to Ursula. Tell her the news about Bert. She'd want to know since she put up his bail on the first count."

"You have something in mind, don't you?"

"Darling, I'm an old mystery writer." She tugged at Isabel's arm. "Come on."

Together they walked across the bridge and around the side of Ursula's house. After Diana rapped the brass knocker, it took several minutes before there was a shuffle of footsteps and Ursula opened the door with a confused expression. "What a surprise."

Diana introduced Isabel, and they followed Ursula into the living room. "Can I get you something to drink?"

"No, thank you," Diana answered for both of them. "We were walking to the beach, and I thought it might be a good idea for you to meet my daughter since you've been kind enough to host her wedding reception."

Ursula frowned. "Penny just left. I thought we were meeting tomorrow morning?"

"I know, but I thought an extra visit might be pleasant. I hope that's okay."

Ursula sat in her chair and motioned them to the couch. "Pleased to have you." She looked at Isabel. "Penny told me how you and Grant met in the war zone. I'm a little embarrassed that I gave your mother a difficult time about Grant. I thought she was cavorting with a young man."

Isabel laughed. "Mom's good-looking enough for him to fall for her."

"All right, you two, that's enough talk about me while I'm present."

Ursula smiled and leaned back. "It's nice to have a happy event after all the terrible things that have happened of late. Cora's murder was a shock. Never seen Penny so unsettled. You found the body, Diana."

"I was supposed to pick up your painting that Gloria owned. Cora had it for safekeeping. That's why I went to her house. I'm sorry, but the painting had been slashed, ruined."

Ursula's face paled. "My painting? Why?" She put her hand to her mouth, then let it fall to her lap. "How was Cora killed?"

"A knife. It must have been sudden, perhaps a fight. From what I saw, Cora must have been killed shortly after she call Grant to pick up the painting."

"Lucky you weren't killed, too." Ursula shook her head. "One bad thing after another." She rubbed her forehead as if she had a headache. "I'm sure my painting has nothing to do with the crime."

"I disagree. The paintings are the lynchpin to Gloria's murder, and perhaps Cora's as well." Diana maintained a relaxed outward appearance, but inside every fiber was taut. "You loved that piece of land, didn't you? And then the Feeneys built the Victorian. Why did you paint another one with the Victorian in the scene?"

Ursula shrugged. "Money, pride, anger. Who knows? The point is I did. That woman was crazy."

Isabel sat forward. "Sorry to break in on this conversation, but I thought Ursula should know that the police have proof that Gloria killed Grant Cranston's parents in a hit and run years ago."

Ursula blinked. "Her Impala?"

"How did you know?" Diana asked.

"It was a scandal years ago. I had moved to New York, came back occasionally and got the local paper. Since I had my own, shall we say, run in with the woman, and she was a neighbor, I followed the story."

"They found her Impala in the pond this morning with its front end damaged." Diana said. "She apparently drove it into water to hide it, then claimed it had been stolen."

Ursula nodded. "She deserved to die."

"Murdered? I don't think anyone deserves that, do you? The victims and the perpetrators always pay," Diana said. "Even an innocent like Bert gets roped into the maze. I'm glad you put up his bail. Unfortunately, the district attorney has added murder to the indictment. He's back in jail."

Ursula plucked at the edge of her fuchsia-colored scarf. "Why did he have to tamper with the crime scene? If he'd only left it alone."

"But he didn't. The real murderer will go free, and an innocent man may go to prison." Diana stood, walked to the French doors and looked at the pond. "The crime scene was interesting. A shovel anyone could have wielded, bits of canvas in the yard that Bert covered with a flagstone and a frame with a torn piece of canvas hidden in the shed." She turned and gazed at Ursula. "What do you think it all means?"

Ursula's eyes narrowed. "No idea. You're the mystery writer."

Diana turned to look at a painting on the wall, her back to Ursula. "I like to weave tales and sometimes they're close to the truth. I spoke to your agent, Mr. Franklin. You and Gloria had words while he was here to appraise your paintings."

"Everyone knows I disliked the woman, along with most of Quamscutt."

"True." Diana fingered the frame of an oil painting hanging on the wall. "Poor Bert."

"Oh, posh. He hasn't been convicted yet. There's time, don't you think, Diana? It's been over a year. I doubt if a few more days will make a difference."

Diana turned to face Ursula. "You could be right, but in the end, who knows? He may be more psychologically vulnerable than we think. Guilt is a terrible burden." Diana studied the landscapes. "Do you think Cora's murder is related to your paintings that Gloria owned?"

"How should I know?"

Diana shrugged. "I thought you might have an idea."

"I'm sure Chief Nelson will figure it out." Ursula looked at her clasped hands in her lap as if they might tell her something. She straightened in her chair and raised her chin. "Too many lives have been lost and more could be ruined. I can't turn back the clock."

"I don't want Bert to suffer because of his poor judgement, do you?"

Ursula stared at Diana, but she said nothing.

"Justice will win out eventually, no matter how we hide from it. I have faith that most people are good, but do rash and stupid things." Diana motioned to Isabel with a nod that they should leave. "We'll see ourselves out. Thanks for allowing us to visit. We'll see you and Penny tomorrow to talk about the reception. Is that all right?'

"Of course." Ursula hesitated, then added, "I'll look forward to it."

Isabel and Diana left and walked down the path to the pond. At the path's junction to the beach, Isabel pulled on her mother's arm, forcing her to stop. "You and she were talking in code. What was it all about?"

"The murder of Gloria Feeney."

"I know that, but there was something else."

"Do you mind having your wedding reception in the home of a murderer?"

Chapter 34

Friday morning Diana and Isabel stood on the porch talking with Grant before they left to meet Penny at Ursula's. "I'm glad your interview with Glenn went well," Diana said. "What did he say about my not being here?"

Grant grinned. "He wants to meet with you next week."

"When will his article be in the paper?" Isabel asked.

"Tomorrow. Said he had to gather some other facts first. He promised not to interfere with the wedding, but I'm not sure the photographer will honor the arrangement."

Isabel took his arm. "Forget it, Grant. If he comes, he comes." She laughed. "Maybe we should invite him to take photos, pay him, so we'll have a good wedding album."

"Now there's a thought," Diana said. "And not a bad one, either."

"Oh, shit. Women, what are you saying?"

"We're saying invite the enemy in and then we have some control," Isabel said.

Grant shook his head. "You don't remember the battle for Troy?"

"This is different."

"Is it? The media can distort anything."

Diana interrupted them. "If he gets paid for the pictures, it puts a different spin on his ability to print them without your say-so."

Grant held up his hands in surrender. "Okay, I'll call the guy. But I'll insist on a contract."

Isabel and Diana waved to him from the bottom of the porch steps and walked to Ursula's. "I called Sally Tuttle," Diana said. "I'll pick her up in Providence while you meet your dad at the airport. She'll stay with us at the house. As you said, there are plenty of rooms."

"Maybe Grant should turn the place into a guest house," Isabel said. "He'd get a steady income. What do you think?"

"Who would run it with both of you away in the military?"

"Grant's due for a promotion to Major. It's unlikely they'll send him back into a combat zone after his injuries." She squeezed Diana's arm. "I have another two years."

"What will you do after your tour of duty?"

"I'm not sure. Marrying Grant makes a difference. We'd like to have kids, but not while I'm in the military." Isabel shrugged. "We'll have to see where we'll be assigned and make a decision accordingly."

As they neared Ursula's front door, Diana held back. "This could be an awkward meeting. We'll pretend our visit yesterday never happened unless Ursula brings it up."

Isabel shook her head. "As if it isn't going to be awkward anyway."

After knocking, they waited until Penny, dressed in beige chinos and a yellow sweatshirt, opened the door. "Welcome to the venue for your wedding reception." Her flushed face radiated with a smile. As she led them to the living room, she said over her shoulder, "After we chat, I'll contact the caterer. She's super. Ursula won't even know a party was held here."

"There'll only be eight of us," Diana said.

Penny turned to face them. "Actually, nine. I invited Marlene. I hope you don't mind. She's been so distraught, and I thought this event might cheer her up." Her expression beseeched them to agree. "I know she's hired help. It's your wedding reception, Isabel. Is it okay?"

"Fine with me. She must be depressed with her husband in jail."

"Did you ask Ursula if it was all right," Diana asked. "After all, it's her house."

"Oh, I don't think it'll matter to her. After all she's paying for Bert's lawyer."

"Oh. I hadn't heard. That's wonderful. Where's Ursula?"

"The beauty salon. She wanted to look her best."

"I thought the whole idea was to have the four of us discuss the details of the reception and get better acquainted." Diana searched Penny's face to determine if she had a hidden agenda.

"She said you came over yesterday, and there wasn't much point in her being here." Penny turned to Isabel. "She likes you."

Isabel chuckled. "Is that good?"

"Ursula is very opinionated, so the answer is yes. She's looking forward to the party."

"Will she be at the church?" Diana asked.

"I'm not sure. I told her I'd pick her up, but she hasn't decided. Charlie is going to meet me there. Can you believe all the problems he's had lately. It all has to do with that horrid Feeney house. Grant should burn it to the ground. That would be a good gift, wouldn't it?" She glanced at Isabel. "Sorry, I shouldn't have said that. But that place is the epitome of evil."

Isabel peered through the French doors at the pond and the Victorian before she said, "It's not the house, but the people."

"I know that." Penny's words snapped out. "But it's symbolism. The history is terrible. Ursula told me about Mrs. Feeney killing Grant's parents. He must be devastated."

Isabel shook her head. "Not really. He's relieved to finally know the truth."

"What's Grant going to do with the house?"

"Mom and I were talking about that on the way over here. I suggested he turn it into a guest house. He'd have an income stream."

"Who would want to stay there?"

Diana grinned. "It might be a draw. A mystery tour kind of thing."

"That sounds awful." Penny's eyes widened, her face paled.

Isabel glanced at her mother. "I think it's a brilliant idea. With all the publicity, it would be advertisement for the town. Build up tourism. Maybe even invite mystery writers to lecture."

Penny scowled. "You don't live here. That monstrosity is evil and to use it as a tourist attraction would be a travesty. Cora was wrong to rent it, wrong to fix it up. She had that horrid painting of Ursula's. The one with the Victorian house that spoiled her view. She had no business keeping it. That house should have been left to the fate of the weather or whatever." Penny's hands clenched. "It's not a house, it's a temple of evil and that painting is a symbol of all the horror it represents."

Isabel took a few steps back. "I'm only chatting, Penny. Grant's the one to decide about what he'll do with it, not me, not Diana. Don't take offense, please."

Penny looked from Isabel to Diana. "Of course. Sorry. I get worked up about the place."

"What did you think of Cora's gift and her note?" Diana asked.

"What gift? What note? What are you talking about?"

"Didn't your husband tell you? When I was at the shop you recommended and Maxine heard about Cora's death, she gave me the gift Cora had bought for you. Charles came by my place and picked up the box."

"I haven't seen Charlie. Lately, he practically sleeps at the station. There's never been so much crime in Quamscutt. It's that damn house." She glared out across the pond at the Victorian, threw open the French doors and walked out onto the porch. "Let's sit outside and talk about what you want the caterer to serve."

Although Diana wanted to pursue the note and the gift, she couldn't find the right opening and let it slide. For the next hour they enjoyed the sunshine and discussed the wedding and the menu. By lunch time, Ursula had still not appeared.

"We should get back." Diana stood. "Isabel and Grant are picking up my husband at the airport and I'm getting Sally Tuttle."

"Oh, what time?"

"Dad's plane gets in at ten, but Grant and I are having dinner in town beforehand." Isabel turned to Diana. "I forgot to ask you, Mom. Maybe you and Sally can join us for dinner."

Diana smiled. "You and Grant need time together."

"So no one will be home tonight?" Penny asked.

"That's right." Diana frowned at the question. "Why do ask?"

Instead of answering, Penny turned to Isabel. "I never asked about your wedding dress. Maybe you shouldn't have it at the house. Brides aren't supposed to have the groom see them in it before the wedding."

"Too late for that. Grant was there when I bought it." She gave Penny a hug. "Glad to have you as a friend."

"Me too." Penny hugged Diana and waved goodbye to them from Ursula's doorway.

On the path home Isabel nudged her mother. "Penny really has a thing about the house, doesn't she?"

"More than I thought. And that picture. Despite how busy her husband is, I would have thought he'd have questioned her about the note and gift from Cora." Diana walked on and then paused. "As Police Chief, it's his duty to question her, even though she's his wife."

"You of all people should know that questioning the other half is a declaration of war."

Diana smiled at her daughter. "Remember you said that when you're married."

"Got it. But seriously, the Chief could have someone else in the department question her. I don't know her, but she was upset. Is she normally so on edge?"

"Strung tight, I'd say. Her interest in Cora's murder, the gift or the note was muted. Why wouldn't Charles have given her the present?"

"Maybe he did."

"Then why did she deny it?"

Diana didn't like where her intuition was leading her. Had she been wrong to put so much focus on O'Reilly? Had her dislike of him biased her? No. O'Reilly knew about the drugs Sam had stashed in the house. He was guilty of that. Her assumption about Ursula was spot on, or was it? Penny was protective of Ursula, hated the Victorian as much as Ursula hated it. And what about Cora? Penny seemed angry with Cora because of the painting and her part in fixing up the house.

With this new perspective, Diana had to reevaluate her assumptions concerning the slashed paintings.

Chapter 35

That night Grant, Isabel, and Diana gathered in the living room before leaving for Providence when Isabel answered a call from Sally Tuttle. "Are you sure?" Isabel glanced at her mother. "Of course it's all right. One more won't be a problem. Do you know how to get here? Okay. We'll look forward to seeing you and Professor Horowitz at the church. And of course at the reception afterward. Bye."

"What was that all about?" Diana asked.

"Sally's attending a conference in New York with her professor. They'll come to the wedding and the reception, then drive down to the city. Looks like you're free tonight, Mom. Why don't you join us?"

"It's better the two of you go. You haven't seen your father in a long time and Grant needs to get acquainted with him. I'll call the caterer and tell her there will be one more."

Isabel, dressed in blue slacks, stood by the fireplace. "You and Dad have to talk."

Diana's jaw tightened. "Paul and I do not need an audience. Stay out of—"

"Okay, you two," Grant interrupted. "I'm going to be the arbitrator here. Diana stays home. You and I will go out to dinner as planned and then pick up your dad. There's no point in arguing." He gave Diana a kiss on the cheek, then beckoned to Isabel. "I want some alone time with you, Isabel."

She took his hand and smiled. "My bossy husband-to-be." She glanced at Diana. "Sorry, Mom. I'm a nag."

"You inherited the trait. Go along and have a good time. I'll wait up for you."

"It'll be close to midnight," Isabel said.

"I think I can stay awake till then. Take my car." Diana tossed her keys to Grant and shooed them out the door. "Enjoy yourselves."

After they drove off, Diana poured herself a glass of wine and settled in the chair by the fireplace revising the notes that she and Police Chief Nelson had discussed. She soon became bored with her futile attempts to make sense of the clues and put them aside in favor of having dinner. As she washed her dishes, her thoughts turned to Paul. What would his attitude be toward her? Could they repair their marriage? She missed him and needed him, but did he feel the same way? It would take time to heal the rift, and he'd need options about the sleeping arrangements.

Tossing the dishtowel on the counter, she went upstairs to make the bed in one of the extra rooms at the front of the house. She dusted and vacuumed and put out fresh towels in the bathroom. Back downstairs, she turned off the kitchen lights and went to her room to decide what to wear. Earlier that afternoon, her visit to the beauty parlor had done wonders for her hair and nails. Like a teenager on her first date, she felt nervous. Silly. After all, they'd been married almost twenty-eight years. Their marriage had gone flat, excitement gone, arguments over simple things. They had lapsed from love to a quarrelsome friendship. She wanted more. Did he? It was important that Paul not only saw her looking her best, but understood how her attitude toward Isabel and Jeffrey had changed. Would any of that matter to him?

With hours to spare, she took a shower. Afterward she withdrew one outfit after another from the closet and laid it on the bed. She tried on several, then stood in her bra and panties. Overdressing would be a mistake. Finally she chose light gray slacks and a powder blue silk blouse. As she buttoned her blouse, she heard a bang from upstairs. Odd. Had the wind come up and a shutter was loose? She frowned, shoved her feet into loafers and went to the bottom of the stairs to listen.

Nothing. Had she imagined it? Perhaps the noise came from outside. She remembered how she had heard Grant's screams through the heating duct. They had put traps in the attic for rodents. Perhaps that was what she'd heard. She had no intention of entering the attic to find out. Still a cursory inspection might be in order. If she found a dead rat, she'd let Grant dispose of it. At the top of the stairs she flipped on the light and stopped in the middle of the hall. The door to Grant and Isabel's room opened.

Penny stepped out with Isabel's wedding dress over her arm.

Diana gawked. "What…what are you doing here?"

Penny stared at her. "You're not supposed to be home."

"But I am." Diana took a step forward, but hesitated when she noticed Penny's dilated eyes. "Why are you here? How did you get in?" Penny didn't respond to the litany of questions. "What are you doing with Isabel's dress?"

"I wanted to keep it safe, surprise her."

"No. Isabel will handle everything herself, thank you. Put it back."

Penny wore a fierce and angry expression. "If that's how you want it, but you'll be sorry." She stepped back into the room.

Diana followed and watched her hang the dress back up. "Thank you. Now explain what you're doing here."

Penny turned toward Diana. "Everything will be fine. I'm Ursula's guardian angel and I've taken care of everything. Nothing and no one, not even you, can hurt her now." Penny moved to the side table and fingered a small metal sculpture. "It's pretty, isn't it? Unlike this house. Does it belong to Grant or was it Gloria's? Perhaps a memento. We don't need to have anything like that in here, do we?" She picked it up, cradled it in her hand. "It's heavy. You know I killed Cora, don't you?" She walked toward Diana.

The confession caught Diana by surprise. As Penny walked toward her, she backed up. "Penny, you're acting very strange. Please put that down and we can go downstairs and talk." She pointed toward the door and in the split second that she looked away, Penny swung the statue. Diana raised her arm, too late. She felt the blow.

Diana awoke on a bed in a dimly lit room. Her head throbbed. She tried to get up but her wrists were tied to the wrought iron bed frame with thick rope. Her vision blurred. She blinked and the room came into focus. It was the room she'd prepared for Paul. The clock on the bedside table read: ten forty. Too early for Grant, Isabel and Paul to return. Smoke seeped under the closed door, curling into the room. It spun like cotton and engulfed her. She screamed and strained against the ropes. They held firm, cutting into her skin.

She screamed, terror clawing at her. Her throat became ragged from the smoke and her yells for help. She continued to yell and yank at the ropes. Using her feet for traction on the mattress, she scooted back against the headboard, hoping to get leverage and alleviate the tension. Impossible. The ropes remained taut. Anger and fear raged through every wail of despair. "God, I don't want to die this way," she pleaded.

"You won't have to." The voice came from a figure looming in the doorway. He stepped forward. He was dressed in black leather. The blade of his knife glinted in the fire's light. Smoke from the open door formed a halo around his blond hair.

Her eyes widened. She cringed, waiting for him to plunge the knife into her chest. There would be pain, but it would end. What a fool she'd been. Naive to think she could bargain with murderers. She bit back a cry of fear.

He moved fast. With two quick slashing motions, he slit the ropes that bound her to the frame.

She stared at him, dumbstruck.

"Come on," he said. "We don't have much time. The house is engulfed in fire."

She sat up, the ends of the rope dangling from her wrists. When her feet met the floor, her knees buckled. He put his arm around her waist, and they stumbled through the smoke and down the stairs.

The kitchen was a sea of flames. The first floor was full of dense smoke. He pushed her down onto the floor in the living room and they crawled toward the front door. He fumbled with the knob, then stopped. "The minute I open it, the air will suck the flames toward us." He pointed to the window. "We take a few steps back, crash through the window sideways, stay low, and run for the pond."

He coughed. "Got it?"

She nodded.

His arm tightened around her. They crawled backward, then stood and ran bent over, but as they hit the window, the house exploded throwing them forward and down the steps onto the sand. Glass shards and timber pelted them. Flames swept over their heads. He pulled her up. They ran toward the pond and plunged into it, submerging their bodies into the cool water.

Gasping for air, Diana felt raw, scorched, dazed, standing waist deep in water that reflected the red glow of the fire. She pushed her singed hair away from her face. A wall of flames soared skyward. Like a slow motion film, the walls quivered, then sank inward, sending sparks and smoke into the air.

Sirens pierced the night. Diana looked at her savior. "I owe you my life."

"I might remind you of that at another time." He put his hand on her arm and guided her through the reeds along the shore farther up the road and away from the fire.

One hundred feet up the shoreline, they clambered out. A firefighter led them to a waiting ambulance. EMT personnel put a blanket around each of them and cut the rope off her wrists. "You need stitches," he said. "We'll transport you to the hospital."

"I need to call my daughter."

"I'll have one of the police officers call her," O'Reilly said.

"She'll think something awful happened."

"Well, hasn't it?"

"Yeah. Okay, but explain that I'm fine and tell Grant the house is gone."

Chief Nelson walked up, looking haggard. "Thank God, you're all right."

"I'm alive thanks to O'Reilly. Where's Penny?"

"I don't know."

"She started the fire. Tried to kill me."

"What? No! Not Penny." Nelson shook his head in utter bewilderment and rubbed his hand across his face. "What was she thinking?" He turned toward O'Reilly. "What were you doing here?"

"I'd been talking to Hetch and needed to speak to Mrs. Bellfore. Thought I might catch her at home. When I arrived, smoke was billowing out the open back door. I called it in. I heard screams and went in and found Mrs. Bellfore tied to the bedposts."

"Penny did that?" Nelson asked Diana.

Still dazed, she managed a nod.

"Looks like that leather jacket of yours protected you from the worst of the fire," Nelson said.

O'Reilly looked at his jacket, now in shreds, and pealed it off, flinching as he did so.

"Are you well enough to help out or should you go to the hospital along with Mrs. Bellfore?" Nelson asked and turned to the EMT. "What about it?"

"I'll bandage his hands, but he should be checked out by a doctor."

"I'll go to the hospital later. I'd like to stick around for awhile and search for clues as to how the fire was started."

"Since Penny seems to be involved, I can't lead this case. I need someone who knows what they're doing."

"You'll have my best work on this one."

"You're always thorough. It might be the last case for both of us." Chief Nelson walked off to talk to the fire captain.

"Diana, go to the hospital." O'Reilly wiped his face with a towel. "I'll have Officer Daniels get your statement later."

"I'm indebted to you. My thanks seem to be inadequate to the situation."

He sighed. "I understand you think I've been an ass if not a criminal, but we can discuss that later. Go to the hospital." As an EMT bandaged his hand, O'Reilly smiled at Diana. "You look like hell."

"You don't look so good either."

"Yeah, well, it comes with the territory." He took off his ripped shirt and struggled into one an officer brought him.

"No longer enemies I hope," she said.

"I never thought we were." He buttoned his shirt and ran a hand through his hair.

She looked at her shredded silk blouse and torn slacks. "I need to change, too." She stared at the smoldering mass of rubble. "I guess a shopping spree is in order." She put her hand on O'Reilly's arm. "Why were you at the house?"

He stood next to the ambulance. "Like I told the Chief, I came to talk to you. Hetch called me about your deal."

"Good timing." She backed up against the gurney and let the ambulance crew take over.

Chapter 36

When Isabel, Grant, and Paul visited Diana at the hospital, it was one in the morning. To Diana they looked beautiful, healthy, safe. That's all that mattered.

Paul leaned over, put his arms gently on her shoulders and brushed his lips against hers. "Don't you know an author isn't supposed to become part of the story?"

"I've missed you," she said.

"Same here," he whispered in her ear. A wisp of his brown hair fell across his brow. "You scared me. I realized I don't want to lose you."

Diana clung to him, breathing in his smell. "I wanted to look my best for you. Instead I'm encased in chic bandages, and my hair must look like mice nested in it."

"You're alive. That's what matters." Paul grinned. "I've seen you look worse, like the time you slid into the mud puddle."

"You would remember that." She glanced past Paul to Isabel and Grant. "Things are in a fine mess with your wedding tomorrow. I'm so sorry."

Isabel pushed past her father, and with tears in her eyes, she hugged Diana gently. "Thank God, you're okay. I can't believe Penny would do such a thing."

Grant stood behind Isabel. "Don't worry about tomorrow, Diana, we have everything under control."

"Of course you do. You're Marines." She leaned back against the pillows, feeling woozy. "They gave me pain medication and a sedative. It's difficult to focus."

Paul shook his head. "You aren't invincible, my pet. You have twelve stitches in your skull, cuts on your arms and back, and burns on your legs. Naturally, they gave you something to make you dopey."

"Is that a pun on how stupid I was?" She tried to smile, then glanced at Grant. "What about the house?"

"Nothing left. The arson investigator thinks Penny must have put rags on top of the stove to start the fire. It ignited the gas line running to the water heater. You're lucky you got out before the explosion."

"Where is Penny?"

"They haven't found her." Isabel said. "And Ursula's been admitted to this hospital, too. Heart attack."

"God, what else can happen?" Diana mumbled.

"You rest, honey," Paul said. "They're keeping you overnight. We're going to a motel. I'll come tomorrow morning and bail you out."

"Sounds like I'm in jail."

"You would have been safer there." He brushed his lips over her forehead. "Sweet dreams."

"I wish. Nightmares are more like it."

"Get some sleep, Mom. We'll see you in the morning. I'll buy some clothes for you."

"Oh, Lord, your wedding dress?"

Isabel smiled. "Would you believe it. Penny put it inside Grant's truck along with his suit. I don't understand what she was thinking. Why would she raze the house but save our wedding clothes?"

"I found her in your room with your dress over her arm. I know she hated the house, but she has to be insane to set it on fire."

"It makes no sense that she tried to kill you." Grant said. "I thought the two of you got along. Were friends."

"She killed Cora."

"Cora? She killed Cora?" Isabel asked.

"She confessed just before she hit me. The slashed painting fits into what she said before she struck me." Diana fingered the bandages on her temple. "Penny admired Ursula and would do anything to protect her. In Penny's distorted view Ursula's oil landscapes, like the house, needed to be destroyed. I don't know why she thought that. She said something like no one can hurt Ursula now. I took care of everything. I killed Cora. That was the last thing she said to me." She sighed.

Grant rubbed his hand across his face. "But with her attempt on your life and the destruction of my house, killing Cora fits the scenario."

"Poor Chief Nelson," Isabel said. "He must be devastated."

"He put O'Reilly in charge of the investigation," Diana said. Grant's look of disgust surprised her. "O'Reilly saved me, didn't you know that?"

"No. We just heard you got out of the house and were in the hospital," Isabel said.

Paul put his hand on Isabel's shoulder and nudged Grant. "We'll discuss everything tomorrow. Diana needs sleep." He smiled. "We have a lot to talk about." She started to speak, but he put his finger tips on her lips. "Later."

After they left, Diana faced the wall and cried: for herself, for Penny, for all the people ensnared in the murders and intrigue around the Victorian on Potters Pond.

Through the night, nurses came in and out of her room at odd hours. In the morning, Diana was served oatmeal, toast, and scrambled eggs. The coffee was drinkable, the eggs rubbery, the toast cold. Did the staff eat this stuff?

When a nurse came in, she asked, "Is it possible for me to visit another patient. She had a heart attack, and I'm a good friend."

"What's her name?"

"Ursula Von Reiter."

"She was admitted to intensive care last night. I'll see how she's doing and let you know."

Diana leaned back against the pillows. Not a satisfactory response, but under the circumstances it was the best she could hope for. It was an hour before her door opened again, but not to the nurse.

"How are you feeling?" Detective O'Reilly asked.

"Better than last night. From the circles under your eyes, I suspect you didn't get any more sleep than I did. Hospitals are not helpful to a good night's sleep."

He pulled a chair up near the bed and relaxed into it. "I need to ask you questions about last night."

"And I need answers about your involvement with Sam."

He gestured with both hands for her to stop. "You'll learn soon enough. I need information about Penny Nelson."

"Have you found her?"

"No."

"Could she have been in the house?"

"They haven't found a body in the rubble."

"Ursula might know where she is. Have you been able to talk to her?"

"Who's doing the questioning here?"

She smiled. "Sorry. Habit. I'll answer your questions." She told him what had happened before he'd rescued her and that Penny had confessed to killing Cora."

"Her fingerprints were found at the scene and with your testimony that she confessed to the crime, she'll most likely be convicted. Right now, she's wanted for attempted murder and arson. That's a big load on Chief Nelson's plate."

"How's he taking it?"

"Like a veteran cop. Setting up a search team, canvasing the area, sending out an APB and interviewing all the people involved, including you."

"Ah." She was about to explain her ideas about Gloria's murder when Officer Daniels stuck his head in the door.

"Sorry to interrupt, Detective, but Chief Nelson wants Mrs. Bellfore to come to Ursula Von Reiter's room."

O'Reilly stood, frowning. "Why Mrs. Bellfore?"

"It was Von Reiter's request."

Diana rang for a nurse, who helped her into a wheelchair, and O'Reilly took her to Ursula's room. When they entered, Chief Nelson was standing at the window that looked out over the town of Quamscutt.

Ursula's hair played out in tufts against the pillow. Her recent visit to the beauty parlor had turned it brighter red, hiding the white. Her faded blue eyes shone like pinpoints of lights from her wrinkled face. She looked all of her eighty-five years.

Tubes and wires connected her to a machine that beeped out her heart rate, blood pressure, and pulse rate. She turned her head toward Diana, then pulled the air tube from her nose. "I heard what happened. I'm glad you survived." She wheezed and put the tube back in.

Chief Nelson turned to face them, his face gray and drawn, his mouth pinched. "Miss Von Reiter requested you be present, Mrs. Bellfore." He nodded to Detective O'Reilly. "I'd like you to stay, too." He took a step toward the bed. "We're all present to hear what you have to say."

"I always did like an audience," Ursula said. "I'm sorry the story ended so badly for Penny. She was too caught up in my life, but why she suddenly snapped, I can't say. I think she knew the truth of Gloria's death." Her blue-veined hands trembled and plucked at the white sheet. She gazed at Diana. "I was wary of your instincts to solve murders, so I tried to be your friend. You know the saying, keep your friends close but your enemies closer. You've been right all along. I hadn't planned to kill Gloria. You met my agent Franklin, didn't you Diana?"

"Yes, I spoke with him at the art show of your paintings."

"Franklin visited me and we went to see my paintings that Gloria had. While we were there, she and I argued about how her house blocked my view. After all those years, I still couldn't let it go. It was a stupid thing to fight about. I think he was glad to leave. After he left town, I visited her the following week to discuss my paintings, thinking she didn't want them, and I could buy them back. She laughed at me. Can you imagine?" Ursula coughed, put a tissue to her mouth, then continued, "She became irate, tore my landscape off the wall, got a knife from the kitchen and ran out to the backyard. I followed her. She slashed my painting. Why would she do that? I was confused, angry. No, I was unhinged watching her. I grabbed the nearest thing at hand, a shovel. I didn't think. I picked it up and swung. She toppled forward."

Ursula's eyes blurred as if she were back at the scene of the crime. "It was raining. I stood over her, thinking she deserved to be in the mud. Then I noticed her hair was getting wet, but it wasn't from the rain, it was blood. I panicked and ran back to my house and was sick to my stomach. Penny came over the next day, and I told her I had the flu. After Gloria's body was discovered, I think Penny guessed I was the killer."

Ursula turned her head toward Chief Nelson. "It wasn't Bert. He was stupid to cover up the scene because he thought Marlene had killed her." She closed her eyes. "So long ago. The picture of Gloria in the mud has haunted me like a repetitive nightmare."

Diana looked across Ursula to Chief Nelson. He pursed his lips, then said, "I'll have your confession typed up for you to sign."

"You'd best hurry," Ursula said. "Not sure how long I've got." She sighed. "I always worried about my reputation. It doesn't matter now. Maybe my paintings will increase in value because the public will learn I'm a murderer. How amusing would that be?" She moved her head side to side slowly. "Diana, do you know a good lawyer?"

"A public defender will be assigned to you if you don't have one," Chief Nelson said.

"Not that kind of lawyer. I'm guilty, but I think death will allow me to escape the law. I need a lawyer to make changes to my will."

"I'll find one for you." Diana reached out to hold the woman's hand.

"Thank you." Ursula smiled and closed her eyes. The Chief nodded and Detective O'Reilly wheeled Diana out of the room.

In the hallway O'Reilly handed his cell phone to Officer Daniels. "Get this confession recording typed up at once and bring it back here for Miss Von Reiter's signature." He turned to the Chief. "I don't think we need a guard at her door, do we?"

"We'd better. It's protocol. Keep the media away and no visitors except her lawyer."

"Got it. Anything further on your, I mean, on Penelope?"

The chief shook his head, then turned to Diana. "Any ideas of where she could have gone?"

"She loved to walk along the beach."

Back in her room, Diana moved to the chair by the window and thought about Ursula. But her reverie was short-lived. Her door opened and a strange man, dressed in a gray business suit, entered. "Mrs. Bellfore, I'm here to speak to you about Detective Joe O'Reilly." He walked over and pulled out his identification. "I'm with the DEA."

She frowned. Were the feds on to O'Reilly?

"I can't go into details because of security issues for those concerned and because of our on-going investigation. Detective O'Reilly has been working with us."

She leaned back and sighed from relief and surprise. "I was so sure he was a corrupt cop."

"He couldn't tell you."

"What about Sam Feeney's involvement?"

"I'm not at liberty to tell you any more."

"Then I'll tell you what I think. O'Reilly had to allow Sam to remove the drugs from the house so we could follow their path to Phil Yukovitch and learn how he laundered the money. Yukovitch might be blind, but he's somehow involved with a drug cartel."

"You can surmise anything you like, but you must not speak to anyone about your ideas, O'Reilly's involvement, or this conversation. I need your promise that nothing I've told you will leave this room and that you will no longer talk about this matter to anyone. That means friends, relatives, or business persons you deal with. And you will not use any of this information in a book, fiction or otherwise."

She took a big breath. "I understand. But I have one question. Does Chief Nelson know this?"

"Yes, but he is under the same strictures as now you are."

"I see. Do you want my promise in writing?"

"We don't want a paper trail. However, please be advised that if you break this agreement, my department with prosecute you." He studied her. "Are we clear?"

"Very. I'm glad O'Reilly is on the side of the law."

He bowed, smiled and left the room, leaving her to contemplate how assumptions can be so wrong.

Chapter 37

Several hours later Diana dressed in clothes Isabel had bought. "You're going to have to go on a shopping spree," Isabel said, pulling out a lipstick for Diana. "I think this is the color you like. Sorry I didn't get you more makeup but I wasn't sure you could use anything due to the bandages."

"Right. Lipstick will have to do."

"Dad's downstairs waiting. They told him an orderly would take you out." She glanced at her watch. "I've got to be at the church, but I can wait."

"Go, for heaven's sakes. It's your wedding day, and you don't need to fuss over your mother." Diana gave her a kiss and shooed her out of the room. She sat on the edge of the bed, wondering if she should try to see Ursula one last time. Her thoughts were interrupted by the orderly, who wheeled her out to Paul, standing by his rental car.

"Ah, the queen of mysteries is ready for her coach," he said.

"You keep that kind of language up, and I'll have grounds for divorce." She stood, put her hands on his chest and leaned close to him. "But I won't let you get away easily."

"Is that a promise?" He slid his arm under hers and helped her into the front seat. "We're meeting Isabel and Grant at the church. Isabel thought they should change the reception locale, but Ursula called the pastor and requested that they go ahead and hold it at her house. Something about good to come out of the bad."

"If Isabel and Grant are comfortable with the venue, it shouldn't matter."

Paul closed the car door, went around to the driver's side and got in. "We have time to get a bite to eat." He drove out of the hospital parking lot.

"I'm not hungry, but I need to use your cell phone."

"Now what?" He slipped it out of his pocket and handed it to her.

"I made a commitment." She punched in Max's number. After a few rings, he picked up.

"This is your favorite author, Diana."

"Not your cell phone number. What's going on? I heard the old Feeney place burned to the ground."

"I don't have time to explain, but I need a lawyer to write a will or change a will, I'm not certain which."

"Wow. You in trouble?"

"No. Well, I was, but I'm not now. The lawyer is for Ursula Von Reiter. She needs one ASAP. Can you get someone for her?"

"Can do. You're running up quite a tab with me."

"I guess I'll just have to write another book." After explaining where Ursula was, she hung up and handed the phone back to Paul.

"You're helping a murderer?" He pulled away from the curb and drove out of the parking lot.

"Although she murdered Gloria, it wasn't premeditated. A violent reaction to an act of destruction of her creation."

"I'll remember not to criticize your work." He glanced at her with a grin.

"You're in a chipper mood. Want to let me in on the secret?"

"I quit my position at the college."

Diana frowned. "You're happy about it?"

"God, yes. It was past time, and the recent events gave me the nudge."

"What about your students? You can't leave them in the lurch."

"They're in good hands. George has been wanting to teach my classes and since he's spilled the beans to you, I thought it fitting." He drove down a side street and turned onto Route One. "I found out what you did. About the girl, Sally Tuttle, who claimed I'd made sexual advances toward her."

"I'm sorry, Paul. I shouldn't have interfered, but when I learned you wouldn't defend yourself, I couldn't stand by and do nothing."

"You can be my defender anytime, and I'll be yours. I'm just sorry I wasn't able to save you from a burning building, and it took a corrupt cop to do it instead."

"You know about O'Reilly?"

"You aren't the only snoop in the family. Yeah. I talked to Hetch. Seems O'Reilly needs to own up to his culpability."

"I'll wager they'll both go free."

"What aren't you telling me?"

"It's need-to-know. Sorry. It's not the ending I expected, but life is not a novel."

She put down her window and let the crisp fall air wash over her face. The pills had taken the edge off her pain, but she throbbed with a dull ache. "So many lives destroyed."

He pulled into the church parking lot. "Beautiful setting." He turned off the engine. "Can we start over again, Diana? Make it work."

"I'll do everything I can to make our marriage what it should be and once was."

He sat quietly for a while. "Remember how we said we'd like to live overseas for a year? How about a trip to Italy? We could find a suitable rental. We've saved for a rainy day, I'll have my pension, and selling the house will allow us to do it."

She smiled. "I like the idea." She leaned toward him, and they kissed, laughing at how the gear shift got in the way. "Come on, let's get our daughter married."

After the ceremony, they drove to Ursula's where the caterer had set up a lovely dinner, thanks to Penny. There was an awkward moment, when Sally and Paul met, but she apologized, and he accepted her contrition. Sally and Professor Horowitz stayed for a short time. Marlene and Bert left immediately afterward. He was out on bail, but the district attorney seemed willing to make a deal before the case went to trial.

From Ursula's porch, the view across the pond of the burned remains of the Feeney house was a grim reminder of the tragic events. But it was the shadow of Penny's actions and her disappearance that hovered over the wedding celebration. Despite that, everyone put on a game face, and after the Schukarts left, Isabel suggested a walk on the beach.

Diana, who had drunk her share of champagne thought it would be a good way to end the day. "I think I can struggle through the dunes." She giggled, then put her hand over her mouth. "If I collapse, the sand will be soft."

"Are you sure you're up to it?" Paul stood next to her.

Diana leaned against him. I need the fresh air. Let me settle with the caterer first."

Paul pulled out his checkbook. "Under the circumstances, I believe I'm the moneybags for this event. You haven't got a check book or a purse."

"I knew you were good for something." She sat on the white couch while he went into the kitchen.

"Mom, are you sure about coming? After all you just got out of the hospital."

Grant put a coat around Isabel's shoulders. "Diana, maybe you should stay here, relax."

"Paul and I are driving home tomorrow, so I'd like one last look at the ocean. At least I can sit on the dunes and watch the sun go down."

Paul came back in the room. "All set."

The two couples left the house and walked down the path toward the ocean. When they turned west along the shoreline, the autumn sun shone like a beacon reflecting off the blue water. It was cool and the breeze lifted sprays of white. Grant and Isabel walked ahead hand in hand.

"They're good for each other." Diana held onto Paul's arm. "With new and different assignments, it'll be difficult for them." Her breath came in puffs, her pace slowed.

"They'll manage," Paul said. "We did." He motioned toward a mound of dry sand. "Let's sit here for a while."

"Good idea. I'm not doing as well as I thought." She smiled. "Must be the champagne."

"And the pain pills. The combination isn't good, but my scolding couldn't stop you."

"My daughter doesn't get married every day, and murderers don't confess every day."

"What about O'Reilly? Do you plan to testify against him?"

"I don't think I'll have to. He's not the bad guy I thought he was."

"I thought you didn't like him."

"I didn't...don't. He's arrogant, pushy, but he saved my life. I even sympathize with Sam. He was young when he was drawn into the cocaine deal. He carried a load of guilt about ratting out the others who were involved."

She turned to him. "I'm sorry. I keep going on about the situation here in Potters Pond and haven't talked about us." She put a hand to his cheek. "I love you. I want us to be together always. I'm to blame for our arguments."

"We both share the blame. You've changed...for the better. We can make it, Diana. You and I need to talk more and...make love more often." He pulled her to him.

She responded and they fell back onto the sand clasped in each other's arms. She enjoyed his ardent kisses that she thought she'd never experience again. She caught her breath and felt the sand in her hair. She squinted at him. "God, I feel like I'm in the movie *From Here To Eternity*."

"We could move down to the water to make it exactly the same."

"Not on your life." She smiled before her mouth met his again.

Chapter 38

Three and a half months had elapsed since Diana and Paul left Potters Pond. She stood in the center of their Philadelphia home's empty living room. Memories of family gatherings spiraled around her, yet she was ready to move on.

Paul, dressed in a parka against the December cold, came in from outside with a pile of mail in his hand. "Last delivery. All the mail will be forwarded to Jeffrey from now on." He handed two envelopes to her.

"Oh." She turned one letter over and smiled. "From Hetch." She tore open the flap, walked to the window seat, sat and read out loud. "Dear Miss Nosy." Diana grinned and looked over at Paul. "He loves to call me that."

"Should I be jealous?" Paul unzipped his parka. "Go on. What's the news?"

She held the letter up to the dim daylight that came through the window and read. "I thought you might like to know that Sam got probation, sold the business and moved to Boston. Sam told me that Phil was blackmailing him and threatened to expose his involvement with the hidden cocaine. Sam would have lost the business, everything. I don't know what happened to O'Reilly. No legal action has been brought against him. He moved away, but I don't know where he went. You probably know the city refused to accept Charles Nelson's resignation. None of what happened was his fault. His wife's body was found washed up on the beach. I'll miss your visits. Shelly's doing great and thank God I have her. Thanks. Yours, Hetch."

She put the letter back in the envelop. "It's nice he wrote. He's a good guy."

"The other one's from your private-eye friend," Paul said, as he stood by the cold clean hearth.

"Hope it's not another bill." She opened it up and scanned a news clipping he'd included. "Nope, just news and Ursula's obituary." She read Max's letter. "Listen to this," she said. "Ursula left her house to the town of Quamscutt to be used as an artists' retreat. Money from the sale of her paintings will be used to fund art scholarships."

"So, some good came out of her crime." Paul glanced at their suitcases in the hall. "You ready for Christmas in D.C.?"

She nodded. "It'll be good to be with the kids. It's been a long time since we've all been together. Imagine, we have a Major for a son-in-law and a First Lieutenant daughter together at the Pentagon. Who would have thought that possible? I hope Jeffery and David's flight doesn't get canceled."

"They'll make it, but if we don't get out of here soon, we might get stuck in the storm."

They picked up their two remaining small bags, locked the door behind them and walked past the *Sold* sign. While Paul stowed the bags in the trunk, a car drove up. He glanced up and muttered, "Beatrice."

Diana sighed, but moved toward the driver's side of her mother's car.

Beatrice put down her window, her usual quarrelsome frown in place. "Were you going to drive off without saying goodbye?"

"We saw you last night at dinner," Diana said. "There didn't seem much point."

"I don't know why you couldn't all be here with me for Christmas. After all I won't see you for a long time. What will I do alone?"

"We invited you to come to D.C. for Christmas."

"You know I have a bad heart and shouldn't travel."

At seventy-four her mother was in excellent health and didn't have a heart problem. It was another of Beatrice's way of trying to control Diana. This time she refused to be drawn into a confrontation or an argument. Beatrice, however, would not relent and continued her litany of complaints. "Running off to Italy in the winter isn't logical, and you'll be too far away from me. What if something happens to me? You haven't thought about me at all."

Diana and Paul hadn't told Beatrice they were going to rent a small home in the Caribbean for two months before they embarked for a long stay in Italy.

Beatrice gripped Diana's gloved hand. "And the grandchildren haven't even called, and I wasn't invited to the wedding. No one cares about me." She sniffled and gazed into Diana's face with a forlorn cocker spaniel appeal.

The act no longer carried weight with Diana. "Mother, we've had this conversation before." She looked at Paul who stood by their car. "We've got to leave. The storm you know." She gave her mother a quick kiss on the cheek, squared her shoulders and walked away.

CPSIA information can be obtained
at www.ICGtesting.com
Printed in the USA
FSOW03n0209020317
31260FS